RETRIBUTION

Katie Reus

Cover art: Jaycee of Sweet 'N Spicy Designs
JRT Editing
Author website: http://www.katiereus.com

Publisher's Note: This is a work of fiction. Names, characters, places, and incidents are either the products of the author's imagination or used fictitiously, and any resemblance to actual persons, living or dead, or business establishments, organizations or locales is completely coincidental.

Retribution/Katie Reus. -- 1st ed.
KR Press, LLC

ISBN-13: 9781942447047
ISBN-10: 1942447043

eISBN: 9781942447030

For Carolyn Crane. Thank you for giving me the extra push I needed with this book.

Praise for the novels of Katie Reus

"...a wild hot ride for readers. The story grabs you and doesn't let go."
—*New York Times* bestselling author, Cynthia Eden

"Has all the right ingredients: a hot couple, evil villains, and a killer
action-filled plot. . . . [The] Moon Shifter series is what I call Grade-
A entertainment!" —Joyfully Reviewed

"I could not put this book down. . . . Let me be clear that I am not
saying that this was a good book *for* a paranormal genre; it was an
excellent romance read, *period.*" —All About Romance

"Reus strikes just the right balance of steamy sexual tension and nail-
biting action....This romantic thriller reliably hits every note that
fans of the genre will expect." —*Publishers Weekly*

"Prepare yourself for the start of a great new series! . . . I'm excited
about reading more about this great group of characters."
—Fresh Fiction

"Wow! This powerful, passionate hero sizzles with sheer
deliciousness. I loved every sexy twist of this fun & exhilarating tale.
Katie Reus delivers!" —Carolyn Crane, RITA award winning author

Continued...

"A sexy, well-crafted paranormal romance that succeeds with smart characters and creative world building."—Kirkus Reviews

"*Mating Instinct*'s romance is taut and passionate . . . Katie Reus's newest installment in her Moon Shifter series will leave readers breathless!" —Stephanie Tyler, *New York Times* bestselling author

"Both romantic and suspenseful, a fast-paced sexy book full of high stakes action." —Heroes and Heartbreakers

"Katie Reus pulls the reader into a story line of second chances, betrayal, and the truth about forgotten lives and hidden pasts." —The Reading Café

"Nonstop action, a solid plot, good pacing, and riveting suspense." —RT Book Reviews

"Sexy suspense at its finest." —Laura Wright, *New York Times* bestselling author of *Branded*

CHAPTER ONE

March 1ˢᵗ

Declan Gallagher glanced up from his stack of paperwork when his intercom buzzed. It was close to seven and he should be at home, sipping on a beer right now. Some days he missed working for the CIA more than others. The thought of being stuck in a third world shithole for an op sometimes held more appeal than being stuck behind a desk.

"Mr. Gallagher, there's a Vernon Nash here to see you. I know you told me not to bug you after six, but—"

Vivid memories of Cairo swam before him. "Send him in, Blair. And go ahead and get out of here."

"If you're sure..." she hedged.

"I'm sure. Don't worry about coming in early tomorrow either. You've been working too hard so I'll see you later."

"Thanks Mr. Gallagher. Have a good night."

As the intercom disconnected, his office door opened. The last time he'd seen Vernon, two armed terrorists had been holding a pistol to Declan's head, ready to blow him away. In those days Vernon hadn't been Deputy Director of the FBI's counterterrorism division. He'd simply been a field agent stationed in one of Egypt's

Legal Attaché offices. And Declan had been a cocky agent for the CIA too secure in his paranormal abilities that he thought he'd been invincible. If it hadn't been for Vernon, he'd be dead.

Declan stood and held out a hand. "Vernon, good to see you. It's been a while."

"Coming up on a decade." Vernon pumped his hand once then dropped onto the leather chair facing Declan's desk.

"What brings you to Miami?" He shifted his stack of papers to the side.

"You do. I arrived about an hour ago."

So this wasn't a social call. "You need a place to stay?"

His friend shook his head and Declan couldn't help but notice more than a few new gray streaks in Vernon's brown hair since the last time he'd seen the man. "No, but I need a favor. And it has to be off the books."

He leaned back in his chair, interested. "Lay it on me."

"For starters, the Lazarev brothers are dead. Supposedly of natural causes, but what're the chances of each of them dying of heart attacks." It wasn't a question.

"Shouldn't that be the CIA's problem?" Gosha, Kirril, and Sergei Lazarev were all filthy pieces of shit. They ran drugs, women, and weapons, mostly in Europe, but they occasionally served the United States with information. Or rather, they had.

"Yes and no. What I'm about to tell you is classified."

Declan nodded, his interest even more piqued. He still had top secret clearance and even if he didn't, he had a feeling Vernon would tell him anyway. "Understood."

"I didn't take much notice of Gosha's death, but when his brothers died within months of each other, I got a buddy of mine with the CIA to send me their files."

"Why?" The Lazarev brothers were known in certain circles but they operated mostly in Europe and the horn of Africa. And they weren't involved in domestic terrorism. The FBI shouldn't care what happened to them.

Vernon cleared his throat but his stubble-covered face was expressionless. "I've been watching them for the past two decades. It's personal."

Okay then. Declan just nodded.

"Twenty years ago the Lazarev brothers were connected to Yasha Makarov. They did a lot of low-level work together. Mostly as hired guns."

Declan gritted his teeth at the mention of Yasha Makarov. The older Russian had been living in Miami for the past few years and he did nothing but wreak havoc wherever he went. He ran drugs up and down the East Coast and probably had a farther reach than that. Many of Declan's clients frequented the same establishments as Yasha and simply being in the same room as the mobster increased any security threat.

Vernon continued. "I know what the reports say, but I think the Lazarev brothers were murdered and I think the people who killed them are after Yasha. I'm fairly certain they'll be in Miami in the next couple weeks."

Declan leaned forward and placed his elbows on his desk. "What's the problem then? Yasha is...evil." There wasn't another word he could think of to aptly describe the man. And he'd seen his fair share of human atrocities over the years. Declan wasn't sure what it said about him, but he'd be more than fine if Yasha ceased to exist.

"It's more complicated than that. Word on the street is he's moving girls now with his drugs."

The drugs weren't new, but moving people? "Girls? You're sure?"

A short nod, his expression grim, Vernon said, "Sure enough. He's been talking with some movers from Eastern Europe in the slave trade. We need him stopped before he can think about growing bigger."

"So let the unsanctioned hitters take him out." Win, fucking, win, as far as Declan was concerned.

"I can't."

There was more to it, Declan read it on his friend's expression. "Can't or won't?"

He sighed and rubbed a hand over the back of his neck. "Rumor is he's moving in a new shipment soon. We're not sure how or when exactly, but it's soon and it will be through Miami. He's selling virgins to the highest bidder. We need more information to save those girls and to bring down his entire op. If he dies before we do that..." Vernon shook his head. "He plays things close to the vest. We can't risk him getting killed until we know more details."

"So, take out his assassins. Or, pay them to back off temporarily." Declan hadn't been out of the game that long that he didn't remember how things worked. Two years ago he'd given up his job as a Black-Ops agent in The Agency to start his own security company, but some things never changed. A bullet in the head or a cash payoff were standard operating procedure.

"It's more complicated than that. The CIA officially doesn't think anyone killed the Lazarev brothers and so far, they haven't made the connection between them and Yasha. Their deaths aren't monumental so I think they're just being written off as a bad luck story. Karma and all that shit."

"How'd you make the connection when a team of trained analysts couldn't?" Declan frowned at his friend.

Vernon opened his briefcase and pulled out a thick manila folder. Out of the folder, he withdrew pictures of two attractive women and slid them across Declan's desk.

Declan tapped his finger on one of the pictures. The women were obviously related but he knew he'd seen one of them somewhere before. "She looks familiar."

Vernon nodded. "That's Alena Brennan. She does a lot of modeling. You've probably seen her Campari ads. And if you missed those, she was in the news a couple years ago. Some scandal involving the Prince of Morocco."

"What about the other one?"

"That's Nika, her sister. From what people say they're as different as night and day. She got her Master's in Technical Communication from Columbia. Does a lot of freelance web design and unlike Alena, she's not into the party scene."

"Nika." The woman's name rolled off his tongue. Her sister was gorgeous, but Nika was...striking. It was the only way to describe her. Caramel hued flawless skin, sharp cheekbones, dark brown hair she left natural and curly and startling green eyes that seemed even brighter against her darker skin. The freckles dotting her nose and cheeks gave her an almost innocent quality. He almost snorted at the word. *Innocent.* No one was innocent. Realizing he was staring, he met Vernon's gaze. "So you think *these two* are your assassins? Why the hell would they want to kill the Lazarev brothers?"

The older man's jaw tightened a fraction as he pulled out another file and slid it across the desk. Vernon adjusted his tie and nodded toward the manila folder. "Open the file and look at the date stamps on those pictures."

Declan flipped it open and scanned various pictures of the Lazarev brothers. Some were taken in nightclubs and some were in restaurants. In one picture, Alena and Nika Brennan were clearly visible. He looked up. "Where were these taken?"

"Germany, Egypt, and the last one—the one with the women—is from the Bahamas. Right before the last murder."

"So what?"

Vernon slid another file across the table. "Look at the flight manifests for the women. They've been in each city at the time of each murder. It can't be a coincidence."

"Maybe, maybe not. If what this says is true," Declan tapped on Alena Brennan's dossier, "then she's little more than a socialite *and* she's made a lot of money from modeling. All this could be random. Those types of people always seem to travel in packs, staying in the same circles. And you still never answered my question. Why would they want to kill these men?"

Something akin to pain flashed in Vernon's eyes, but it was gone so quickly Declan wondered if he'd imagined it. "I just know that my gut tells me they're somehow involved in this."

He was lying. Declan was sure of it. The FBI director had no business getting involved in this unless it was somehow personal. But he knew when to back off. So he would, for now. "Okay, fine. I'm going to play this hypothetical game. Say these two women are assassins. What's the connection between the Lazarev brothers and Yasha Makarov?"

"They did a lot of work together years ago for the Belov family."

Declan glanced at the file again. "If what this says is correct, that was before these two girls were barely old enough to walk, so there's no clear personal connection. And it can't be about money considering how much this one makes." He tapped on Alena's picture. "So even if the brothers and Yasha were connected years ago, what's the connection with these women?"

Vernon cleared his throat. "Andre Makarov will be coming to Miami soon. I know you've helped out his security detail when he's in town and I'd like you to keep an ear to the ground."

Okay, so Vernon was apparently ignoring his question—and it was just feeding Declan's curiosity more. Maybe it's what his friend planned on. He sighed. "That's all you need from me?" Andre Makarov might be Yasha's son, but the two were nothing alike. If anything, Andre barely tolerated his gangster father.

Vernon shook his head. "I've got it on good authority that the Brennan sisters are headed to Biloxi as we speak."

Andre owned a few casinos in Biloxi. He also owned some in Vegas. Could be a coincidence. Declan glanced down at their file. "Says they own a home in New Orleans. It's not far from Biloxi."

"They're staying at the Ivy."

"Shit." That was the casino where Andre spent most of his time. Hell, from what Declan knew about the man, he practically lived there. He preferred the Gulf Coast to the desert. If the women did want to kill Yasha, this would be the way to get to him.

"My thoughts exactly."

"You think they're going to try and get to Yasha through Andre."

Vernon shrugged and started gathering his files. "It's what I would do if I was in their position. Yasha is damn near impossible to get to with his security. Something happened a year ago to spook him—before you ask, I don't know what it was, I just know the rumors. He's tightened his security even more. A pretty woman would mean nothing to him. Using Andre as a go-between is the perfect angle."

"You don't want me to keep an ear to the ground, you want me to spy on these women," Declan said quietly, understanding *exactly* what Vernon wanted. Vernon knew about Declan's abilities and that was why he needed him. This wasn't just a normal favor.

"Yes. I need you to get *close* to one of them. I don't care which and I don't care what you have to do to get your information. It all has to be off the books. We've had a problem with leaks lately and I can't take the chance we lose those women. Those girls. I'm going to be your only contact for this."

"You don't have much intel." Part of the reason he'd left the CIA was because he was tired of the cloak and dagger bullshit. The other reason was something he didn't like to think about. Now he had no choice.

Vernon snapped his briefcase shut. "You know I wouldn't ask if I had anyone else to turn to. You have a personal relationship with Andre. He knows you used to work for the Agency and he also knows you're more than a trained security professional. Your company is the best. Besides, you owe me."

The last few words cut through the air with all the subtlety of a fifty-cal rifle. His friend had to be desperate if he was calling in a favor. When Declan had been barely twenty-two his cockiness had almost gotten him killed. If it hadn't been for Vernon, he'd be six feet under in a nameless grave. The man was right, Declan owed him. "Fine. I'll call Andre this week. Put out a few feelers and see if he needs extra security when he's in town. I can't promise he'll hire me, but I'll make a hard pitch." Without making it seem like a hard one. All part of the game.

A tired smile played across Vernon's features as he stood. "Don't worry about his security. He'll be calling you. Trust me."

Declan knew better than to ask how Vernon knew that. In truth, he didn't want to know. Less knowledge gave him plausible deniability. He stood and shook hands with Vernon before settling back into his custom-made leather chair. As he massaged his temple, he flipped open the file Vernon had left on his desk and delved into the dossier on the Brennan sisters.

If he wanted to find out more about them, he'd have to get into their heads. And to do that, he'd have to break all his rules. As he stared at the pictures of the two women, he tried to decide who would be the best target. The thought of getting inside Nika's head turned him on and that surprised him.

Imagining walking through her dreams and tapping into her most intimate thoughts was a strange aphrodisiac. Something he didn't think was possible. He'd been born with the ability to tap into other people's thoughts, but only during their dream states. Since he'd retired from the CIA he hadn't put his dream walking gift to use.

The last time he'd walked through a woman's dreams, she'd almost killed him.

CHAPTER TWO

Declan pushed open the glass door of the dingy diner and glanced around. Almost immediately he spotted his brother in one of the booths. It would be hard not to. He was six foot flat, but he had wide, linebacker shoulders. Sitting down, he looked huge. As Declan neared the table a grin broke out across Riley's tired face.

Wordlessly, Riley stood and pulled him into a tight embrace. He had a sleeve of tattoos on both arms. He'd done the designs for all of them and tatted some himself too. Since he owned three tattoo places, two in Miami and one in Orlando, he was a perfect walking advertisement.

"Looking good."

"You're such a liar." Riley chuckled as he sat back down. "I'm fucking exhausted. Been working for eighteen days straight. I don't even know what day it is," he muttered, glancing at the screen of his cell phone.

With at least three days stubble and a faded T-shirt that appeared a few decades old, his brother actually did look one step up from a homeless person. "So what's up? You sounded tense on the phone."

Declan waited until their server took his order and left before talking. "I can't go into detail, but in the near future it looks like I'm going to be taking a job for Andre Makarov." Possibly.

Riley lifted his shoulders. "You've worked for him before."

"There's someone he's going to be traveling with soon and I need to get into their head."

"Their or *her*? Is that what this is about? A woman?" His brother's mouth pulled into a thin line.

Declan gritted his teeth. He'd never been able to hide much from Riley. "Yeah."

"How long are you going to let that bitch's ghost haunt you, man? You've been denying who you are for too long."

Ignoring his brother, Declan took a sip of the coffee placed in front of him. The place might look like a dump on the outside but they had the best coffee and pie in the city.

Riley just watched him intently, his dark eyes flashing with impatience. "So who is this woman?"

"I can't say."

"Why do you need to get into her dreams?"

"I can't say."

"You can't say a whole hell of a lot," Riley muttered. "Thought you left all that cloak and dagger shit behind."

Declan bit back a smile. "Sorry, man."

"Listen, I know it's been a while since you've gone dream walking, but—"

"Two years." Which was why he'd called his brother.

"Fine, it's been *two years*. What are the chances that you get into another psychic's head? And even if this woman is a psychic, what are the chances she's as powerful as Madelyn?"

"Yeah, I know." But the truth was, he wasn't sure how slim the chances were. In his previous line of work, like seemed to be attracted, or at least pulled, to like. Wasn't sure what that said about him.

"Can you decline the…job? Or whatever it is?"

"I owe someone a favor. A big one."

Riley nodded once, as if that explained everything. Gallagher men took their promises seriously. "Then suck it up and do it."

"That was really fucking motivational," Declan muttered.

Riley leaned back as the waitress returned carrying their burgers, a grin tugging at his lips. "What can I say? I'm good. Been thinking about taking up motivational speaking."

Declan declined an offer of more condiments. When the server left, he flicked a glance up as the napkin holder slid away from the wall and landed in between their plates. He narrowed his gaze at his brother. "Why are you doing that in here?"

Riley grinned in the obnoxious way only a younger brother can do. "Some of us actually practice our gifts. Don't want to get rusty."

Declan didn't respond, but Riley was right. His brother had honed his telekinetic powers years ago. Hell, all of his brothers were in control of their skills. Declan was the only one who hadn't put his gift to use in a while.

On a logical level he knew he needed to get over his shit and do this job. The thought of immersing himself back into that dream world made him break out in a cold sweat in a way looking down the barrel of a loaded weapon never had.

* * *

Declan laid against his pillow, staring at the ceiling. He told himself to stop being a pussy and do what needed to be done. Bringing the picture of Nika Brennan to eye level, he stared at it and fought back the jump of desire that stirred deep in his gut. He had a job to do and he couldn't afford to screw this up. Especially not over a woman. A *very* pretty woman with electric green eyes. Putting the picture down, he closed his eyes and focused all his mental attention on her face and what he'd learned about her from her dossier.

Dark curly hair, bright green eyes, creamy caramel skin. Delicate, slim build...

Loud, Caribbean music pumped through speakers. Bright colors swirled everywhere, smiling, tan people. An Asian woman snorting cocaine, a black woman dancing...

The scene dissipated so quickly he felt as if he was falling through space. Then he was standing at the edge of a four-poster king-sized bed. A hotel room. He took in his surroundings. A glance out the window and he saw the Chrysler Building. New York.

It took a fraction of a moment to realize he was being watched. All his senses went hyper alert as his gaze locked with the woman sitting straight up in the middle of the bed. It was *her*. Nika Brennan.

"Who are you?" she asked.

His blood ran cold. He was in her dreams, but she was actually aware of his presence. That had only happened once before and it hadn't ended very well for him. Normally he saw dreams play out in random bits and pieces and he gleaned information from digging. He needed to tread carefully. "Who do you want me to be?" *He kept his voice low, seductive.*

Her dark eyebrows raised in what looked like amusement. "I really must be losing my mind if I'm imagining sexy men in my dreams," *she murmured.*

"You think I'm sexy?" *he asked.*

She let out an indelicate snort. "Even my fantasy man needs his ego stroked. Freaking men," *she murmured.*

"If you don't want to stroke my ego maybe you can stroke something else." *He was playing with fire, but it was impossible to pull back in this woman's presence. Everything about her was bright and vivid. Not just physically, but psychically, like she was surrounded by an otherworldly light. He'd never seen anything like it.*

She let out a sharp bark of laughter. The sound was throaty and unexpected and sexy as hell. It had his dick at full attention. "And he's a smartass too."

"Why are you staying in a hotel room?" He had a lot of questions so he figured he'd start small. He wasn't sure why or even how she was aware of his presence and he didn't want to scare her in case she could kick him out of her head. Or worse.

"You're my fantasy man. You tell me." She slid off the bed and walked toward him. His cock pulsed once, as if it had a mind of its own, when he realized she wore blue boy-short panties and a matching skimpy tank-top that showed just enough skin to drive him wild. As she came to stand in front of him, she reached out and placed her hand on his chest.

When she did, he realized his shirt had disappeared. She must have projected that she wanted it gone. The feel of her hand against his chest was so real. His skin warmed and heated to a low burn under her touch. Her eyebrows rose in surprise when they made contact. Unless she was a consummate actress, she was just as surprised as him. Okay, that was a good thing.

Feeling almost drunk with the need to touch her, he reached out and cupped her cheek. She let out a soft exhalation at the contact and he didn't miss the way her nipples hardened underneath her top.

Or the way her full lips slightly parted. When she moistened them with her tongue, he groaned. He hadn't realized he made the noise until she smiled.

"This is the best dream I've had in a long time," she murmured and stepped closer to him. Slowly, sensually, she slid her hands up his chest and wound them around his neck. "What are you doing in my head, mystery man?" she asked, the question a whisper.

He was pretty sure she wasn't looking for an answer. Her eyelids dropped seductively as she zeroed in on his mouth. As if drugged, he started to lean forward, ready to capture her *mouth with his. Just one taste. That's all he wanted. No, one taste wouldn't be enough. He was rational enough to know that. His heart raced wildly. He had to get out of her head before he did something stupid.*

Wake up, wake up, wake up.

His eyes flew open with a start, his heart pounding against his chest in an erratic tattoo. But he was in his own bed. Alone. He pushed his comforter off, groaning as it dragged against his erection. It might have only been a dream, but his reaction to her was real enough. Too damn real.

At least now he was prepared. Next time he got into her head, he wouldn't be taken by surprise. She obviously thought she'd conjured him up so he planned to use that to his fullest advantage.

CHAPTER THREE

March 9th

Nika opened the door of the plush hotel bathroom and stepped out to find her sister smoothing on cherry red lipstick in the mirror. Lipstick that screamed *look at me*. Which was exactly the point. "You look amazing," she murmured.

"Thanks." Alena turned to look at her, a megawatt smile plastered on her face. Of course the smile didn't reach her eyes.

And that depressed the hell out of Nika. It seemed the closer they got to their goal, the more detached they both were from it. As if they were denying what they had to do. Or maybe it was just Nika who wanted to deny it. After years of planning, everything was finally falling into place. So why didn't Nika feel any sense of impending relief? Instead, all she felt was doom. Dark and depressing. And her damn dreams—or nightmares, she wasn't sure—didn't help either.

"You sure you're ready to do this, Alena? Sometimes I think..." As she sank onto the California king-sized bed, she clenched her jaw to keep from saying the words aloud. She'd only been saying them for the past year. It wouldn't do any good to repeat herself. Her sister would never change her mind and she was tired of nagging.

"You think what?" The lipstick tube dropped to the dresser with a clatter.

She met her sister's shuttered gaze in the mirror. "Maybe we should just walk away," she whispered.

Alena's full mouth pulled into a thin line and for a split second, her dark brown eyes flared with rage. "You think that fucker deserves to live?"

God, the rage was always there with Alena, a living breathing thing Nika swore she could see swirling around her sister. Nika swallowed and shook her head. "No. I don't want to lose you too." For so long it had just been the two of them. She couldn't imagine life without her sister. Refused to.

Expression softening, Alena strode across the suite to sit next to her. The bed barely moved as she took Nika's hand. "You're not going to lose me. I promise."

Alena hadn't broken a promise to her since she was five. In her gut, Nika knew that no matter what she said, her sister wouldn't back down from this. She could scream and threaten to leave, but even if she did make threats, Nika knew her sister would never believe her. Because Nika would *never* walk away from her. Hell, she *couldn't* walk away from Alena.

Sighing, Nika stood and placed her hands on her hips. To get through this she'd be faking it every step of the way. Something she'd learned to do from a young age. "Let's get this over with. What am I wearing?"

Her sister stood and drew back the mirrored closet door. She reached in and pulled out a strapless emerald green dress that would cover Nika's ass by about two inches. "It matches your eyes."

Nika took the dress from her outstretched hand and suppressed a grin as she held out the shimmery scrap of material. "No one's going to be looking at my eyes."

"Exactly. I guarantee Yasha's son will notice us tonight." Alena flashed her toothpaste commercial smile in that familiar way.

She couldn't help but notice that her sister didn't call him by his first name. He was simply Yasha's son. As if that somehow detached Alena. "And if he doesn't?"

"He will." Her sister dismissed the question with a flick of her wrist and turned back to the closet where she rummaged for something to wear herself.

A secret part of her hoped he wouldn't notice Alena, but the realistic part of her brain knew he would. Nika was pretty. She could admit it. Men occasionally did double takes. But pretty girls were a dime a dozen. Especially for a man like Andre Makarov, Yasha's son. He might look twice at her, then dismiss her just as quickly.

Alena however, was beauty and grace personified. Thanks to their mixed heritage they'd both been blessed with smooth skin and high cheekbones, but everything about her sister was intensified. Their mother had been a beautiful, petite Russian woman and their father a tall, large British man with ebony skin. They'd both taken after their parents, but Alena had large, exotic eyes, naturally full lips that didn't come from injections, and a killer body thanks to daily Pilates. It ensured that they'd at least get the man's attention.

Not to mention they had a secret weapon. Nika. Even if he could ignore her gorgeous sister, he'd likely take notice when they started to rake in hundreds of thousands of dollars at his casino. She just hoped things wouldn't get that far.

As Nika brushed on mascara she chuckled when she saw what her sister picked out. The wisp of red material that was supposed to be a dress was pure sex and sin. "You trying to give the man a heart attack before we..." The laughter died on her lips as she realized what she'd been about to say. Clearing her throat, she bunched her dark, out of control hair at the back of her neck. The curls were riotous as always. Normally she just pulled it into a ponytail. "Should I wear it up or down?"

Thankfully Alena ignored her first comment. "Definitely down. Turn on the curling iron and flat iron and I'll style it for you. Smooth out some of those wild curls and flip them at the ends."

By the time her sister was finished, Nika's curls were softer and framed her face. Alena had flat ironed her own dark hair so that it was sleek and shiny as it fell down her back. Like an inky waterfall.

"Remember, after tonight, all talk in this room," her sister motioned with her hand, "is scripted."

"I know, I know. We need him to invite us—or you—to Miami on his next trip." They'd only gone over it a hundred times, but her sister always felt the need to re-peat things.

If Andre did notice her sister tonight, then they had to assume that he'd be running their backgrounds and checking up on them. If he was anything like his father, they had to act on the assumption that he would bug their room. Which meant they could only make boring small talk unless they were absolutely sure they weren't being watched.

Alena's phone started to buzz when they both grabbed their clutch purses.

"It's your agent," Nika said without thinking. Since she hadn't been born with her gifts some things she was still figuring out—on a daily basis—but this was something she always just sort of knew.

"Showoff." Alena grinned as she pulled out the phone, then silenced the ringer. "That never ceases to amaze me," she said, putting it back inside her purse.

Alena linked arms with her as they headed out the door. On the way to the elevators Nika could feel the pent up energy humming through her sister.

The Gulf Coast city of Biloxi was smaller compared to Vegas, where Makarov's other casinos were, but Nika liked the area better. It had less of a garish, bright-lights atmosphere. And they had the perfect cover for being here. They owned a home in New Orleans and this was only an hour and a half away. It was one of their stops on their way home after a recent bout of traveling. At least that was their cover story.

"We're so damn close to finishing this, I feel it," Alena whispered.

Nika just nodded, her thoughts split between the mystery man from her dreams and the whole situation she and Alena were in now. Damn that sexy man she'd imagined. And yes, she realized she was cursing a figment of her own mind. She seriously needed to get laid or something.

She gave herself a hard mental shake. After this job, Nika hoped her sister would finally find some peace. They'd already tried to kill Yasha once. Hopefully this time they'd succeed.

For all her premonitions and visions, Nika never saw a glimpse of her or Alena's future. Not even a peek. And that was a scary thing indeed. They might have an advantage over the Makarov family, but the one thing she feared above all was that no matter how much planning they'd done, Yasha Makarov was ruthless in a way she and her sister never would be. No matter what Alena seemed to think, there were certain lines she knew her sister wouldn't cross. It stood to reason that his son was just the same. Hell, one didn't build an empire of casinos without making some enemies.

As they strolled down the hallway, a door to one of the other luxury suites opened. Two flashily dressed men about their age stepped out. Out of the corner of her eye, Nika watched one elbow the other.

One of them let out a low whistle, but neither she nor Alena bothered to turn in their direction. The elevator dinged almost the second they arrived in front of it. Despite her sister's promises, and despite the edge they had, a trickle of sweat rolled down Nika's spine.

"Smile," her sister ordered, as they stepped into the mirrored elevator.

"Hold the door," one of the men called from the hallway.

Nika smiled and waved as she pressed the button to close the door. Her sister snickered at the annoyed protests that were silenced as the doors whooshed shut.

Seconds later, the doors opened on the first floor. Music, cigarette smoke, and loud voices immediately greeted them. A sharp contrast from the mellow elevator music.

"Blackjack tables," Nika said, already knowing what her sister was going to ask. They'd definitely get lucky there. She could feel it straight to her bones.

Their heels clacked on the marble tile of the lobby as they made their way to the casino area. When they passed a big cluster of quarter slots, Nika's eyes were drawn to a shabbily dressed man sitting in front of one of the machines.

His despair was so acute, it surrounded him like a dark cloud. The back of her neck prickled as she watched him. Unexpected tears sprung to her eyes as a vision of him holding a pistol in his mouth flashed in front of her.

"Damn it," she muttered under her breath.

"Nika." Her sister's warning tone and the intensity of the grip on her arm didn't stop her from halting by his chair.

She leaned over the guy's shoulder and tried to ignore the suffocating scent of body odor and stale cigarettes. He looked at her in surprise, his dull eyes flashing with momentary interest. Nika tapped the unoccupied machine next to him. "Play this three times, then go home to your wife. And for the love of God, stay away from the roulette tables."

"What?" He swiveled in his chair.

But she'd already turned back to her sister.

"What are the odds that loser listens to you?" Alena rolled her eyes and shook her head.

"That, I don't know." But Nika had to try and help the guy.

As they continued walking, the sound of excited shouting behind them caused a few people at the slots to turn toward the noise.

Her sister glanced behind them, but Nika didn't bother looking. She knew what she'd see.

"Ten thousand. Not bad. Now how about we quadruple that?" A silvery laugh rolled from Alena and Nika bit back a grin.

If it was up to her sister, they'd have hit up casinos a long time ago. As they strolled toward the nearest blackjack table, a few men turned and moved out of the way when they saw Alena.

Nika pressed a nervous hand to her stomach as they took a seat. She just hoped this plan worked. If not, and Andre Makarov thought they were counting cards, they'd end up kicked out on their asses. Unless he was like his father. Then... yeah, she didn't even want to think about that.

* * *

Andre Makarov stared at the private video feed streaming from the flat screen on his office wall. Using the remote control, he zoomed in on the dark-haired woman on screen. She was so petite yet also curvy. Everything about her was vibrant from her wide eyes to her bright smile.

His throat clenched as she leaned in and said something to one of the patrons at the Blackjack table. Whatever it was, it had the man laughing. Andre couldn't remember the last time a woman had turned his head. Hell, he couldn't even remember the face of the last woman who'd shared his bed. Which said more about him than he wanted to admit.

Instinctively, he glanced at the photo of his deceased wife. Tall and thin with a short platinum blonde bob. And of course, she was unsmiling. His gaze reverted back to the screen and a deep-seated—unexpected— hunger hummed through his veins. *Mine.* He wasn't sure where the word came from but fuck him, he felt it.

Andre pressed his intercom button. "Barry? You still out there?"

"Of course, boss."

"Can I see you for a moment?"

When his assistant stepped inside, Andre nodded to the screen. "I'd like you to have security ask that woman to join me at Tsuki's."

Barry frowned and looked back at him. "Is there a problem, sir? Do you think she's cheating?"

"No. I'd simply like to speak with her." His approach was likely arrogant. He just didn't care. He wanted to talk to her now.

"Of course...you do know who she is, correct?"

When Andre shook his head, Barry picked up a cigar magazine from the stand by the door and flipped it over. "Her name is Alena Brennan."

That's why she looks so familiar. Her hair was pulled back tight against a face that was slimmer, more hollow looking in the picture—no doubt airbrushed. He preferred the real life version. "Thank you, Barry. After you make the call, get out of here. It's too late for you to be here anyway."

"You sure?"

Biting back a smile, Andre nodded. "Just because I'm here, doesn't mean you have to be here too."

The younger man smiled. "Thanks, I'll see you tomorrow."

As Andre flipped off the live video, he called Tsuki's. The hostess picked up on the third ring, which meant they were probably busy. "Chiyo?"

"Yes, Mr. Makarov."

"Is my table available?" He knew it would be, but he asked because Chiyo would get flustered if he simply showed up unannounced.

"Of course, sir."

"I'd like a bottle of Dom and two glasses waiting for me. I'll be down in a few minutes."

"Right away, sir."

Andre glanced at the silver-framed photograph on his desk one more time, then slipped it into his top drawer. Two years had passed since she'd died and he wasn't a fucking masochist. It was past time for him to get over his unfaithful wife.

CHAPTER FOUR

Nika glanced behind her and Alena. A small crowd of men and women had gathered around them. Mainly drunks. Some worse off than others. The stench of booze and one woman's overpowering musky perfume was nauseating. And the pockets of misery surrounding some of the people were enough to make her want to lock herself in their room and never come out.

"Damn it Alena, it's time to find another table. We've been here over an hour," Nika murmured low enough for only her sister to hear.

"We're up two hundred thousand." Alena didn't even glance at her, her gaze riveted to the table.

Nika gritted her teeth at her sister's attitude. Her spidey sense—as Alena loved to call it—was on high alert. The hair on the back of her neck stood up. They'd been noticed by someone who worked at the casino. She felt it bone-deep. After her sister won yet another hand, the table cheered and the dealer shot them a hooded look.

Nika squeezed Alena's leg and this time, she wasn't taking no for an answer. "It's time to take a break. *Now.*"

Her sister started to argue, but she stopped when they made eye contact. "Okay, okay."

Gathering her chips, she stood. Nika moved to help her, but before they'd picked them up, two men wearing gold nametags that simply said *Security* appeared. They weren't rude or outwardly threatening, but the dark expression in both of their eyes sent a chill snaking down her spine.

And Nika hated that. Normally she got a feel for people right away, but these two were like Greek statues. As if their heads were completely empty. Not too comforting.

"We were wondering if you two ladies might come with us." The tallest dark-haired one spoke. Even though the statement was perfectly polite, there was an almost threatening undertone to his words, belying that it was an order, not a request.

"Why?" Alena put a perfectly manicured hand on her hip and frowned.

Nika noticed the dealer closing the table. As he did, the other people quickly dispersed.

"Andre Makarov, the owner, would like to meet you."

"What about my money?" her sister pouted, in full-on actress mode.

The tall one nodded behind her. "Our pit boss will take it to the cages for you. Don't worry, it will be waiting when you come back."

Alena glanced at Nika, who shrugged nonchalantly, just as they'd practiced. A meeting with Andre Makarov was exactly what they'd wanted. She just hadn't expected it to happen so quickly. Either karma was on their side tonight or she was about to kick their asses.

Nika felt as if jagged razorblades were attached to the bunched knots in her stomach. It almost hurt to breathe, but she forced one foot in front of the other and followed the two men in dark suits across the plush red carpet.

One of her mother's favorite sayings—one of the few things she actually remembered about her mother—played in her head. *Be careful what you wish for.*

A trickle of sweat rolled down the side of her face but she didn't dare swipe at it. Even though the security guys were in front of them, she didn't want to draw any undue attention to herself. Especially since she guessed they were being watched on the casino's camera system.

They stopped in the lobby of a posh Japanese restaurant within the casino. "If you wouldn't mind waiting here?"

"Do we have a choice?" Alena huffed as the two men disappeared behind a crimson curtain next to the hostess stand.

Nika inwardly sighed at her sister's bimbo, socialite act. It might be necessary but it was still annoying. Right now, she just wanted to run away and live a normal life with normal friends. Unfortunately, she doubted it was possible. She didn't even know what normal was anyway. She'd never had it.

"Ms. Brennan." Nika and Alena turned at the sound of a deep, gravelly voice. One of the security men held back the curtain as Andre Makarov—their enemy's son—strode from the interior of the restaurant.

He was just as they'd seen in his pictures. Dirty blond hair, incredibly pale blue eyes, Slavic bone structure, well over six foot, and very fit. He might be wearing a dark blue, two-button—no doubt custom made—jacket, but underneath the expensive suit was a ruthless man. Or at least that's what they'd heard. He certainly looked confident.

"Which one of us are you talking to?" Alena asked.

"Ah." For a split second the man's step faltered as he walked toward them. "You are Alena Brennan, correct?"

"Yes, and this is my sister, Nika." Alena motioned with her hand.

He flicked a quick glance in Nika's direction before turning to frown at one of his men. Just as quickly he looked back at Alena. "I apologize. I did not realize you were here with anyone. I simply wanted to ask you to dine with me tonight."

"That's fairly presumptuous for a man I've never met."

"You must excuse my manners—"

Nika cleared her throat, ready to make a quick escape. This was better than they could have hoped for. And she could sense that Andre didn't have any dark motives. She still wasn't sure how she knew, but she felt that familiar tingling of sensation again telling her. "Alena, I'm not feeling well so if you'll excuse me..."

Andre quickly swiveled in her direction, a surprisingly concerned expression marring his handsome features. The vibes from him were sincere too, as if he was actually sorry. That was interesting. And unexpected. "Ms. ah, Nika. I didn't mean to offend you. I'd be pleased if you'd *both* join me for dinner."

"We've had a long day and I'm exhausted." Nika leaned over and kissed her sister on the cheek before turning back to him. "Make sure my sister gets back to our room at a decent hour."

Without giving him a chance to respond, she strode from the restaurant. Alena would have no problem handling herself with Andre Makarov. If anything, her sister would perform better without Nika there.

People rushed by her in a blur as she made her way toward the elevators. She hadn't been lying when she said she was tired. All this traveling was taxing, and she had no desire to make small talk for hours. Not to mention being in a casino seemed to increase her sensitivity to people. She was picking up all sorts of depressing emotions and it was draining. Tension knotted her neck and lower back as the elevator opened onto her floor.

For the past week she'd been assaulted with incredibly vivid, incredibly erotic dreams and it had left her in an almost permanent weakened state. Which might explain her hyperawareness to the people around her. A very sexy, mysterious man had invaded her deepest sleep. It was as if this dream man had come out of nowhere and latched onto her mind. Everything about him was real from his spicy, masculine scent to his strong, callused hands.

And he visited her dreams every single night. She woke up tired, panting, and half the time, unfulfilled from his kisses and caresses. It was like he was keeping her on the hook, which she knew, sounded insane even as she had the thought. The man wasn't freaking *real*.

She slipped her keycard into the door and waited until it closed behind her. Since she expected her sister back in a few hours, she didn't put the extra latch in place. After washing her face, she stripped out of her dress and tugged a T-shirt on before sliding under the soft sheets.

Just sleep. No dreams. She repeated the words over and over as her head sank deeper against the pillow.

No dreams...

Nika sat up in bed and pushed the sheet off her. It fell to her waist, exposing her breasts, but she didn't care. Her mystery dream man had seen her naked more than once. She was so far beyond caring about a little nudity at this point.

"I know you're here." As always, there was a slight echo to her voice in this dream state. A reminder that in her dreams anything could happen, but she was still safe and in control.

She was in her hotel room, and while things were the same, the atmosphere was different. Like a photograph that hadn't fully developed. The edges of the air were thick and hazy. It was the only way she was sure of her current reality.

From the shadows stepped the man who brought her pleasure and frustration. Taller than her by almost a foot, his jet-black hair mirrored his dark, enigmatic eyes.

Eyes she'd gotten used to looking into the past week. It was stupid, this weird addiction she seemed to have for her fantasy man. And part of her wondered just how fictitious this man was.

Years ago, when she'd started researching the paranormal, she'd stumbled onto an entire world of people with different gifts and abilities. Empaths, healers, those with telekinetic powers—she was still wrapping her mind around that one. She'd never met someone who could enter dreams before, though she had heard rumors of night walkers. They were supposed to create nightmares, but so far her mystery man hadn't done that. Just the opposite.

She rolled onto her side, facing away from him. "I don't want to play tonight." Okay, that was a big fat lie. She wanted to feel his hands and mouth on her body and stroke him everywhere in return, but she was too mentally taxed after tonight.

The bed didn't dip, it never seemed to in dreams, but she felt him slide in behind her. Well, she sensed him, more than felt anything until his big body moved flush against hers, his chest against her back. "Rough day?" The question was sincere.

Which just made her feel crazier that she'd conjured him up. Still, she answered. "Yeah."

"Want to talk about it?"

Yes. "No." Saying out loud what she and her sister were going to do made her feel even crappier.

"Want me to leave?" His big, callused hand slid across her stomach, moving downward until his fingers skittered over her mound.

Instead of answering, she rolled over so that she was facing him. He immediately adjusted his hold before he cupped her once again, his hand so damn possessive it made her shudder.

Slowly, he stroked his middle finger along her slit. They hadn't even kissed yet tonight, but he touched her body with a wicked familiarity she was getting far too accustomed to.

She reached for him, wanting to shove his dark cargo pants down his legs. Why was he even dressed anyway? He stopped her before she got very far, his hand moving lightning quick to circle her wrist.

"No touching," he murmured before he captured her mouth with his.

Her tongue danced against his even as she tangled her fingers through his dark hair. No touching? Screw that. She was going to touch tall, dark and sexy all over. This was her dream.

As if he read her mind—for all she knew he did—he chuckled against her mouth before pulling back.

"You're killing my restraint." A soft growl emanated from him and she couldn't help but find it incredibly hot.

"Forget restraint." She started to slide one of her hands down his chest but he moved quickly and she found herself pinned underneath him.

Exactly where she wanted to be. She rolled her hips against him. This was her dream and her rules. She could do whatever she wanted with no consequences.

"You going to keep teasing me tonight?"

"Teasing?"

"All buildup and no release." She felt her cheeks warm up at the statement, which was ridiculous.

He watched her for a long moment, as if contemplating something. There was indecision in that dark gaze, then *something she couldn't quite define.* "Hold on to the head-board."

"Why should I?" she demanded.

He just watched her, the lust and heat in his gaze scorching.

She did as he said and wasn't exactly surprised when silky bindings appeared around her wrists, securing her hands in place. Just as quickly her clothes disappeared, as if they'd never existed at all. Oh yeah, things were about to get interesting.

They hadn't played with restraints before and she'd definitely never done so in real life, but she felt safe with him. This was her dream, she reminded herself.

"If you don't like them, think them away," *he murmured, his head dipping down to one of her breasts.*

She arched her back, trying to push her nipple farther into his mouth. If she had imagined him, she'd done a damn good job. With his wicked tongue and fallen-angel face, he was sex personified.

He flicked against her nipple, teasing it into a hard peak until she was panting and tugging against the bindings. She'd wrapped her legs around him as he teased her, digging her heels into his back.

She was already slick and impossibly turned on. And she didn't even know his freaking name. This whole situation should feel wrong, but everything he did had her trembling for more.

He moved to her other breast, then lower, lower... She rolled her hips insistently when he settled between her open legs, crouched like a predator about to devour his prey.

She didn't exactly mind being his prey. Not when he was watching her with a hunger so intense, she felt it all the way to her core.

Keeping his gaze pinned to hers, he slid a finger down her slit, feeling how turned on she was.

"This is for me." A statement, not a question. There was so much intensity behind those few words, his eyes looking midnight dark in the hazy room. Oh yeah, she could easily see him as a fallen angel as she watched him.

Before she could blink, he'd moved, dipping his head between her legs, his mouth sucking on her clit. There was nothing gentle about it. He slid his tongue over her pulsing bud with a raw intensity that had her crying out and rolling her hips, begging for more.

It was too much and not enough. When he slid two fingers inside her, she almost came undone. It was like the last few days had been building to this and she was about to push right over the edge with almost no buildup.

He began moving his fingers inside her, thrusting in a gentle rhythm that seemed so at odds with the intensity of his tongue.

That was all it took. The orgasm punched through her with practically no warning, sharp and striking all her nerve endings as she writhed underneath him.

This was what she needed so desperately, even if she hadn't realized it. Pleasure continued to pummel through her until she finally collapsed against the sheets, her breathing ragged.

As she did, the bindings fell away, but she could barely move her body, much less her hands. Watching him through a hooded gaze, she found his eyes on her too. He still crouched between her legs, all sexy predator.

Something in his gaze made her sit up. When he didn't say anything she drew her knees up to her chest and wrapped her arms around them. She wasn't great with words or people.

Normally she didn't feel the need to fill silences but right now was bordering on awkward. "Why do you keep visiting me... Are you real?" She hadn't planned to ask, but needed to know.

"What do you think?" he murmured.

"Can't you just answer the question?" When he didn't respond, she continued. "Fine, then who are you? I want a name."

"Tell me what you think." Tingles skittered over her body at his words.

He was a master at evading her questions. Something she'd noticed from the beginning. He only asked, but never answered. And it was beginning to drive her mad. If he really was a fantasy, he wouldn't be so obnoxious. Would he? "Are you a night walker?" The question just popped out.

Something unexpected flashed in his eyes. For a split second, he appeared almost angry. "Night walkers are vile, vicious creatures. I'm not one of them."

But it was odd that he knew what they were. "Then what are you?"

"Maybe I'm a figment of your imagination." Back to the casual, seemingly unconcerned man. But she knew that reaction of his hadn't been conjured up from her own thoughts.

"If you are then you'll disappear when I close my eyes."

"Why don't you find out?" His words sounded almost taunting.

Even though a trickle of fear slid through her veins that he actually would disappear, she closed her eyes...

Nika sucked in a breath as her eyes snapped open. Her sheet was damp from her sweat but she still had on her T-shirt and underwear unlike in her dream. She pressed a shaky hand to the middle of her chest. Her heart beat an erratic rhythm. She should be relieved that her mystery man had left her in peace, but disappointment buzzed through her, sharp and unexpected.

Her sight and gifts were limited but she knew there were others out there like her. She should have *known* he wasn't just a figment of her imagination. There was no way he was, not after that night walker comment. So what the hell was he doing, just visiting her dreams for sex? If a man looked like that he didn't need to go trolling dreams. Sitting up, she scrubbed a hand over her face. She didn't know what to think now.

At the sound of the door handle jangling, she nearly jumped out of her skin until she heard Alena's voice.

"You awake?" her sister whispered.

"Yeah. That was quick." Nika wasn't sure what time it was, but she knew she hadn't been asleep that long. Through the dim light streaming in from the cracked bathroom door, Nika could make out some of her sister's movements.

Alena dropped her purse onto the chaise lounge in the corner before slipping her shoes off. "Quick enough to get a breakfast *and* lunch invitation tomorrow. If all goes well, we'll be sipping *mojitos* in South Beach in no time."

"Perfect," Nika muttered before rolling onto her side and closing her eyes. According to their intel, Andre didn't plan to head to Miami for another couple weeks which meant she'd be stuck in Biloxi that whole time. Maybe not though. Maybe she'd just head to their home in New Orleans and let her sister stay here with Andre if things went that far between them.

As she sank into the bed, a little voice told her she wouldn't have another dream tonight.

The realization brought a strange sadness. It settled deep inside her, weighing as heavy as an anchor. And there wasn't a thing she could do about it. While her sister knew she hadn't been sleeping well, Nika had kept the details of her dreams to herself. She didn't know why and couldn't explain it, but something in her gut had told her to keep what she knew about her mystery dream man a secret.

She closed her eyes once again. As she drifted to sleep, a darkness tugged at her. She tried to force her eyes open, to stay awake, but it was impossible.

This wasn't normal. Wake up, damn it, she tried to order herself. She suddenly sucked in a breath as something tugged her under. It was as if she was being sucked out to sea by a powerful undertow. Foolishly she tried to grab onto something, anything, but smothering darkness pulled her under.

Suddenly she found herself in a dark room. A little girl, maybe ten years old, clutched onto a teddy bear.

"Help me," she whispered.

Nika blinked once, looking around her surroundings. She wasn't in the hotel room but...near a tree. No, a cluster of them. She was in the woods. Her surroundings started to become clearer, like a photograph coming into focus. A half-moon hung high in the sky and crickets sounded in the distance. She focused on the little girl again. "Who are you?"

"Help me," she whispered again.

Oh God, this couldn't be happening again. "Where have you brought me?"

"I can't stay long...you must start listening to us...we need your help..."

With a gasp, Nika surged back to reality. Breathing hard, she rolled over and saw Alena curled up in the fetal position, sound asleep.

She was in the hotel room and okay. Everything was okay. She pressed the heels of her palms to her eyes, trying to banish the truth of what had just happened. If those manic dead people thought they could start haunting her dreams again, she was going to lose her mind.

It was only a nightmare. That was all. It wasn't a spirit talking to her again. It just *couldn't* be. She'd put all that behind her years ago. Sighing, she rolled onto her back and sent up a silent prayer that she actually got some uninterrupted sleep. No sexy man to taunt her and no dead people who wanted to haunt her.

CHAPTER FIVE

Two weeks later

Nika stretched her legs out and shifted against the leather seat of the plane to face her sister. Alena's eyes were closed but Nika knew she wasn't sleeping. Reaching out, Nika plucked the earphones attached to the mp3 player in her sister's ears.

Alena's eyes flew open. "What's up?"

"You dragged me on this flight, you get to entertain me." Normally she'd just read on her ereader, but she was too anxious about the flight. It wasn't freaking normal for people to rocket through the air at hundreds of miles per hour in a steel tube.

Alena lifted a dark eyebrow. "Entertain you? Like what, do magic tricks?"

"Come on, you want to play gin rummy?" For a couple hours Nika could pretend that this was just a fun trip to Miami with her sister's new boyfriend and that they were just having a good time. But only for a little while. Once their plane landed, she knew reality would crash over her head. The past two weeks Alena had spent in Biloxi so Nika had headed to their New Orleans home and gotten a lot of work done. Fortunately, or maybe unfortunately, her mystery man hadn't visited her anymore.

A tiny smile played on her sister's lips. "Gin rummy, you're such an old lady," she said, snickering. "You know you're going to win anyway. Cheater."

Okay, yeah, she did win a lot because of, well, her gift she guessed. "Don't make me start whining."

"I think I've got a deck of cards in my bag. Be right back."

As her sister got up and headed toward the back of the Cessna, Andre emerged from the pilot's cabin. Nika instinctively tensed when he sat on the long leather bench that paralleled her and Alena's bucket seats. He'd been perfectly polite and she couldn't get over the guilt gnawing at her insides. Every time she looked at him, she feared he could see what she was thinking. Unlike her sister, the constant lying didn't come as easy to her.

"Has your flight been comfortable? Do you need anything else?" he asked.

"Yes and no. The flight has been perfect." She really hated how courteous he was. Ever since the night they'd met, he'd gone out of his way to be extra nice to her. The first couple days she'd stayed in Biloxi before heading home, he'd asked her to breakfast, lunch, and dinner with him and Alena. And it wasn't just for show. The man treated her as if she actually existed. Something Nika couldn't say for her sister's past flings.

He crossed one of his long legs and shifted against his seat. "I appreciate you agreeing to come to Miami. Your sister said she wouldn't travel anywhere without you. It's nice that you could come."

"You might not say that if I hurl on the descent," she said dryly, not exactly joking. The only good thing about infiltrating the man's life was that Nika didn't have to pretend to be someone else. She and Alena had been forced to lie over the past year, but this time, they could be themselves and it was refreshing.

To her surprise, he laughed. "Have you been to Miami before—" Andre frowned as his satellite phone rang. "Excuse me," he said, already answering. "Yes…Are you sure the threat is credible…Are the vehicles armored…Just make sure we have extra security."

Nika's stomach twisted as she digested his words. She glanced out one of the small circular windows in an effort to appear as if she wasn't eavesdropping. Clear blue sky was all around them, but she couldn't block out Andre's conversation. It was obvious the man had increased his security. The only question was, why. *Could he know what they were doing?* No. She shook the thought away.

"Hey." Alena's hand on her arm caused her to jump. "You okay?"

"Yeah, fine."

"Good, I found those cards. Are you ready to—"

Nika cut her off as Andre set his phone down. "Did you say heightened security? Is everything okay?"

He nodded, but didn't seem overly concerned. "There was an unconfirmed threat against my life so we've heightened security. It's standard for when I travel to

Miami. Don't worry. The security firm I've hired is the best. The owner is ex-CIA and he's personally heading up our security detail. He knows what he's doing, trust me. If you'll excuse me, I need to speak with the pilot." Before he walked to the front, he leaned over toward Alena.

Nika stared out the window again. The last thing she wanted to watch was her sister make out with Makarov. She already felt bad enough that her sister was using her body to get close to this man. Despite what the tabloids said, Alena rarely took lovers and she hated that her sister was doing this. She hated everything about the entire situation in fact.

"What the hell was that?" her sister whispered as Andre disappeared behind the pilot's door.

Out of habit, Nika glanced behind their seat, but the rest of the cabin was empty. She'd thought it strange that Andre had opted to fly without security but now she understood why. Men were already waiting for them in Miami. "He was talking about increased security. We have a right to know what's going on."

Alena's lips pulled into a thin line.

"Did you hear what he said about the head of his security team?" It appeared as if they might have gained a new problem, but her sister seemed completely unaffected.

"Yes, he's ex-CIA so that's wonderful for us. More protection in case we need it."

Nika gritted her teeth at her sister's words. She knew what her sister was doing and she understood. That didn't mean she liked it. They had to consciously operate as if someone was listening at all times. Which meant she couldn't argue with her sister even if she wanted to.

The plane dipped suddenly so Nika grappled for her seatbelt. "I didn't realize we were so close," she muttered. For how often they traveled, Nika hated the landing more than anything. Every single time she feared they would crash.

The overhead intercom buzzed for a second, then the pilot's voice came over the radio. "We should be touching down in about fifteen minutes for an early arrival. Looks like clear skies and a temperature of sixty-eight degrees. Please fasten your seatbelts as we prepare for landing."

Gripping her armrest, Nika tried to focus on anything other than the vision of their plane plummeting toward the hard earth at a thousand miles an hour. Twisted metal, burning debris, the smell of burning flesh. She squeezed her eyes shut as if that could somehow block out her thoughts. Even though she knew the chances of crashing in a plane were slim compared to the chances of dying in a car crash, her heart pounded wildly against her chest.

When Alena squeezed her arm, Nika's eyes flew open. "Thanks."

As her heart rate returned to normal, Nika reminded herself that they had a hell of a lot more to worry about than a plane crash anyway. Like the fact that they could be killed if anyone discovered the real reason they were going to Miami.

* * *

Declan scanned the surrounding area of the private airport as he walked around the nose of the twin engine Cessna. Black tarmac surrounded them for at least three hundred yards on all sides. He'd picked the most deserted area of the airport for Andre's landing. Unless a sniper was hiding on top of one of the airport storage facilities—and Declan had cleared them all—Andre was safe. Safe being relative considering Declan still didn't know the real intentions of the two women in the plane with him.

Declan's skin tingled and burned at the thought of meeting Nika Brennan face-to-face. After their last meeting weeks ago, he'd forced himself to stay out of her head. As a dream walker he'd always tried to use his gift to help others. When he'd been inside her head, he'd felt himself growing attached to her. Protective even. It had been a foreign, disturbing experience.

With the exception of their erotic games, her mind was locked up tight. Occasionally he'd get flashes of random scenes of violence but nothing made sense and she didn't think about *anything* in her dream state long enough for him to latch onto. As if she was purposely blocking her mind.

And he still couldn't figure out *what* she was. Maybe she was psychic, but then again, maybe not. The last psychic he'd encountered had been nothing like her so he had no way of gauging. When she'd asked him if he was a night walker, he'd known it was time to put some distance between them. Unfortunately all he wanted to do was touch her, hold her, kiss her. Wipe away those frown lines when he could tell she'd had an upsetting day.

He'd been in so many individual's minds over the years he'd lost count. No one ever remembered his probing. Until Nika. When he'd worked with The Agency, one night he'd be invading a known terrorist's dreams and the next morning he'd be interrogating the suspect who was none the wiser.

Each night he spent with Nika, he'd been fascinated that she remembered everything about their encounters. He couldn't know for sure if she'd know him in real life until they met.

After Vernon had given him the files on the Brennan sisters he'd done some extra research. From what he'd uncovered, the women's lives were an open book. Alena modeled occasionally and partied regularly. Nika had traveled with her sister since graduating college but she'd been a very serious student and did a lot of freelance web design. From her portfolio, she was damn good. They had money from a trust fund and traveled whenever they felt like it. Which was quite often. A few weeks' vacation in Antigua, then off to The Hamptons.

Next, Europe. They definitely didn't stay in one place for long. Which made them very hard to track. Despite their travel, Nika seemed to work a lot, seemed to enjoy what she did. Her portfolio was impressive.

Nothing in their files suggested either of them should know anything about the paranormal, though. The words night walker weren't something Nika could have pulled from thin air. Yet, she'd asked him with absolute certainty.

Her question and their strange dream encounters suggested there was a hell of lot he didn't know about her or her sister. And that had put him on high alert.

"Boss, the place is locked down. The warehouses are secure and the rooftops clear," Clay Lamos said, as he came to stand next to him.

"Good." Declan checked his SIG one more time before he tapped his earpiece, turning on his communicator.

"Where'd you hear about this threat against Makarov anyway? You sure it wasn't meant in connection with Andre's father?" Clay had been with Declan since he'd started Gallagher Security.

Even though Clay had been in the Navy, he and Declan had worked missions all over the world together when Declan had been with the CIA. Although he trusted the man with his life, Declan was playing this one close to the chest. No specifics. "It's credible. I got it from one of my old sources. There's a threat against him and possibly one of the women he's traveling with. I don't have hard intel though."

As far as he knew there was no threat against the women but he was covering all his bases.

Clay nodded and pointed at one of the other men before he started giving instructions. While he ordered the men into position, Declan spoke into his mic. "The area is secure. The passengers can now disembark."

"Roger." The pilot waved once at him from the window before disappearing from sight.

As the airport employees rolled the retractable stairs toward the plane door, Declan and Clay followed and stood at the bottom.

Raw anticipation hummed through him at the thought of seeing Nika in person, especially after their last encounter. He could still remember the way she felt beneath him, the way she tasted and the way she sounded when she came. He bit back the twinge of disappointment when Andre appeared in the doorway first. Damn, he felt like a randy teenager with his first crush.

Wearing one of his trademark Armani suits, Andre stepped down with Alena Brennan holding onto his arm. The pictures Declan had seen of her didn't lie. The woman had an old Hollywood kind of beauty. She wore tight, dark jeans, three-inch knee-high boots over them, a belted coat and oversized sunglasses to match her overdone hair.

"Declan." Andre smiled as he descended the stairs. "Thanks for taking this job on such short notice."

"Anytime. We've made some last minute changes on the route. I'd like to go over them before—"

"About that," Andre glanced at Alena, then back at Declan. "Give me a second, there's something I want to go over with you, too."

Before Declan could protest, the other man walked a couple feet away with Alena in tow and just out of earshot from Declan.

Declan frowned, but his attention was immediately diverted as Nika stepped out.

"Now *that's* the kind of woman I wouldn't mind waking up to every morning," Clay murmured beside him as she descended the stairs.

A primal surge of protectiveness swept through him. She might not belong to him, but he'd be damned if any one of his guys made a move on her. "She's off limits."

Surprise on his face, Clay nodded. "Understood."

As Clay headed to talk to one of the airport security, all Declan could focus on was the woman coming toward him. She clutched the side rail and held up a hand to block out the sun. Everything about her was a sharp contrast to her sister. She wore jeans, a plain white T-shirt, a fitted military-style leather jacket, and flat shoes that looked like ballet slippers. And her dark hair was pulled back into a simple ponytail.

When she reached the last couple stairs, he stepped forward and held out a hand to assist her. "Let me help you," he murmured.

Her head jerked at his voice. When her pretty mouth formed a small 'O', he realized she was noticing him for the first time. She yanked her hand back as if afraid to touch him and before he could react, she tripped over her feet and pitched forward, right into his arms.

Her hand splayed against his chest as she tried to get her footing and he attempted to get his body under control. Her fingers dug into his skin for a moment and he had to bite back a groan. What he wouldn't give to feel her claw her fingers down his back as he thrust into her. An exotic, rich scent that reminded him of cool Florida nights surrounded him. Fuck him, this wasn't remotely professional, but he couldn't seem to force himself to care.

Touching her in her dreams was nothing compared to holding her for real. She was petite and soft in all the right places.

His heart pounded mercilessly against his chest as her body meshed against his. As if his hands had a mind of their own, they settled on her hips—as if he had a right to actually touch her. His fingers flexed around her possessively. Something primitive kicked in and he had the sudden urge to grasp her and pull her tighter against him just to feel her warmth. For a split second her hold on him tightened, but just as quickly she shoved away and out of his embrace.

"Are you okay?" He kept his voice low, not wanting to embarrass her.

"I'm fine," she muttered. With her darker, caramel hued skin it was hard to tell, but she was definitely blushing. Her cheeks had a bright flush to them. More than anything he wanted to take those too-dark sunglasses off and see the expression in her eyes. In her dreams, those green eyes of hers were electrifying. He wondered if they'd be the same in reality.

"Nika, are you all right?" Her sister was by her side and shoving him out of the way before he could think of a halfway decent response.

"Yeah, I'm fine. Just embarrassed." She let out a light, self-deprecating laugh. He realized she was avoiding looking at him.

He frowned, not liking that at all. Did she remember their dreams too?

Her sister continued talking. "Andre wants to take me to lunch, just the two of us. You wouldn't mind driving back to his villa without me would you?"

"It's fine." Nika seemed more resigned than anything as she spoke.

"There are already rooms set up for both of us and you'll be with his bodyguards the whole time." Alena flicked her wrist in Declan's direction, but Nika didn't follow the motion.

Declan watched as her jaw clenched, but instead of arguing like he expected, she nodded. "Fine." Her voice was tight, annoyed.

Leaving the two women alone, Declan strode toward Andre, who was talking on his phone. As he approached, the other man muttered a quick goodbye then slid his cell phone into his jacket pocket.

"What's this about going somewhere special for lunch?" Declan asked. That wasn't part of the security detail he'd been prepped for.

"I've worked a lot the last couple weeks and I want some alone time with Alena. I'll take one of your security details with me, but I want you to make sure her sister gets back to my place."

Warning bells went off in Declan's head. If the woman wanted to kill him or kidnap him, or whatever she had planned—if anything—this would be the time to do it. Andre had been insulated at his casino, with heightened security there all the time. Maybe their plan was to get to him in Miami. "That's not a good idea. You've had too many threats lately."

"Your concern is noted, but I always have threats and it's just lunch." There was an edge to the man's words.

Declan nodded once. Andre was his client and he didn't argue with his clients unless they were putting themselves in imminent danger. "Okay, I'm heading up your detail though."

"No, I want you to go with her sister. Alena's very protective of her and I told her you were the best. I can't tell her I'm giving Nika second best now."

Declan mentally sighed, but outwardly kept his expression calm. "How well do you know this woman?"

Andre's features went carefully neutral. "I don't allow someone into my house without checking them out first. You know that."

"I do know that, but you hired me to do a job. You're my priority."

Andre raked a hand through his normally immaculate blond hair, the action out of character for the polished man. "I know and I...I'm sorry but the woman is driving me crazy. She's so hot and cold, I can't get a read on what it is she even wants... And you don't fucking care about that." He straightened abruptly, all business again. "I want some time alone without any interruptions."

In the end, Declan knew Andre could do whatever he damn well pleased. Declan's guys were the best so he wasn't worried about that, but he wanted to be the one protecting Andre. Still, he knew when to push and when not to. If he pushed too hard, Andre could let him go completely. "I'll take care of her sister for you."

"Thank you."

Declan briefed his men on the change of plans before getting into the back seat with Nika. Against his better judgment he watched as Andre left with Alena and four of his men. Two were ex-special forces and the other two were former members of the FBI's hostage rescue team so he wasn't worried about their capability.

He glanced up front as Clay put the SUV into drive, then looked at Nika's profile. Normally he drove but he didn't want his attention divided from her. She hadn't said two words since she'd gotten in the vehicle and she still hadn't taken off her sunglasses.

The need to see her eyes surprised him. Pictures were never the same and he knew that she was purposely ignoring him.

"How long do you plan to stay in Miami?" Declan asked.

She lifted her shoulders, the action jerky instead of casual as he assumed she wanted. "I'm not sure."

"I think your sister might be a while. Andre wanted to make sure you were taken care of, so is there anything you'd like to do? Shopping or sightseeing?" He shifted his leg so that their knees were almost touching.

"I'm fine, thank you." She turned toward the window and crossed her legs away from him, effectively dismissing him.

His hand clenched against his leg as he had to restrain himself from reaching out and cupping her cheek. From touching and exploring her the way he had in their dreams. He didn't have a right to touch her, even if every fiber inside him said he did.

Forcing his unprofessional feelings on lockdown, he shifted back in his seat and faced the road. Maybe the intoxicating woman was a psychic after all. One way or another, he was going to find out.

CHAPTER SIX

Alena crossed her legs away from Andre and fiddled with her seatbelt strap. Right now the only weapon she had was body language and psychological games. The man was confused as hell about what she wanted and she could tell it was driving him crazy. She felt really guilty, but she needed the advantage.

He wasn't a playboy. She'd done enough research to know that. And the past couple weeks spent with him had only confirmed the truth. Still, he was used to getting what he wanted, especially when it came to women. Right now he wasn't. And it was making him crazy.

"Your sister will be fine." His deep voice so close to her ear caused her to turn toward him.

She sucked in a quick breath to find him inches from her face. So far he hadn't pressured her to sleep with him. He certainly wanted to, but the man had been incredibly respectful. She knew he was restraining himself, holding himself back, but he desperately wanted to sleep with her. That wasn't arrogance on her part, she could see it every time he looked at her. The lust in his eyes was potent and scorching. Unfortunately, she wanted him just as bad. The realization had been unexpected. "I know, I trust you," she murmured.

In response, he reached out and tucked a loose strand of hair behind her ear. Even though she had plenty of motivation to lie to him, it was impossible to deny her attraction to the man. When he touched her, her body simply reacted. Like a switch flipping on, heat bloomed in her lower abdomen and she hated it. Hated that the son of her enemy could make her want so much when previous lovers had barely stimulated her, even during sex.

Instead of kissing her mouth, he nipped her jaw. "I have a room prepared for you, but I'd like you to stay in mine tonight." And there it was. Right out in the open.

The plan was working so much better than she could have wished. So why was she feeling guilty? He was a means to an end. That was all. She couldn't afford to get soft now. She placed a hand on his chest. "Maybe."

She felt, more than saw the tension humming through his body and her answer did nothing to appease it. He didn't respond though. He sucked her earlobe between his teeth and gently bit down. She held back a moan as heat pooled between her legs. He got her so slick and turned on and they'd hardly done anything.

Out of the corner of her eye she could see the driver glance at them in the rearview mirror and she couldn't fight the inexplicable wave of shyness that rolled over her. She modeled seven to ten months out of the year and was used to taking her clothes off in front of strangers. She didn't want anyone seeing her and Andre intimate though.

"Andre," she whispered.

Sighing, he dropped a chaste kiss on her lips and leaned back, but his shoulders were taut with tension.

"So where are you taking me?" she asked, needing to fill the silence.

"It's a surprise."

"I hate surprises."

The corners of his mouth curled up slightly. He looked adorable like that. "That's too bad."

"Is that right?"

He shot her a sideways glance. "Say you'll share my room and I might tell you."

"Are you trying to blackmail me?"

"Is it working?"

"I don't think so." She bit back a smile at the frustrated expression that crossed his face. He looked like a kid who'd been told he couldn't open his Christmas presents.

Andre opened his mouth to say something when his phone rang. When he looked at the caller ID, he frowned. For a moment she thought he might not answer, but then he sighed and slid his finger across the screen. "I told you not to call unless—What? *Damn it.* No, I'll be right there. Give me ten minutes. I'm not that far away."

As he hung up she knew they weren't going to lunch. Part of her was disappointed but another part of her was glad. All this time she'd been spending with him was wreaking havoc on her conscience. She needed to focus and remember the plan.

"I'm sorry, Alena. There's a problem down at one of my warehouses and—"

She pressed a finger to his lips. "It's business so don't apologize. I get it." And she did. Probably more than most.

Relief and surprise crossed his face. "I'll make it up to you tonight. I promise." He leaned forward. "Stop the vehicle."

"Sir, I don't think—"

"You're taking Miss Brennan back to my villa and I'm catching a ride with them." He motioned toward the SUV behind them. "It's a simple change of plans. Don't make me ask for another security team."

"Of course, sir." The driver glanced in the rearview mirror then pulled off onto the side of the road. He keyed his radio and started talking to someone in the other vehicle, letting them know what was going on.

Andre pressed a tender kiss to Alena's forehead. "I'll only be a couple hours."

Something foreign inside her twisted but she ignored it. She leaned closer so that her lips touched his ear. "I'll have my stuff moved into your room."

His pale eyes darkened at her words but he didn't respond. For a moment he looked like he wanted to, but instead he just slid from the vehicle. When the door shut behind him she had to stop herself from jumping at the sound.

Tonight was it. Once she slept with him there'd be no going back.

"This is reckless," the driver growled as he steered back onto the road.

The dark-haired man in the passenger seat shrugged. "He can do whatever the hell he wants man."

The driver muttered something she couldn't hear clearly, but it earned a chuckle from the other guy.

"What were we supposed to do? Restrain him?"

An odd possessiveness jumped inside her as they talked about Andre. Alena cleared her throat, reminding them she was there.

Instantly the vehicle went silent. She relaxed against the leather seat and stared out the window, forcing her mind to calm. After a few minutes she plucked her purse from the floorboard. She wanted to let her sister know she was on her way. As she reached for her cell phone, her entire world shifted in a sharp, violent twist.

Even though she was strapped in, her body jerked as her head slammed into the window. The strap pulled painfully against her chest and pain fractured in her skull as she tried to gain her bearings. Had they been in an accident?

The two guards in the front seat shouted something but she couldn't make out the words. Everything was too fuzzy. "What's going on?" she mumbled or at least she thought she said it out loud.

The SUV jerked again and this time she managed to brace herself with an arm as the vehicle violently jolted.

A scream tore from her throat as glass and metal crunched all around them.

Her world started spinning out of control. Nausea bubbled up. Was the vehicle rolling? She reached out a hand to brace herself on the seat in front of her but grasped air.

Suddenly everything jerked to a halt and an eerie silence descended inside the vehicle. She pressed a shaky hand to her temple. When she looked at her fingers, they had blood on them. Struggling against her seatbelt, she leaned up and tried to check the driver's pulse. She couldn't reach him though.

His head lolled to the side almost unnaturally, but it looked as if he were breathing. From her position it was too hard to tell. The other guard unstrapped his seatbelt and swiveled to look at her. It was as if everything was happening in slow motion.

Shaking her head, she tried to get a grip on her surroundings.

"Are you okay ma'am?" The dark-haired guard asked.

"I think so. What's...what's going on?"

"A semi-truck clipped us—" He abruptly stopped talking as he focused on a point behind her head. "Get down!"

Instinct beat out curiosity. She threw herself down on the seat.

Loud pops surrounded them as glass shattered everywhere, covering the inside of the vehicle. Just as suddenly the noise stopped. She didn't want to move. Was too afraid. But she knew she had to. She tried to lift her head, to push up, but everything swam in front of her. She stared down at the leather seat, but it was all blurry.

Voices, male voices, seemed to be saying something in the distance, but she couldn't make out anything. Maybe she'd lost more blood than she realized. She couldn't hold her body up and collapsed back against the seat as darkness sucked her under.

* * *

"Where exactly is Andre's place?" Nika's sexy voice filled the interior of the SUV.

Declan glanced at her, surprised by the question. He'd expected silence the rest of the drive. "It's in a gated community near Star Island." Before he could elaborate, his cell phone buzzed. One of his security team. "Yeah?"

"They fucking ambushed us! Andre left about ten minutes ago for some emergency but the girl is gone and we're completely immobile." Kevin's hoarse voice cut through the line. "We need an ambulance."

His mouth went dry. "SITREP, now." He might not be in the Corps anymore, but some things stuck with him. He needed a breakdown of what the hell was going on.

"A semi-truck and a fully armed Humvee came out of nowhere, boxed us in, and shot out the engine."

"Where's Andre? Is he alive?"

"He's not even here. They must have planned to take him but he left when he got a call."

"Wait, what? *Who* took her?"

Though she couldn't hear Kevin, Nika straightened at Declan's words. There was no doubt he meant her sister.

"Oh my God! Someone took—"

He held up a hand, needing her silence while he got all the details. To his surprise she was quiet but he could feel the fear rolling off her. She was completely still, watching him intently. He kept her in his periphery, not wanting to look at her face and get distracted. He forced himself to tune her out as his guy continued.

"Boss, we don't know. They wore masks, non-descript fatigues and carried M-4's. Fucking assault rifles."

"Fuck," he muttered. At least they'd been wearing masks. That meant they might want to keep her alive.

"What's going on?" she shouted as she gripped his forearm.

Ignoring her, he asked, "Did they say anything? Make any demands?"

"No, just that they'd be in touch."

"Is anyone else injured?"

"Ethan's hurt, but it's from the crash. If we get him to the ER soon he'll be okay. The only time they opened fire was when they blew out the windows and the engine. Boss, I recognized a tattoo. At least one of the guys is ex-military. Special Forces. These guys are pros."

They'd have to be to do something like this in broad daylight. Andre's lunch trip had been unplanned. Which meant somehow they'd been watching and waiting for him. Or they had an inside source. Even thinking of the second option made Declan see red. "Where's Andre now?"

"He's with the other team."

"Is there a chance the woman was involved?" He ignored Nika's inhalation of breath next to him. She'd be starting to figure out part of his conversation by now.

"Anything's possible but I don't think so. She was injured, bleeding. She was unconscious but breathing. It sounded like they planned to ransom her or..." He didn't finish and Declan didn't need him to.

Alena Brennan was a beautiful woman. These shitheads could have taken her for any number of reasons. Shit, shit, shit.

"Shit boss, I'm fucking sorry."

"We'll discuss this later." He wouldn't blame two guys for not being able to take on an assault team, but Declan wanted to know why his team hadn't called him to let him know the change of plans. That was unacceptable protocol and he ran a tighter ship than that. He reined the question in for now. There'd be time enough for that later. "We're on our way."

"What the hell is going on? My sister's gone? Where's Andre? Is she hurt? Who took her? We need to help her!" She machine-gun fired words at him, her grip on his arm tight and unforgiving as her short nails dug into his skin.

"I need you to be quiet," he said calmly. "I'm going to find out who took her but I need fucking quiet while I track..." He trailed off as he got to work. He was good at tuning people out and right now he had to ignore her. As he'd been talking to Kevin, he'd retrieved his tablet and had already pulled up his company's GPS program. Declan logged the location of Kevin's vehicle. His men were on a deserted stretch of road that ran parallel to I-95. Ethan had been the lead driver. Why the hell had he even gone that way? They'd been sitting ducks. "They're here." Declan held out the device for Clay, who simply nodded and took a sharp turn toward the nearest exit.

He started to call the team protecting Andre when a tight grip on his arm stopped him.

"What the hell is going on?" Nika's voice was softer now, but a raw, thrumming panic threaded through each word. When he faced her, she stared at him without her sunglasses as a barrier. Fear was clear in her startling green eyes, sharp against her caramel skin. Whatever her and her sister's plan—if they even had one—this hadn't been part of it. He'd seen enough terror on the battlefield to know that hers was real. She loved her sister and was worried for her. He definitely understood that kind of love and loyalty.

A momentary wrench of compassion squeezed his heart. He had a job to do and comforting her wasn't part of it. But he covered her hand with his and squeezed.

"Someone ambushed the vehicle your sister was in. She was kidnapped but she wasn't their main target so it's likely they don't want to hurt her. They were wearing masks, which is definitely a good sign. It means they want to keep their faces hidden from her because they're not planning to kill her." He couldn't be absolutely sure, but for now he'd lie to Nika. "They said they'd be in touch, which is also a good sign. They'll likely want to ransom her." At least he hoped so. "I'm going to do whatever it takes to get her back."

"You swear?" Her voice cracked, sending an arrow straight through his heart.

"Yeah, I swear." Somehow he squeezed the words out even as he wrapped an arm around her shaking shoulders. *Never make promises you can't keep, son.* That was something his father had taught him years ago. Long before he'd joined The Agency. Emotional entanglements could get him killed. Something he knew, something he lived by. For some reason it was hard to give a shit when he looked into the most beautiful, haunted green eyes he'd ever seen.

God, she felt so fragile in his arms and he hated it. To his surprise she hugged him back, her arms going around him in a tight grip for just a second before she pulled away and straightened. "Please find her." Her voice cracked again.

"I will."

CHAPTER SEVEN

Nika paced along the plush carpet of one of Andre's guest bedrooms. Oh God, her sister was gone.

Taken.

And they hadn't called the police. She thought she might understand why but she needed to talk to Declan about that. She scrubbed a hand over her face, hating this feeling of powerlessness. Alena had been taken for who knew what purpose and was out there right now. Her sister had been trained by their uncle but still, she had to be scared. Anything could be happening to her right now.

Iciness flooded through Nika. They needed to find her. Declan had sworn he would.

Then he'd dumped her in this room. She didn't know who he was exactly, but she knew there was more to him than met the eye. A lot more. It couldn't be a coincidence that the man haunting her dreams looked *exactly* like the head of Andre's Miami security team.

Everything about him was the same, right down to the slightly crooked bottom tooth and the almost invisible scar near his left eye. The man was even better looking in person—in an edgy, rough sort of way—and that in itself was unnerving. Dark hair, espresso colored eyes, pronounced cheekbones, broad jaw, and even broader shoulders.

But his stare. God, his stare was enough to make her nerve endings sizzle with the memory of what he'd done to her with those full lips and strong hands. Their last encounter had been more than intense. An unwanted shiver rolled over her skin. She shouldn't even be thinking about that when her sister was missing.

Oh God, her *sister*.

Clasping her hands against her stomach, Nika forced herself to stop pacing and to *think*. She couldn't have a breakdown right now. Not when Alena needed her most. It seemed impossible, insane even, that Alena had been kidnapped, but unless her sister had planned another operation without telling her, they had a very serious problem. In her heart, Nika knew her sister would never put her through this torture. Since they were kids Alena had gone out of her way to look out for her. No, this was a real kidnapping.

Well, she wasn't going to sit here and do nothing. Shrugging out of her leather jacket, she tossed it onto the bed and opened the door. One of the security guys was at one end of the hallway with his back to her.

Luckily for her, the palatial two-story villa would be easy to get lost in. If Andre and his men thought they could keep her cooped up while her sister was fighting for her life, they were out of their minds. She was going to be kept in the loop on everything that happened.

Keeping her eye on the security guard, she rushed to the other end and disappeared around the corner only to find another hallway that looked exactly the same. Oversized gold-framed paintings hung along the walls and a string of dark wood doors lined the corridor.

Last she'd seen, Andre and the head of his security had been downstairs arguing. If she could find out what was going on or something about Andre's father, now would be the time to do it. For all she knew that bastard Yasha was behind this. Maybe he'd figured out who they were. That seemed like a stretch, but she couldn't disregard anything at this point.

Her heart pounded against her chest as she tried the first door. It quietly swung open into an obviously unused guest bedroom. The next door opened just as silently but that room wasn't empty. *Oops.*

The sexy, powerful looking security guy stood at the end of a large bed, cell phone in hand. When their gazes connected, his dark eyes immediately narrowed. "I'll call you back," Declan growled into the phone before touching the screen. "What the hell are you doing?" he demanded.

Nika had learned that sometimes the best thing to do was go on the offensive. "No one's telling me anything and I want to know where my sister is and what's being done to find her!" She felt a little crazy yelling, but couldn't stop herself. She'd shout this whole house down to get answers.

He rubbed a hand over his face and his voice was much softer when he spoke again. "We're doing everything we can to locate her."

Forcing herself to remain calm, she took a deep breath. "I want to know what's going on. No one is telling me anything and I'm not going to sit by and do nothing. If you don't tell me, I'm calling the police. In fact, why haven't you called the police yet? Or the FBI. Don't they handle kidnappings?" She wasn't actually sure what the laws were but on TV that's usually what happened. And yeah, the fact that she was using television as a guide was ridiculous, but it was all she had at this point.

"We're not involving the police. The kidnappers have already made contact with *strict* instructions and I'm going to follow them. I've handled this type of situation before. They're calling back in half an hour with their demands."

Her heart rate kicked up at the news. "They've made contact?" And no one had thought to inform her? "Alena's okay?"

"Yes, she's okay." Sighing, he walked past her and shut the door. "Sit."

"What?" She edged away from him, trying to avoid any contact. Being this close to him she felt exposed, both emotionally and physically. Even though it had only been in her dreams, the man had touched and kissed every inch of her. And she'd freely let him. Maybe she should feel shame, but the only shame she experienced was that she was even thinking about it while her sister was possibly hurt somewhere.

He pointed toward the bed. "Sit and listen. Please."

The please surprised her so she did as he instructed. Sinking onto the gold duvet, she wrapped her arms around herself and stared at him. "Well?"

"I'm only going to ask this once. Are you or your sister involved in this in any way?"

Anger punched through her like a physical blow. Her hands balled into fists, but she answered, understanding that he probably needed to ask for protocol. *"No."*

"I had to ask. I'm sorry." He didn't sound the least bit apologetic. He glanced at his watch, then back up at her. His dark eyes locked with hers, silently probing. "I'm meeting my team downstairs in less than a minute so listen carefully. We are *not* contacting the authorities in any capacity. If you do, you'll be putting your sister in danger. I'm a trained negotiator and two of my men are former members of the FBI's HRT. Ah, Hostage Rescue Team. Like I told you earlier, the men who took your sister wore masks, which likely means they don't plan to kill her. They wouldn't have bothered hiding their faces otherwise. As soon as they make contact again, we're going to start the negotiating phase. From this point forward, it's all about who has the most bargaining power. If I let you listen in on their call, do you promise to keep quiet?"

"Yes." She knew if she didn't, he'd kick her out and probably lock her in a room somewhere. She hated feeling helpless and wanted to be kept part of this as much as he'd let her. Unfortunately she realized he held all the power right now.

Something unreadable flashed in his dark eyes, but just as quickly, it was gone. "I need to make a private call. It's why I'm up here in the first place. Wait in the hall for me and I'll escort you downstairs in a moment."

Wordlessly she nodded and headed for the door. Even though his demeanor was rough and abrupt and more than a little rude, his deep voice had a strange soothing effect on her. After the door shut behind her, she sagged against the wall and closed her eyes. The man seemed so certain that the men who'd taken her sister wouldn't harm her. But he couldn't know that for sure.

* * *

Declan pulled out his cell phone and called Vernon Nash again. It went straight to voicemail.

Again.

He'd been calling non-stop since they'd arrived at Andre's villa and the FBI director hadn't picked up once. If this had been part of Vernon's plan, there was going to be hell to pay.

Frowning at the lack of response from the man, Declan slipped his phone into his pants pocket and opened his bedroom door. Her eyes widened with a fraction of hope when she saw him, as if she thought he'd learned something in the last sixty seconds. But she didn't say anything, just watched him carefully. She was skittish, but all his instincts told him she had no knowledge of her sister's kidnapping.

Still, she might have an ulterior motive for being here and the fact that he'd caught her sneaking into his room didn't look good. Until he could prove it, however, she was simply a concerned family member and he was going to operate under that assumption. And for all he knew, she remembered those damn dreams and she was wary of him. Or worse, afraid. He frowned at that thought.

"Do you have an idea who might have done this?" she asked as they headed for the stairs.

"Not yet." But he was damn sure going to find out.

"Andre has to have a lot of enemies. Don't you have any hunches or leads?"

"Until we start any sort of dialogue, I know as much as you do. We'll get your sister back." God, he hoped that was true. He placed a hand at the small of her back as they walked. It was stupid to touch her, but he didn't remove his hand. Touching her felt instinctive and natural and if he was honest, he liked it a little too much. He needed to protect this woman on a primal level.

Nika bit her bottom lip as he held open the door to Andre's office. He tried to ignore how vulnerable and tired she looked, but it was damn near impossible to push back the unwanted protective urges she brought out in him.

The two desks had been pushed together and they'd brought in another table to complete the triangle. Their laptops and tracking system had been set up. Now all they needed was for the kidnappers to make contact. If they'd waited for the Feds to get involved it would have taken too long and in his experience, Alena had a better chance of surviving without their involvement. No fucking politics or anything else getting in the way.

"Why don't you sit here?" Gently taking Nika's elbow—and trying to ignore the heat in his abdomen—Declan guided her to an unoccupied chaise lounge by one of the windows.

Andre was clearly surprised by Nika's presence, but didn't protest it so Declan assumed the man was fine with her here.

Wordlessly she did as he asked, but the fear shining in her eyes was bright. Even though what they'd shared was only in their dreams, he had an undeniable yet primitive urge to take her in his arms and comfort her. All his instincts told him not to trust her but he still couldn't shake that protective feeling.

"It's going to be okay. I promise." The second the words were out of his mouth, he wanted to take them back, but it was too late. He needed to *stop* with the fucking promises. If he couldn't keep them... The thought made him want to rip his heart out.

Surprise flared in her eyes, but it was obviously what she needed to hear. "Thank you," she whispered.

Forcing his legs to move, he joined Andre by one of the desks.

"How's Nika holding up?" Andre asked low enough for his ears only.

"She's genuinely scared. I could be wrong, but she's not involved in this."

Andre scrubbed a hand over his face. "I can't imagine either one of them being involved. It doesn't fit with their financial or personal profile."

Declan nodded in agreement. When the phone rang, he put in his ear piece and glanced back at Nika. He placed his forefinger over his mouth and she nodded. The last thing he needed was her going irate or saying anything at all.

"This is it guys." He answered on the third ring. "Andre Makarov's residence."

A mechanical voice came over the line. "Who is this?"

"My name is Declan Gallagher. I've been hired by Mr. Makarov to negotiate."

"I said no police."

"I'm not the authorities. I own Gallagher Security. We're a private firm with no ties to local law enforcement. You must know who I am since you took Alena Brennan from my guys." Something he was beyond pissed about. He should have been there with her and Andre. And his guys should have known better than to take the route they had. It didn't make sense. Right now he couldn't question the lead driver since he was in the damn hospital.

A slight pause followed. "Our demands are simple. We want twenty million dollars. Half in bonds, the other in small, unmarked bills. Mr. Makarov has twenty-four hours to get the money."

Declan glanced at Andre, but his expression was neutral. He was remaining quiet as they'd discussed. "You want twenty million for a woman he's dating? A woman you obviously kidnapped by mistake?"

"Unless Mr. Makarov wants her murdered like his late wife, he'll have the money. Tell him to check his personal email. Twenty-four hours, not a second more. I'll be in touch the same time tomorrow."

"We need proof of life—"

The phone disconnected before Declan could finish. "Damn it...Did we get a trace?"

Odell Dunn, a genius with computers, shook his head. "Sorry boss. He or they have some serious encryption. I thought I was getting close, but... you don't care about the details. I wasn't able to trace it. I'm going to see what I can do with the number, see if I can locate it now and find out who it belongs to, but if I'm guessing, he'll take the battery out immediately and guaranteed it's a burner."

Declan gritted his teeth, but nodded. He'd expected as much. Now he focused on Andre, whose face was pale, but the man looked pissed. "You need to pull up your email, Andre."

Odell moved from his seat and let the man sit. Declan looked away as Andre typed in his password. There was one new message from a sender called Mr. X.

Real clever.

"There's an attachment," Andre said quietly, as he clicked on it.

Declan's gut twisted as he imagined what they could have sent. The fact that the man had mentioned Andre's dead wife might signify that this was personal. At least on some level. It also meant they'd done their homework. It wouldn't be hard to find out his wife was dead, but not many people other than immediate family knew the circumstances surrounding her murder. They'd kept it very private. Declan knew because he'd made it his business to know.

As soon as a video stream popped up, the quiet buzz of the room turned to dead silence. Alena Brennan's arms were pulled above her head, her wrists cuffed to some sort of pulley system. She was fully clothed in jeans and her top, but her jacket and boots were gone. Her arms had been tugged high enough that she was on her tiptoes, stretched out, and she had a nasty looking bruise on the side of her face. That could have been from the accident though. Declan made a mental note to ask Kevin. The camera was somewhere above her and she kept looking around the room, as if she were unaware she was being recorded. She looked afraid, but not as if she was panicking. At least that was good.

"Oh my God!" At Nika's voice, he glanced over his shoulder to find her standing next to him. Damn, he hadn't even heard her move.

Declan stepped in front of her, positioning himself between her and the computer screen. "This is just a scare tactic. They want us to know they're serious. It's not in their interest to hurt her."

Her eyes were wide, horrified. "Did you see her face?"

"That's from the accident." At least that was what he was telling her. Declan placed calming hands on her shoulders but she shoved him away as she sidestepped him. Her green eyes filled with unshed tears and for the first time in as long as he could remember, he wanted to comfort a woman.

"I can get maybe half of the money," she said, turning to face Andre, completely ignoring Declan. "My sister makes really good money modeling and I can access some of her funds. I've also got some savings. Not as much as her, but I'll give you everything I have. But the other half..." Her voice broke on a sob. A few errant tears rolled down her cheeks but she swatted at them angrily.

Andre shook his head, his expression hard, but clearly not directed at Nika. "Nika, whatever they want, I'm going to pay. I don't need your money."

"What?" She looked as shocked as Declan felt.

They'd barely scratched the negotiation phase.

Andre cleared his throat and glanced at Declan. "I need to speak to you in private."

"Everyone out," Declan ordered. He lowered his voice when he spoke to Nika. "Everything's going to be okay."

She didn't respond, just swiped at more tears as she left the room. Once everyone cleared out Andre collapsed back onto the chair, his calm façade starting to crack.

Declan leaned against the edge of the desk. "What are you going to do?"

"What choice do I have?" His voice was harsh, raspy.

"You're willing to pay that much for her?" Declan kept his voice neutral.

"You'd rather I let her die?" There was an angry bite to his question.

"That's not what I meant. First, do you have that kind of cash lying around?" As the negotiator and head of security, he had to know everything at this point.

Andre nodded sharply. "I've got the bonds and some of the cash."

"Some?"

"I'm…going to ask my father for the rest."

"Andre—"

"You heard what they said. I'm not letting another woman die!" His loud voice reverberated off the walls, reminding Declan that Andre had a lot of personal demons he was probably battling right now.

The kidnappers were obviously playing on Andre's only weakness. His wife had been murdered because of him. Well, because of his association with his father,

Yasha. "I didn't think you even talked to your father anymore."

"I don't, but he'll give me the money," Andre said so matter of fact Declan didn't doubt it.

"It'll come with a price. You must know that. He'll want a favor in return."

Andre shrugged, but the action didn't come off as casual. "Maybe, maybe not. I have the rest of the money, I just can't get my hands on it within twenty-four hours. I'll pay him back within a week."

"What about Kiley?" Andre was private about his life but Declan was aware that Andre's half-sister hated their father.

"It's not like I'm going to bring him to my house in Vegas. Kiley is never going to know about this. No one is, except you."

Declan scrubbed a hand over his face, hating the thought of involving Yasha Makarov in anything. "Where is your sister anyway?"

"She's in Vegas, but I contacted her about the threat as soon you called me about Alena. She's going to increase her own security. If there's a problem, she'll come to Miami or I'll set her up somewhere else."

As another thought set in, Declan frowned. "You said you have the ten million in bonds?"

"Yes."

"Exactly or more?"

"Exactly."

"Is that common knowledge?"

"No. It's sort of a failsafe for emergencies. A few of my financial advisors and my sister are aware, but I don't broadcast it."

"What about your assistant? Anyone else you can think of?"

Andre's mouth pulled into a thin line. "I hired a man named Barry Green about six months ago. He handles a lot of the day to day operations at the Ivy when I'm not there, but I don't think he knows about it. Or he shouldn't."

Declan mulled over the information. The assistant could be innocent, but he was near the top of Declan's suspect list since he was so new. "Okay, make a list of anyone who might have knowledge of your financials and of any possible enemies. Any business deals gone wrong in the past five years, anything you can think of." Five years was a little far to go back, but Declan knew that people could be very patient. "I'm also going to want phone records from your main offices for the past six months."

"No problem. What are you looking for?"

"If there's a connection between the kidnapping and someone you work with, I'm going to do a search. I don't know that we'll be able to pinpoint a connection before they schedule the meeting but we'll try. Either way I'm assuming you want this investigated."

He nodded once. "Someone is going to pay for this." Andre's voice was low, deadly, and almost guttural.

Declan pushed up from the desk. "I'm going to send Odell back in here and run the diagnostics on the video. See if he can pick up any outside noise we might be able to use. Maybe they left personal metadata. I doubt it, but we'll run every program possible on it. After I check on Nika, I'm going to make some calls around town to see if anyone has heard anything about a kidnapping."

Andre nodded and pulled out his own phone, no doubt to start making calls to his financial people and unfortunately, his father.

He opened the door to find Odell and three of his other guys waiting, but no Nika. As soon as he rattled off instructions, he went in search of the woman who was now haunting his waking thoughts. It was likely stupid, but the need to comfort Nika after seeing the pain on her face was eating away at him from the inside out. It would just take a couple extra seconds, he told himself.

CHAPTER EIGHT

Declan's heart raced he descended the stairs for the second time. Andre's house was big, but it wasn't that big. He couldn't figure out where the hell Nika had slipped off to. Security hadn't seen her leaving through the main gates and none of his guys had seen her head out of any of the exits so she had to be here. Besides all her stuff was still in her room.

"Any luck boss?" Clay asked as he reached the bottom stair.

"No, have you heard from Kevin?" Clay was fielding calls for Declan as he tightened things down at Andre's.

"Yeah, doctor said Ethan is out of surgery and should be able to talk in a few hours. As soon as the meds wear off. Kevin's with him for now."

Declan hated that he wasn't there. "Keep me updated. And tell Kevin to head out soon. He needs to get a few hours of sleep. I'll send more guys to the hospital." And he planned to go himself as soon as he could. Ethan Ford, the driver of Andre's vehicle had suffered a serious head wound. Declan was concerned but he also wanted to know why Ethan had taken an out of the way route when they were ambushed. It certainly hadn't been part of his orders. Kevin hadn't known why either but Ethan had been team leader so he hadn't questioned him.

When Declan pushed the swinging door to the kitchen open, he paused at a scuffling sound. Glancing around the Mediterranean style room, he frowned as he took a step farther inside. An exotic, almost tropical scent that didn't mix with the braids of garlic hanging from the iron pot rack tickled his nose. He'd recognize it anywhere. "Nika?"

"Yeah?" Her tired, sexy voice rolled over him.

"Where are you?" He glanced toward the closed pantry door.

"By the window."

He found her sitting in the corner of the small breakfast nook. Her back was against the wall and she had one hand wrapped around the wine glass sitting on the circular mosaic table. She looked at him with red-rimmed, glassy eyes. He could see the feeling of helplessness in her gaze and it clawed at him.

Declan pulled one of the bar top stools from the wall and sat across from her. "Have you been in here the whole time?"

"Yeah. I hope Andre doesn't mind that I opened this." She nodded to the long-stemmed wine glass and open bottle of red wine.

"He won't care. Have you eaten anything today?"

She shook her head. Her green eyes filled with tears but they didn't spill over this time. She looked so small and lost as she stared at him. That stupid need to protect her swept through him with an uncomfortable, unfamiliar intensity.

"Come sit at the island, I'll fix you something." He shouldn't be taking the extra time, but fuck it. His guys were all doing what they were supposed to be doing and the place was locked down tight. Without waiting for her response, he picked up the bottle and glass and headed across the expansive room.

He heard her pull out a chair as he opened the refrigerator.

"Why are you being so nice to me?"

Declan glanced over his shoulder. "Is there a reason I shouldn't be?"

"Earlier you asked if I was involved in all this," she muttered.

Biting back a sigh, he pulled out one of the plastic containers. "I was just doing my job. How does turkey and Swiss on wheat sound?"

"It's fine, thank you."

She was silent as he fixed her sandwich. Normally silence didn't bother him but it somehow unnerved him with her. Maybe it was because it felt as if there was something unspoken simmering between them. He was tempted to ask her about the dreams, but held off. Now was definitely not the time. When he was finished, he slid the plate in front of her. "Eat."

She eyed the sandwich as if he'd just given her one covered in mold, but picked it up anyway.

"We're going to get your sister back."

"You can't know that," she said in between bites.

"I'm good at what I do."

"What *do* you do?" she asked.

"I own a security firm that specializes in...clientele with high security risks." There was more to it than that, but that was all she needed to know.

She looked at him thoughtfully for a moment, her green eyes narrowing. "Andre said you used to work for the CIA. Is that true?"

He paused, but nodded once. "For over a decade."

She swallowed hard. "Have you ever dealt with a kidnapping before?"

"Since I started my company, twice."

"What about before then?"

He shrugged, hoping she'd understand what he meant.

"*Okay*, what were the outcomes of the two you can talk about?" Oh yeah, she understood.

Declan cleared his throat. He could lie to her, but something told him she'd know. And for a reason he didn't quite understand, he didn't *want* to lie. "One survived."

Nika dropped her barely eaten sandwich onto the plate and shoved it away. "So Alena's got a fifty-fifty chance then."

She was still in crisis mode, possibly mild shock. Until she came to terms with the situation, nothing he said or did would make a difference. He sat next to her and pushed the plate back in front of her. "Please take another couple bites."

She looked as if she might try, but just shook her head. "I'm not hungry. But I appreciate the effort. My sister is gone, I'm terrified and nothing will change that until she's safe." The strain was already wearing on her; he could see it in every line of her body.

Sighing, he nodded and motioned toward the door. "You look like you're about to pass out. I'll walk you to your room."

She slid off the chair and fell into step with him. Declan was partially watching over her because he was worried, but he didn't plan to let her off his radar again. Once she was in her room, he was placing a guard outside. Nika might not be part of the kidnapping, but she was still an unknown variable. One he'd agreed to watch out for.

Just because she got him hotter than any woman he'd ever met didn't mean he could let his guard down around her. The last woman he'd done that with had tried to kill him. He wouldn't make that mistake again.

* * *

Yasha glanced up at the knock on his office door. "Yes?" he barked out.

"It's me." Dima, one of best men.

"Come in." He'd given strict instructions not to be disturbed so he knew this would be important. Or it better be. When Dima stepped inside, Yasha frowned. "What do you want?"

"Your son is on the phone. He says it's important."

Though surprised, he didn't let it show on his face. Yasha closed the laptop in front of him and nodded at Dima. As soon as the door shut behind his employee, he picked up the house phone. "Andre. It's been a long time."

"Hello, father." Andre's voice was devoid of emotion.

"How are you?"

"I'm... For once tell me the truth. Did you have anything to do with this?" Now there was definite anger, what Yasha was used to receiving from him. It was an emotion he could deal with at least.

Yasha bit back a sigh. His son hadn't talked to him in two years thanks to his meddling bitch half-sister. It seemed things hadn't changed much. "Do with what?"

Andre cursed but didn't elaborate.

"Since this clearly isn't a social call, tell me what it is you want."

"Five million dollars."

Yasha leaned back in his chair. "Why?"

"Does it matter?" That bite of hostility was there, crystal clear.

"I'm assuming you need this in cash so yes, it does matter."

His son was silent so long Yasha wasn't sure Andre would answer. "The woman I'm involved with has been kidnapped and I need the money by tomorrow after-

noon. I don't have enough time to get all the funds together so quickly but I'll be able to pay you back within a
week or two."

"I do not want you to pay me back." Yasha smiled to
himself at the surprising turn of events. This was exactly
the opportunity he'd been waiting for.

There was a moment of silence. "What's the catch?"

"I need a small favor but we'll discuss it in person."

"My phone is secure if that's what you're worried
about."

"I cannot take the chance. I'll be at your house at sev-
en sharp with the money so tell your security to expect
me."

"Fine," he ground out.

"One more thing. Who is the woman you're seeing?"
Technically it did not matter, but he was truly curious
what woman had elicited such a response from his son.

"Will it affect your money?" Andre's voice was a razor sharp edge.

Yasha massaged the back of his neck. It was always
the same with Andre. Even when asking for a favor, his
own son couldn't forgive him. After everything he'd
done for him, Andre still chose that bitch over his own
father. "I'll see you tomorrow."

As he hung up the phone, he locked his office door.
His employees knew to knock but he wasn't taking the
chance of being interrupted. He bypassed the safe hanging behind one of his paintings and ran his hand along
the cherry wood paneling. After pressing the hidden

button he pulled the panel back further when it clicked open. None of his emergency stash had been touched. Not that he'd expected it to be.

He didn't like taking out any of his emergency fund, but in less than a week it wouldn't matter. He'd be richer than he ever imagined. After growing up in the slums of Moscow and clawing his way to the top, he deserved this.

A sharp rap on the door pulled his attention back to the present. After fitting the panel back in place, he opened the door to find Dima standing there.

"What do you want?"

"Is everything okay?"

He shrugged and stepped back to allow the other man entrance. Friends were a luxury Yasha couldn't afford, but Dima was often a sounding board. "Share a drink with me."

"How's your son?" Dima pulled two glasses from the small bar as Yasha sat behind his desk.

"He needs money. A woman he's seeing has been kidnapped but I didn't see anything in your report on him about a new girlfriend."

Dima glanced up from pouring their drinks, vodka bottle suspended in mid-air. "If he's seeing someone, then the relationship is very new."

Interesting. Yasha frowned as he pulled out the file he kept on his son. Since they hadn't talked in years, he had to monitor Andre any way he could. Andre had an unexplainable chivalrous streak where women were concerned, but to shell out millions for a woman he just started dating seemed impossible. And *stupid*. "We're meeting him early tomorrow so I want you to find out what you can on this mystery woman. Where she calls home, who she screws, all known associates, everything."

Dima nodded as he handed him a glass and took a seat across from him.

The liquor warmed him going down. "Do you have the information on the Lazarev brothers I requested?"

"I've got a guy working on it. One of the coroner's reports was harder to obtain. I'll email it to you when he's finished."

He nodded and took another sip of vodka. Yasha hadn't worked with the Lazarev brothers in over a decade, but they'd made a lot of enemies many years ago. For all three of them to die so recently had him paying much closer attention to his surroundings. Because if someone had targeted them, it stood to reason he might also be a target.

CHAPTER NINE

Nika's surroundings came into focus in a haze, but she pushed back her panic. Looking down she saw she wore a starchy hospital gown and was holding onto a pole. There was an IV in her arm attached to it. A low hum from the fluorescent light above filled the air. The sound was mildly annoying, but nausea swept through her, taking all her focus.

On unsteady feet, she pulled open the heavy bathroom door, rolling the IV with her. The room, a hospital room, was dim, as she took a step from the bathroom. And she wasn't alone. She recognized that almost immediately.

There was a shift in the air, a slight movement. Someone was in the shadows, between the bed and one of the windows. Moonlight streamed in, but it wasn't enough to make out the person. The white curtain surrounding the bed was pulled back, the sheets rumpled. She must have gotten up to go to the bathroom.

"What do you want?" she rasped out. When no one answered, she reached out her free hand for the nearest wall. Maybe there was a light switch somewhere. She started to fumble around when the shadow moved from the wall on silent feet.

She couldn't make out his face but he was definitely a man given his build. He had something in his hand. When he raised it, she realized too late it was a gun. Panic bloomed inside her. There was a sound of puffing air, once, twice.

"Nika! Wake up!"

Nika's eyes flew open at the sound of Declan's voice. Her arm flailed up to block her face until she realized he wasn't trying to smother her. "What...where am I?" she asked, though belatedly she realized exactly where she was. She'd been having one of her visions. Or possibly a dream, but she was fairly certain it was a vision. Someone was going to die. Unfortunately there hadn't been any identifiers this time. Sadness welled inside her, but she pushed it away as the remnants of the vision fell away and she settled back into reality. A reality where her sister was kidnapped.

"You're in bed." The light streaming in from the hallway illuminated his broad form. He stood, hovering over her, concern etched on his far-too-handsome face.

Though she knew she was, she still looked down at the gold sheets. Her heart rate slowed to normal as reality set in. She wasn't in a hospital, but Andre's guest room. "What are you doing in my room?"

"Are you okay? I was outside and it sounded like you were choking."

Rubbing a hand over her face, she shook her head, trying to banish the image of that shadow man trying to kill her. "I'm fine. It was just a dream. I was in the hospital and someone tried to shoot me..." She trailed off. *Why was she telling him any of this?* Her brain was still fuzzy and he did not need to be privy to any of her dreams, no matter *what* the content. Especially since she still wasn't sure what he was or if he remembered those wildly erotic dreams she'd shared with him. At this point she was too terrified to ask. "Why are you hanging around outside my room? Are you spying on me? Have you found out something?"

"Nothing new to report," he said with clear concern. Without an invitation he sat on the edge of the bed and completely invaded her personal space. "And showing concern isn't spying."

"Says the man sneaking around my room in the dark." Even though she was fully dressed she pulled the sheet higher against her chest.

Declan leaned over and turned the tableside lamp on. "It's not dark anymore."

Before she could move, his hand cupped her cheek and jaw. The action took her completely by surprise. His callused touch made her skin tingle, only adding to her awareness of how very masculine he was. Slowly and oh so gently, he rubbed a thumb over her cheek and for a moment white hot lust flared in his dark gaze. His eyes became heavy and hooded as he watched her, his desire a palpable thing. It was weird, but at the same time oddly normal, as if he'd touched her before.

"What are you doing?" she asked quietly.

He blinked then seemed to shake himself. Letting his hand drop, he turned the back of his palm and pressed it against her forehead. It took a moment for her to realize he was seeing if she had a fever. Despite her instinctive need to stay away from this man, her insides melted at the sweet action. "You're worse than Alena..." Her sister's name stuck in her throat. *Alena.* At least while she'd been asleep Nika had been able to put her fears to rest if only for a little while.

"Hey, your sister's going to be okay. We're getting the money together and at this point it's just a waiting game. It's not in their interest to hurt her." His hand was on her face again, cupping her cheek.

If he was trying to distract her, he was doing a mighty fine job. Her heart was a drum beat in her throat as she stared into his dark eyes. She should pull away, but couldn't find the strength. Even though his gaze never wavered from hers she could practically feel his heated eyes all over her. Undressing her.

When he leaned forward she had no doubt he intended to kiss her and it took willpower she didn't know she had to pull back a fraction. "What are you?" The words were barely a whisper on her lips.

A muscle in his jaw clenched, but he didn't retreat. "What do you mean?"

"Don't play games. You know exactly what I mean."

Only inches from her face, he smiled. Actually smiled. And the expression was one of pure, male, satisfaction. "You remember your dreams?"

As if on cue, heat pooled between her legs as wildly vivid naked images flooded her mind. Oh yeah, she definitely remembered, even though it was the last thing she wanted to be thinking about right now. Those dreams were seared into her memory forever. She swallowed, almost afraid to answer. Shit! What the hell *was* he?

Maybe he was a sensitive like her. She didn't think so though.

His touch strayed a little lower until his hand was on her neck and he was rubbing against her pulse point in little circles. "What do you remember, I wonder." His voice was low, sensual, and it sent another rush of heat straight between her legs. Maybe she should be embarrassed by how she reacted to him, but she had no choice. Her body simply flared to life, begging to be touched by Declan.

"Everything." The word popped out before she could censor herself.

"Are you psychic, sweetheart?" he murmured as he leaned a little closer, his spicy, masculine scent enveloping her. His voice was liquid sin, but the words hit her like a bucket of ice.

Sweetheart. A term lovers used. And they barely knew each other. Not truly. Because shared dreams didn't count.

Nika pushed slightly against his chest, not hard, but he moved back, giving her space. She felt oddly bereft at the loss of contact as she scooted back against her pillow. His effect on her body completely unnerved her, but she wasn't stupid. "You can't use sex to get answers from me." Or the promise of it. Because it was clear in his gaze what he wanted from her.

Gritting his teeth, he stood and she noticed the way he tried to casually adjust his black pants. Seeing that she'd affected him as much as he'd affected her gave her pleasure. But when she saw that her door was still half open, she cringed. Anyone could have walked by.

"This isn't over." His words came out hoarse, drawing her attention away from the open door.

Of that she had no doubt. But she wasn't going to tell him anything about her that he could use against her or her sister. Declan might want her physically, but he was fishing for something more. It was obvious he didn't trust her but she couldn't figure out if it was just his nature or if he knew something about her and her sister. He *had* worked for the CIA at one time after all. That was a huge red flag. And he'd been in her dreams before they arrived in Miami. That wasn't a coincidence.

Still, he couldn't know their real identity. Her uncle had taken care of their identities a long time ago. And *he* didn't make mistakes. Unless Declan had somehow tapped into her deepest memories. Her heart skipped a beat at the thought. It should be impossible, but... "What do you want from me?" She swallowed hard as she stared at Declan.

"I think that much should be obvious." His voice was dry.

She folded her arms across her chest and leaned back. An ache was spreading through the base of her skull and she didn't have the energy or desire to play mind games. "I'm tired so if you wouldn't mind leaving..."

The corners of his lips curved up into a harsh smile and as he pulled the door shut, he paused. "Sweet dreams," he murmured, before it clicked into place.

Gritting her teeth she punched her pillow. *Sweet dreams, my ass.*

* * *

Heart pounding, he hurried out of one of the hospital exits. The job was done and Ethan Ford was dead. Two shots to the chest, one to the head.

When he was in the parking lot and alone, he fished one of his cell phones out of his pocket and pressed the first speed dial.

Rick, the man who'd hired him, answered on the first ring. "Is it done?"

"Yes."

"Did anyone see you?"

"No. Are you sure you've taken care of the security tapes?" He might not have been actually seen in the room, but security was sure to have recordings of him entering and leaving the hospital at the time of Ethan's murder. And there were cameras in the parking lot as well. Once the death was looked into, it wouldn't be too hard to figure out he was responsible. Rick promised if he took care of Ethan that Rick would take care of the security.

"Don't worry. Everything is being handled. Has Andre gotten the money?"

"As far as I know, he's working on it. I think he's contacting his father for part of the funds. It should be a done deal."

"Good. This might work out better than if I'd taken him." Rick's voice was laced with smug satisfaction.

"How's the woman?" he asked cautiously.

"A little scared, but fine."

"On the video you sent of her—"

"It was staged. She's unharmed and will stay that way. This isn't about *her*."

"Okay." He still didn't understand Rick's hatred of Andre Makarov and he didn't plan to ask. As long as Rick paid him the rest of the money he'd promised, it didn't matter. "I'll contact you tomorrow if there's a problem."

"See that you do."

Sighing, he slid her phone into his pocket. One way or another, this would all be over soon.

CHAPTER TEN

Declan tugged his shirt over his head and tossed it on the chair next to the bed. "Damn it," he muttered to the empty bedroom. His brain fucking hurt.

After visiting Nika's room he'd gone to the hospital to check on Ethan. Kevin and a few other guys had been there, but they'd all left when the nurse in charge informed them they wouldn't be allowed to see Ethan until tomorrow. She'd promised to tell Ethan that they'd stopped by though. Back at Andre's place, Declan had found the man working tirelessly in his office and his own guys were on duty. Odell had run every program they had trying to nail down the kidnappers and Declan had put out every feeler he knew, calling in every favor just to get a lead on a potential kidnapper working in the Miami area. Still, nothing yet. He hated this waiting game. Made him feel useless. And he was trying really hard not to think about what Alena Brennan might be going through. Without knowing the identity of the kidnappers it was anyone's guess. The thought of any female being hurt, for any reason, made him see red.

He was edgy and not himself. It didn't help that the sexiest woman he'd ever met was a few doors away from him. He thought he'd seen a flicker of awareness—or

115

something—when he'd asked if she was psychic, but he couldn't be sure. Her eyes had dilated, but... gauging her reaction wasn't a fucking science. And he hated not being able to trust his instinct where she was concerned. She was clearly different, like him, but he didn't know how advanced her gifts were.

After changing into boxers, and forcing himself to ignore his erection, he slid under the soft sheets and picked up his tablet from the nightstand. He tapped on one of the files he'd saved and started scanning the names of possible enemies Andre had listed for him. Frowning, he focused on one name.

Rick Savitch. Unfortunately Declan didn't have enough information on him to get into his head during his dreams. He knew the rumors about the man, but he didn't even have a picture or a decent dossier giving him intimate details of the man's life. A simple picture would have made all the difference in the world. He'd have something to focus on as he tried to dream walk.

According to Andre, after the murder of Ivy, his wife, Andre had discovered she'd been having an affair with a man named Rick. And Rick hadn't been quiet in his accusations against the entire Makarov family. In no uncertain terms, he'd blamed the Makarovs for her death.

Since Alena Brennan's kidnapping had personal written all over it—even if she hadn't been the intended target—Rick was at the top of Declan's suspect list. Too bad he was a virtual ghost. Declan's best guy hadn't been able to find even the thread of a trail for his current whereabouts. The rest of the list contained almost a dozen names of enemies, but they were all business rivals. Hiring a group of well-trained professionals and trying to kidnap Andre seemed a stretch for a deal gone bad. It could happen though, so they weren't off the list, but they weren't at the top either.

Declan's phone buzzed across the nightstand, diverting his attention. "Declan here."

"Boss, it's Clay."

He frowned, and glanced at the caller ID again. "What number are you calling from?"

"Ah...Listen, I'm at the hospital. There's no other way to say this, but Ethan Ford is dead."

Panic punched through him. He'd just been there. Both the nurse and doctor had confirmed that Ethan had been conscious temporarily and was on the road to recovery. Declan had planned to visit Ethan again as soon as he could get away. "What changed in his status?"

"He was shot. Three times. Two to the chest, one to the head."

Shit. That was professional. "Anyone else hurt?"

"No one even heard anything."

Which meant the shooter would have used a suppressor. This must have something to do with the kidnapping. Declan had no doubt. "I'll be down there in twenty minutes."

"You might want to stay where you are. The cops are on their way and they'll be here before you. I know a nurse who owes me a favor. She's going to try to get me a peek of the video feed before they get here. I'll try to get a copy. If you show up your presence might piss off the cops."

Declan scrubbed a hand over his face. He and local law enforcement had crossed paths more than once because of a security op running into one of their investigations. Not exactly bad blood, but Clay was right. It'd be better if Clay could get a copy and get out. "Try and get a copy before the uniforms show up. Keep me updated. But don't tell any of the guys about this yet. And be careful."

"Will do."

As far as Declan knew, Ethan didn't have any family, but there would still be funeral arrangements to take care of. The fact that Ethan had been killed in the hospital sent up a giant red flag. From the sound of it, he'd been professionally murdered. Ethan hadn't been with Gallagher Security long, but he'd had a strong resume with a military background and no financial red flags. The man had taken a detour while working Andre's security detail on the same day they'd been attacked—for no discernible reason. Now he'd been murdered. It wasn't a far jump to conclude that Ethan had been involved with the kidnappers and they'd killed him to silence him. It would certainly make sense.

Declan scrubbed a hand over his face as he leaned back against his headboard. He needed to keep the rest of his team and Andre protected and find out if there was a mole on his team. Considering Andre was bringing his father into things in just a few hours, Declan also needed to get inside the older man's head.

If he could put it off, he would, but time was running out.

He closed his eyes and focused on Yasha. There was always the possibility that Yasha had been behind this whole mess as a way to get Andre to talk to him again. Declan wouldn't put anything past the gangster. As he honed his energy on the tall, blond criminal, he tried to mentally prepare himself for the darkness he knew he'd face. A man as evil as Yasha was sure to have a dark mind.

A young woman was stretched out on a bed. Crisp, white sheets underneath her. She was blonde, too skinny to be healthy, scars trailed down her arms. Eighteen years old at the most. Her dark eyes were hollow and dead even though Declan could see she was alive.

"Get on your knees," a familiar male voice said. It was Yasha, but he was younger.

Declan wanted to get out of his head, but made himself stay put. People saw the world uniquely so every dream he invaded played out differently. Some were flashes of places and things, others were actual scenes. Like a movie unfolding before him. Just like now.

The girl didn't make an attempt to get up. She mumbled something incoherent and spread her legs. Declan wanted to puke. This was just a sick memory of Yasha's. Occasionally Declan could push people's thoughts in another direction if he concentrated hard enough. It was the power of persuasion. Using a person's subconscious as a tool.

It didn't matter. Yasha's mind was dirty but it was strong. A switchblade appeared in Yasha's hand. He held it to the girl's throat and shouted at her in Russian. Still, she barely moved. He pressed harder and she cried out like a wounded animal. Crimson blood trickled down her soft skin. Yasha shoved a knee between her legs, slamming against her soft, breakable body.

He couldn't watch this. Wake up, wake up!

Reality rolled over Declan as he opened his eyes. Sweat trickled down his face and back. He could only imagine how that would have played out and he didn't want to. Trying to mentally shake the images did nothing.

The only thing that could wipe away the vision was seeing Nika. She was lightness in a way he didn't fully understand. Though it was definitely playing with fire and part of him knew it was a dangerous game he played, he didn't care. He craved seeing her again, even if it was only in a dream state.

He let his head sink against the pillow and focused all his thoughts and energy on the woman down the hall. Growing up, it had taken years of practice to choose whose dreams he walked through. Just like his brothers, Declan had mastered his gift at a fairly young age. Even after two years out of practice, once he'd dipped into her thoughts a few weeks ago, now it came as naturally as breathing.

His body relaxed, his breaths evened out and Nika's face swam before him. Bright, emerald green eyes. Smooth caramel skin. A smattering of freckles that were barely visible covering her nose…

While Declan adjusted to his surroundings, he tried to keep his presence unknown as he drank in the images playing in Nika's head. The reason he hadn't been able to see her dreams was because she'd known *he was there. Even if it was on a subconscious level, she'd known someone was in her head. Which would explain why everything he'd experienced had been happening in real time—relatively speaking. She was trying to protect herself.*

Like an old, silent movie, a vision played out in front of him. Two little girls huddled together in a tight space. A closet? One was older by a few years but they both had dark hair and dark skin. Tears streamed down the youngest girl's face but her head was downturned and he couldn't see the color of her eyes. His instinct told him it was Nika.

"What the hell are you doing here?" Nika's annoyed voice cut through the haze, until everything he saw completely dissipated and he found himself staring directly at her. She sat on the bed, arms crossed over her chest and a scowl marred her pretty face.

"I wanted to see you."

"Then knock on my door like a normal person and stop getting into my head."

"You didn't mind before."

"That's before I realized you were a real *person. I thought you were some illusion I'd dreamed up."*

"Aren't you curious how I do it?"

"Of course I'm curious, but I want you to stop. You have no right to be here. This is an invasion of my privacy."

"You're not supposed to remember my visits," he muttered.

"Oh really? So you visit other women's dreams and what, molest them too? I bet that's how you get your rocks off! Freaking pervert."

"Molest! Everything we've done has been based on your projections. Everything I've done, everywhere I've kissed, was because you wanted it to happen. I have no control over your thoughts."

She threw the covers off and jumped out of the bed. "My thoughts? You're out of your mind."

He bit back a smile, knowing it would only piss her off. "Technically speaking, I guess I am. But according to you, I'm your fantasy. Do you remember saying that to me when we first met?"

Her eyes flashed dangerously. "You're infuriating. Why are you even here? It's not a coincidence that you've been haunting my dreams before we even met."

"How do you know?" he asked.

"Because I don't believe in coincidences and you're surprised I remember you. For all I know, you're involved in my sister's kidnapping!"

"You can't believe that." Things weren't going exactly like he'd planned. Maybe he should just cut his losses, but he couldn't walk away from her. The woman fed some sort of addiction he didn't know he had.

"I don't know what to believe." Sighing, she sat on the edge of the bed and stared at a spot over his shoulder, refusing to look at him.

Emotions he didn't understand warred inside him. If he exposed what he was, it might convince her to open up to him.

Or, it could give her ammunition against him. The last psychic he'd revealed his weakness to had struck out at him at the first opportunity.

If Nika was a psychic, her powers were different than what he'd experienced in the past. If he wanted to get close to her, he had to give her something. "I'm a dream walker, Nika."

Her eyebrows knitted together in confusion. "Is that like a night walker?"

"Not even close. They create violent nightmares. I just watch." *And learn. And in her case, apparently, interact very intimately.*

"Just watch? Like a pervert?" *A smirk played across her full mouth. A mouth he desperately wanted to taste again.*

He ignored the second question. "I watch dreams and memories play out. You...you're different."

She frowned. "What do you mean?"

"I don't see your dreams. I see only you." *And not enough of her as far as he was concerned.*

She stared at him for a long moment. "What if I told you I wanted to see you right now? Not...here, but in your room." *Her voice had taken on a seductive, sensual quality.*

It surprised him but he knew himself well enough that he wasn't going to say no. It wasn't smart and it sure as hell wasn't professional, but...Nika was his. "What's stopping you?"

Declan opened his eyes as he jerked out of the dream state. For a moment everything blurred around him but just as quickly, the dim surroundings of his room came into focus. Either she came to see him or she didn't.

At the sound of the door rattling he automatically reached for the SIG on his nightstand, but he stopped himself. No one would have breached this compound and if they had, they wouldn't be as noisy as her.

His cock instantly lengthened at the sight of Nika stepping into his room. The outside security lights streaming through the blinds were the only source of illumination, but it was enough to see she wore long pajama pants and a skin-tight tank top. She'd been wearing shorts before but she'd obviously changed.

"What kind of games are you playing?" he rasped out. It sounded as if he had gravel stuck in his throat.

"I don't want to be alone tonight and I don't want to talk," she whispered.

His throat seized at her words, but he restrained himself from jumping her. She'd only said she didn't want to be alone. She didn't say she wanted him to jump her and take her on the floor—or up against the wall. Although that wasn't such a bad thought.

Nika knew she was taking a big chance coming to see Declan when he had the ability to invade her mind, but she couldn't stop herself. If she was being honest, she didn't want to stop. Not tonight.

He was the last man on the planet she should be interested in, but now that she'd discovered her fantasy man was real and she knew he was just as talented with his hands in real life as her dreams, she wasn't sure if it was a blessing or a curse.

Wearing simple blue boxers, he looked good enough to eat. Seeing his broad chest and trim waist in her dreams was nothing compared to real life. The smattering of dark hair covering his muscular chest was a stark reminder that he was all man. Everything about him screamed virility.

The few men she'd chosen as lovers had been a lot less physically intimidating than sin-in-the-flesh, Declan Gallagher. An unwanted shiver spiraled through her as she watched him. With a broad, muscular chest and scars nicking him all over, he looked like he had in her dreams. Well, their dreams.

He stalked toward her like a pure predator. His movements were sparse, economical. Everything about him screamed raw power. As he came to stand in front of her, she thought he was going to kiss her. The air between them cracked with electricity and even though sex wasn't her priority right now, she didn't want to be alone.

Surprising her, he leaned down and placed a chaste kiss on her forehead. "Come on. You need sleep." He nodded toward the bed, placing his hand at the small of her back.

She more or less let him propel her toward it, too surprised to do anything else. She'd thought he'd pounce, crush his mouth over hers, help her forget things for a little bit.

But... he headed for the other side of the bed, still half-dressed and slid in.

"You want me to sleep with you? Just sleep?" she asked, still standing on the other side.

He snorted. "I want more than sleep and you do too," he added, "but we're not doing this now. Not with your..." He trailed off and she realized what he wasn't saying.

Not with her sister missing. He was right. She might want him, but more than anything she just didn't want to be alone. If that made her weak, she didn't care.

Following suit, she got into the bed next to him. She expected to feel awkward, but it was the opposite. Laying down she rolled onto her side and wasn't exactly surprised when he settled in behind her and hooked his arm around her waist. He pulled her back against his hard chest and simply held her. She had no problem letting him. He felt like an anchor and she desperately needed one right now.

"You surprise me," she whispered, not wanting to disrupt the quietness of the room. She could feel his erection against her back, but he seemed content to just hold her.

"You're not ready." His voice was raspy.

Ice flooded her veins. "You know that from getting into my head?"

"No. I can feel it in every tense line of your hot little body. I don't want you to be with me just so you can forget about your sister. I want you completely willing. Mind and body. And not in a dream." The last few words were a seductive whisper.

Her mouth dried up and she was thankful her face was turned away from him. She'd thought she had him completely pegged, but was glad to be wrong. Her mind was a battlefield right now with fear for Alena and thoughts of Declan. She felt like a freaking nutcase.

As the seconds ticked by, she allowed herself to settle against him. It was so damn dangerous, but deep down she knew she could get used to his embrace. Too many what-if thoughts raced through her mind, making her insane. She'd thought about what Declan had said and knew he was right about the kidnappers keeping their faces covered. Still. "How long have you known...what you are?"

"You mean a dream walker?"

"Yeah."

"As long as I can remember."

"Does anyone else know what you can do?"

"You're just full of questions," he spoke against her hair, making her shiver.

"That's not an answer."

"My family does, but no one in this house knows what I am or what I can do if that's what you're asking," he murmured.

Oh. "Why'd you tell me then?"

His arm tightened around her waist. "No one will believe you if you tell them. Now no more questions, *a mhuirnín.* I'm tired."

His strong embrace seemed to have a ripple effect over her entire body. She wasn't precisely sure what *a mhuirnín* meant but she liked the way it sounded on his lips. His deep voice was an aphrodisiac she could definitely get used to. Sighing, she shut her eyes and savored the feel of his arms around her as she tried to force sleep to come. In a few hours the kidnappers would be calling and...damn it, her eyes welled with tears as thoughts of her sister in pain or worse flooded her mind. She closed her eyes, trying to banish the images.

Having a breakdown now wouldn't help anyone. They were going to get her sister back. She refused to believe anything else.

* * *

As Nika settled against him, Declan tried to ignore his erection. She had to feel it, but he wasn't going to make a move until the sexy woman was completely ready. Getting physically involved with her on this plane of reality was stupid, but it almost felt like a foregone conclusion. Simply kissing and tasting her would never be enough. She'd awakened something in him he hadn't known existed. The primitive urge to protect her and keep her safe was overwhelming.

Not to mention he needed to figure out where the hell her sister was and if this was all part of some bigger conspiracy. He refused to believe Nika was part of it though. Her terror and fear at losing her sister was real. So much so it was almost palpable. Of course that didn't mean her own sister wasn't using her, hadn't lied to Nika about the kidnapping.

Closing his eyes, Declan focused all his energy on Alena Brennan. Since he couldn't get in Nika's head without being discovered, he had to try her sister. If he could just get into her dreams, maybe he could discover where she was being held. A road sign, a landmark, someone's face. If she retained any of those things in her dream state, it could push them in the right direction and they'd be able to save her.

Nika hadn't said anything about her sister having a gift, but he couldn't be too careful. As he honed all his energy and thoughts on Alena, black edges of his dream state started to overtake him.

"Keep your ears covered," the little girl whispered.

"Why?" the smaller girl asked.

"Because I said so."

A woman screamed in the distance. The sound, like a wounded animal, jarred him to his bones. The scene blurred and shifted. Red paint—no, blood. Everywhere. All over a carpeted floor. On the sage colored wall. The smaller girl started to cry harder.

Suddenly the vision morphed again. Everything dipped and swirled around him before things came into focus. Alena was in the bathroom of what appeared to be a nightclub. There was a urinal. A men's bathroom. A man was there but his back was turned. A needle flashed... darkness swirled in front of him... Now she was on a bed rolled on her side fully clothed... A loud scream echoed in his mind. He saw only red. Bright, garish red, pushing him out of her head.

He opened his eyes with a start, his heart rate kicked up a fraction. Alena might not be psychic but her subconscious didn't want him poking around her memories.

Under his arm, Nika stirred with him, but thankfully she didn't wake up. Staring at her, he could feel himself falling under her spell and wondered what the hell he'd gotten himself into.

CHAPTER ELEVEN

Declan opened his eyes at the sound of a low buzz. He automatically tightened his grip around Nika's slim waist, but just as quickly released her when he realized the source of the sound. Ribbons of the early morning sun covered her face, but she didn't stir as he drew away. He knew she hadn't slept well last night. She'd been restless for the few hours she'd been in here, so he didn't want to disturb her.

Lying on her side, she had one arm thrown over a pillow and her dark hair cascaded softly around her face.

Though he didn't want to tear his gaze away, the incessant buzzing forced him to. Stifling a groan, he grabbed his phone from the nightstand. "Yeah?" he murmured.

"Sorry if I woke you," Vernon Nash said.

"About time you called me back." Declan understood that as Deputy Director of the FBI, Vernon would be occasionally unattainable, but a return phone call wasn't too much to ask. Especially when Declan was doing him a favor.

"I would have called you earlier if I could. The Department of Homeland Security has set up a task force to bring Yasha down. I've been in meetings for over forty-eight hours and was dark for half the time so don't start."

Declan knew better than most that the DHS had a virtual umbrella over all the major law enforcement agencies in the United States. He could only imagine the task force was a smorgasbord of acronyms and bureaucratic assholes. Something he definitely didn't want to get involved with. "Did you get my message?"

"Yeah, but I didn't understand. What the hell is going on with the Brennan sisters?"

Declan glanced down at Nika. She hadn't stirred but she could be faking. Easing off the bed, he shut himself in the privacy of his bathroom. "Alena Brennan has been kidnapped."

"*What?*"

"So you didn't have anything to do with this?"

"Hell no. Is this serious or a scam the women are running?"

"It's real and Andre is contacting his father for part of the ransom." Declan quickly filled him in on what had happened.

"Damn it," Vernon muttered. "We've been watching Yasha and word on the street is he's moving his shipment in four days."

Declan just grunted.

"Do you think the youngest sister will make a move on Yasha if given the opportunity?" Vernon's voice was grim.

"It's...possible. But doubtful. I'm still not sure why you think they're murderous assassins, but I don't see Nika killing someone." Something told Declan that if the women were behind the deaths of the Lazarev brothers—for whatever reason—Alena was the one who'd actually killed them, not Nika. There was a hell of a lot he didn't know about the woman, but she didn't strike him as a killer. She wore her emotions out in the open.

"Keep an eye on them...if you even get Alena Brennan back. Do you need any backup for the exchange?"

"Thanks, but no. We can't risk any law enforcement in this." Declan didn't need or want any outsiders involved in this.

"Have you learned anything *useful* from either woman?"

"No."

"I'm on a timeline. Nothing can happen to Yasha. *Nothing.* We've got to bring him down, save those women. Rumor is, there are kids he's moving too. This operation has to be stopped. Just... keep Nika Brennan on a short leash and away from Yasha."

Declan bit back a response. He knew how to do his job, but he understood the pressure Vernon was under.

Vernon continued. "I'll be in Miami tomorrow joining the rest of my team. Keep me updated."

After they disconnected Declan stripped and turned on his shower. The pulsing jets did little to ease the tension knotting his back and shoulders. The kidnappers would be contacting him in a few hours. He needed to meet with his men and make at least a dozen calls before then. Getting Alena back was the most important thing, but when she was safe, he was going to find out who'd taken her and killed one of his men.

And they were going to pay.

Declan wrapped a towel around his waist and mentally prepared himself to see Nika stretched out on his bed. Last night it had taken all his willpower not to finish what they'd started. His dick still hadn't forgiven him.

When he opened the door, Nika was gone.

* * *

Yasha barely glanced at the hostess as he and Dima entered the supposedly posh restaurant. It was done in all bright gold and red colors with pineapples everywhere. Fucking pineapples. He didn't understand the décor, but the view of the Atlantic was prime.

Not that he cared about any of that. Yasha would be going to see his son very soon with what Andre needed. But Yasha wanted to bring him something more. Unexpected, sort of a peace offering. While he responded to an email, he watched out of the corner of his eye as Dima slipped the woman a fifty. She palmed it smoothly then murmured something too low for him to hear.

It was positive news though, because Dima simply motioned with his head once. That meant his target was here.

Good.

They strode past the few diners, not surprised by how quiet it was. He supposed most people weren't up this early on a Saturday, but the place was open almost twenty-four hours and served breakfast. Some marketing tactic.

Winding his way through the linen cloth-topped tables, he inwardly smiled when his target spotted him.

Manuel's eyes widened a fraction as he shifted against his seat. Immediately he straightened and looked at his breakfast date, a tall redhead who was busy texting. Manuel said something to the woman that had her rising from her seat, phone in hand, without a backward glance. She flicked a look at both him and Dima, but just barely as she made her way to the bar. She'd left her purse so clearly planned to return.

"Yasha," Manuel said, nodding politely as Yasha sat where the woman had vacated.

"You haven't returned my calls." Something that pissed him off. But he didn't let his annoyance show, just kept his voice level. It would throw Manuel off more if he was civilized.

The other man nodded once. "I just got back in town this morning. On a job. Figured it'd be too early for you."

"What kind of job?" he asked, as if only mildly interested.

Manuel was a decent criminal. Fairly small-time, but did well enough to carve out a nice living for himself. He ran the occasional con and did jewelry heists—only out of town—to keep his income steady. For his low-level status, he seemed to have a decent pulse on the city. At least the criminal element.

Yasha occasionally came to him for information even though he knew the man hated him. He could see the fear and loathing every time they crossed each other's paths.

Manuel shrugged in response. "Just work. You know how it is."

Yasha guessed Manuel wouldn't say anything in public about any of his 'work' ventures. Just as Yasha wouldn't. He could never be certain when he was being followed. The FBI and DEA often liked to put tails on him so he was careful about his public persona. "I do know." He waited a beat of silence before continuing. "You're a very knowledgeable man."

Manuel just watched him, not responding one way or another.

Yasha picked up one of the gold forks from the table. He pressed it softly to the top of his hand. "Have you ever seen the damage a fork can do to someone's hand? All those nerves," he said. "I want to know what you've heard lately in regards to me or my son. Anything, no matter how small."

The other man straightened slightly, his entire body pulling taut. Unless he was a complete moron—and Manuel wasn't—he'd understood the not-so-subtle threat.

His lips pulled into a thin line as he reached around for his jacket, which was hanging on the back of his chair.

Dima made a move, as if to pull out one of his hidden weapons, but Yasha held up a hand.

Manuel retrieved his cell phone, swiped in his code, then his fingers flew across the screen. A few seconds later he handed the phone to Yasha. Manuel had typed up a text message but hadn't included a recipient.

Yasha read the message. *Man named Rick was asking about your schedule a few months ago. No last name. Didn't ask me specifically but I heard through the grapevine. Someone must have told him it was stupid to mess with you because the talk died down as quickly as it flared up. He did a few b & e's, all local, with a guy named Spider. Spider's dead and Rick is in the wind.*

"Why is this the first I'm hearing about this?" Yasha asked, passing the phone back to him.

Manuel shrugged. "It was trivial and I had no concrete deets."

Deets. Yasha nearly snorted. "For me, not my son?"

"You."

"Anything else?"

He shook his head. Yasha was good at reading people and while he could never be certain, Manuel didn't appear to be lying. He wouldn't, not out of respect, but fear. Which was fine with Yasha. He'd rather be feared than anything else. "If you hear anything in the future, no matter how *trivial*, contact me." He didn't bother with threats because he didn't have to.

Fear flared in Manuel's dark gaze as he nodded.

Yasha set down the fork and stood, not bothering with any more discussion. It was unnecessary. He'd gotten what he'd come for.

* * *

Declan sat next to Odell, tablet in hand. He'd been digging into the financials of a portion of men on his list of Andre's enemies but had tasked Odell with digging too. "Have you been able to eliminate any from your list?"

Odell didn't look over from his screen. "Only two. They're currently out of the country. Though they could have hired someone."

"No, whoever is involved in this is handling things directly." This whole thing had a personal feel to it. "I eliminated three as viable suspects," he said, frowning as pictures flashed on the screen. He wished he could eliminate more. "Is this what you tagged me to see?"

"Yep. I hacked into an old satellite and managed to pull up some data from yesterday. It's very interesting."

"Damn it Odell, I told you—"

"Don't worry. It won't be traced back to us. I piggybacked onto...You know what, never mind. The feed I got is fuzzy and I lost the signal, but look at this replay." He pointed to the computer.

Although the screen was grainy, they had a decent aerial view of a neighborhood. A large subdivision split into three sections. A semi-truck and Humvee turned into it. "Okay, what am I looking at?"

"What *don't* you see?" Odell asked.

"Holy hell." There were no other vehicles in the neighborhood. None in the driveways or parked on the curb. Even if everyone used their garage, and that was statistically slim, there were no other vehicles at all. None driving through the subdivision. "No cars."

The screen abruptly went black so they couldn't know exactly what direction the vehicles had gone but it was a big start.

"Exactly." A map popped up on screen next. "This is the exact location of the neighborhood. The construction on it and three neighboring ones were abandoned during the construction bust a few years ago."

Declan nodded. Florida's economy had been hit hard not too long ago, with innumerable people losing their homes, construction companies going under overnight and foreclosures popping up in the thousands. They were on the upswing now, but not everyone had recovered from the crisis. "How many homes in this stretch?" he asked.

"Three or four hundred. All unoccupied. And all in various stages of construction. I can't get a live feed but I think this is our guys. I managed to run their plates."

Which would also involve hacking, something Declan ignored because he didn't care.

"The plates are both from cars reported stolen months ago. Probably jacked the vehicles, then switched the plates."

"Good work." Really good. One of these homes would be the perfect place to hide a kidnap victim. He set his tablet in his lap and pulled up the video of Alena he'd saved. "That could be a garage couldn't it." It was more a statement than question.

"Shit. Yep, her wrists are bound to the pulley system. Can't see it completely, but… yeah. That could definitely be a residential garage."

Declan's heart rate kicked up a notch. She could be in one of those homes. There were too damn many to sweep and he couldn't risk sending in a big search party. The kidnappers could just cut their losses and run, which would mean killing her.

"Have you seen Clay this morning?" Declan asked, starting to text the man.

"Yeah, saw him out on the lanai talking on his cell not too long ago. What are you going to do about this?" Odell asked, nodding at the map.

"Keep it to yourself for now." Declan was going to put together two teams to infiltrate the place, but he needed to tell Andre about the lead first and get more information on the neighborhood itself. "I want to know who owns the subdivisions and more importantly I want the architectural plans for—"

Odell smiled widely, the white of his teeth seeming brighter against his darker skin. "Already on it. You telling Andre about this?"

"Yeah, as soon as he's down here he needs to know."

"We're gonna nail these fuckers."

Fuck yeah they were. As Declan opened the French doors to the lanai, he spotted a few of his security guys patrolling the yard, as they should be. Clay leaned against one of the pillars and nodded once when he saw him.

"Thanks Susan, I appreciate your help." Clay spoke for a few more moments before ending the call. His defeated expression told Declan what he needed.

"Any news on the security feeds from the hospital?" Declan wasn't holding his breath for a different answer from earlier. Clay had texted him the news that the videos had been seemingly erased, but a small part of him hoped it was a mistake.

"Yeah, just talked to my nurse friend. Turns out it wasn't a glitch. They think someone came in with a magnet and erased everything. Either that, or someone hacked in and got to the videos that way. Cops are fucking pissed."

"The feeds would be saved offsite though." It was standard procedure for most places now.

Clay nodded. "She said the cops are looking into it now but it might take a few days."

Declan rubbed a hand over his face. They didn't have days. "Ethan had to have been involved with all this."

Clay's lips pulled into a thin line. "Someone was tying up loose ends."

"Tell Odell I want the police report on his murder. And tell him to email me Ethan's phone records." Odell had already run Ethan's records, but Declan wanted to scan everything himself. When Clay simply nodded, he said, "I'll be inside in a minute." As soon as Clay disappeared through the doors, Declan glanced at his watch before calling his assistant's direct line. It was an hour before she was scheduled to arrive at work, but he knew her well enough that she'd be there.

Blair picked up on the second ring. "Gallagher Security. How may I help you?"

"Don't you ever sleep?" he asked.

"Do you?" she shot back.

"Listen, I need you to pull up the GPS logs over the past six months for all the vehicles and I want you to highlight any unusual activity."

"You mean...for your guys?"

"Yeah."

"No problem. Want me to email it to you?"

"Yes, and keep this between us."

"Of course."

Declan reviewed the logs on a semi-regular basis to make sure his men weren't using their company vehicles for too many personal errands, but he'd hand-picked most of the guys who worked for him. As a rule, he'd learned not to trust anybody, but most of his men had had top security clearances at one point or another in their previous professions. They were the kind of men he'd want with him during a firefight.

Unfortunately he needed to reevaluate some things. He hated the thought of spying on his men through their dreams, but what choice did he have. If Ethan had been working against him, there was a chance he hadn't been doing it alone. "And put together a list of eight men—none with ties to this case—with covert infiltration experience." Most of his guys had that, but he wanted the ones with the most experience. "Contact them and tell them to gear up and head to the office. They're on call as of now. I'll let you know more in probably half an hour."

As they disconnected, Clay popped his head outside the French doors. His expression was grim. "Andre's father is here."

Just freaking great. "Where's Nika?"

"In Andre's office."

"Shit...keep Yasha occupied while I talk to Andre and Nika." That man was a monster and Declan didn't want him in the vicinity of her.

"Of course."

Declan found Odell, Nika, and Andre in Andre's office. Odell was running some program and muttering to his computer. Nika sat in the same place as the day before, looking worried and tense. She wore dark jeans again with a green sleeveless top that matched her bright eyes. The shirt molded to her soft curves in all the right places. Something he had no business noticing. She met his gaze, but quickly averted her eyes.

He still couldn't understand why she'd disappeared from his room without a word. The memory of holding her last night was impossible to erase. Keeping his eyes on her, Declan spoke to Andre, who was sitting next to Odell. He wanted to see her reaction when he mentioned Yasha. "Andre, your father is here. Just arrived."

Nika grasped onto the edge of the chaise lounge, and it was subtle, but her breathing kicked up a notch. That answered his question. She might not want to kill him, but she sure as hell knew who Yasha Makarov was.

Turning, Declan faced Andre, who still hadn't responded. "Well?"

"Well what?" Dark circles smudged under Andre's eyes.

"What the hell is he doing here?"

"I told you I was asking him for the money. He insisted on dropping it off himself."

Declan scrubbed a hand over his face. "I think I have a lead—a strong one—where Alena's being held."

Nika jumped up, her expression so filled with hope he felt it like a physical blow. She and Andre both started to respond when the heavy door to the office swung open.

Yasha walked in with three of his men. The tall, blond crime boss nodded at him as he set a duffle bag on the floor next to his feet. "Mr. Gallagher. Nice to see you again."

Declan pasted on a civil smile. He'd hunted down and interrogated terrorists all over the world, but the man in front of him always made him want to take a shower after being in his presence. "If you insist on being part of this, you can stay, but your men will wait in the hall."

One of his guards immediately stepped forward. "That is impossible."

Yasha held up a hand. "Leave us."

"Boss…"

"*Now.* My son will not hurt me."

Wordlessly the three men strode out. Yasha glanced behind Declan at Andre, then his gaze narrowed on Nika who was still looking at Declan. He was glad neither her nor Andre had asked about their lead on Alena's location. The less Yasha knew, the better.

"You're the kidnapped girl's sister? Are you and she trying to con my son?" Yasha barked, his harsh words reverberating around the quiet room.

Every protective instinct in Declan roared to life. In a few steps he stood between them, completely blocking Nika from view before she could answer. "Mr. Makarov—"

Andre stepped forward, cutting Declan off. "Enough, father. You come in here and start interrogating a woman you don't know. It's nice to see some things never change." The two men looked so similar, tall and blond with sharp features, but Declan knew they couldn't be more different.

Yasha's attention zeroed in on his son, his eyes gleaming. "Ah, you remember you still have a father. So *nice*."

Andre's pale eyes flashed angrily. "You can't make anything easy, can you?"

"You think getting this money was easy?" Yasha motioned toward the bag at his feet.

Andre took a menacing step toward his father. "As a matter of fact, I do."

Before the older man could respond, the phone rang. Immediate silence descended on the room as it rang a second time.

"Boss, pretty sure this is the kidnappers. I'm running it, but can't get a lock on the number," Odell said, his fingers flying over one of his keyboards.

Declan didn't have to look at his watch to know they were hours early. He tuned out his surroundings and answered the call, pressing the speaker button. "Makarov residence."

"Is this Mr. Gallagher again?" The mechanical voice streamed over the line.

"Yes. I didn't catch your name last time."

"No, you didn't."

"What happened to twenty-four hours?"

"Since Yasha Makarov is with you, I figured you didn't need the entire time allotment."

Declan's stomach tightened at the implication of the words. He glanced over at the gangster, unable to keep the mistrust out of his eyes. "Who said Yasha is here?"

"Don't play games with me. I know he's there, so I can only assume Andre has all the money now." The stilted mechanical voice raised a few decibels. "You have two hours." He rattled off an address that was vaguely familiar. It took Declan seconds to realize it had to be in the warehouse district.

"We need more time to get the funds together. You're asking for a large amount without giving us any good faith."

"Two hours. Andre must come alone."

There was no way in hell Declan was allowing Andre to go by himself, but he kept talking. The location they'd given was in the exact opposite direction of where Declan thought Alena was being held. "We need proof of life. I want to talk to Alena Brennan now and she better be at the drop point. He doesn't let go of the money until he has a visual of her."

There was an extended moment of silence before Alena's voice came over the line. "Hello?"

"Ms. Brennan. Have you been hurt—"

"Alena!" Nika shouted.

"Nika, it's me, I'm fine. They haven't hurt me, I swear." Alena sounded okay, but Declan couldn't be sure it wasn't a recording.

"Alena, what day is it?" Declan held up a hand to silence Nika as he spoke to her sister.

"Uh, Saturday, I think."

"Do you know where you are?"

"No, they—"

"That's enough." The mechanical voice abruptly came back on the line. "Mr. Makarov, you have two hours to bring the money. Your countdown begins now. As soon as we have the money, we'll give you the girl."

Declan shook his head. "No! That's not negotiable. Either he gets a visual of the woman before he leaves the money, or you don't have a deal. He is not giving twenty million dollars in exchange for nothing."

There was another long moment of silence. "The woman will be at the address given. Andre comes alone or she dies. He will receive further instructions when he arrives."

The line went dead before Declan could respond. He scrubbed a hand over his face. "Did you get anything Odell?"

"No. I was able to trace him further this time, but I still lost the signal."

Declan glanced at Yasha then leaned down so he was close enough to Odell that Yasha couldn't hear. "If you can, reconnect with that satellite, I want you to monitor what you showed me earlier. See if you find any unusual activity." He'd tell Andre about it as soon as Yasha was out of the room.

"My son is not making himself a target for some whore," Yasha snarled.

"My sister's not a whore you asshole!" The abrupt outburst from Nika shocked everyone into silence for a brief moment.

Yasha's eyes narrowed on Nika and he opened his mouth but Declan cut him off.

"You need to either shut the hell up or get out," Declan ground out. With only an hour to map out a plan, he couldn't have anyone impeding them. Without waiting for a response, he turned to Clay who waited silently by the door. "Tell everyone to gear up now."

Clay nodded and exited as Declan focused on Andre. Before he could say a word, Nika's small hand clutched onto his arm in a vise-like grip. "Declan..."

Her eyes rolled back into her head, showing the whites and her body dropped like a sack of rocks. Before she could hit the floor, he snaked an arm around her waist, but her entire body was limp and unmoving.

"Oh my God," Odell muttered.

Laying her onto the carpet, Declan checked her pulse. It was strong. As he crouched next to her, an icy chill rolled over him. "Nika!" When she didn't respond or even flinch at his voice, he gently lifted back one of her eyelids. Her pupils were almost fully dilated. *Hell no.* He wasn't letting anything happen to her.

CHAPTER TWELVE

*N*ika blinked as she tried to focus on her surroundings. Everything around her was fuzzy and faded at the edges.

This was a dream or vision. Vision, she decided a moment later.

Her gut clenched, a sense of impending darkness threatening her. She couldn't explain why, but terror welled up inside her as she looked at the dim, unfamiliar environment.

Glancing around at the muted darkness, she saw what looked like support beams above her and she could hear male voices...nearby.

Blinking she sat up and realized she'd been lying on a bed. Well, a mattress with a couple sheets thrown on it. And she was in what looked like a half-built house. Exposed wooden beams were everywhere, and dust covered the concrete floor below her sock covered feet. Like someone had stopped construction on this place a while ago. A wood plank covered the window in her 'bedroom' or whatever room this was supposed to be. Faint light peeked through a crack in the plank so she guessed it was daylight still.

Standing, she wavered once on her feet as she got her bearings. It was always like this in a vision but she forced herself to get her shit together. This was important, she was certain. Could feel it bone-deep.

As she walked across the room, something dark to her left caught her eye. The wall hadn't been completed in this room, with beams and some plaster the only separator between her and the other room.

She saw a crate marked 'explosives' sitting against a wall. When she took another step forward her eyes widened. There were assault rifles propped up next to it. She wondered if they were loaded.

She could escape if so. Or at least have a chance to.

Nika shook her head, realizing that wasn't her thought, but... this must be Alena's head she was in. Or she hoped. Before the thought had fully formed, she heard the same male voice from before. In the next room, maybe. They were so close, as if the plaster part of the half-wall was all that was blocking them. She didn't move, not wanting to make a sound or inadvertently reveal her presence.

"We're not taking the woman with us!" a man said. He sounded familiar. One of the men who'd helped kidnap her.

"Yes, we are. This is not up for debate." Another man responded, his voice raspy, as if he was tired or maybe a smoker. But, he was obviously the one in charge. Though she couldn't see them, she could tell by his tone. He didn't shout, but the edge in his voice was clear.

"Andre Makarov is dead either way. Why are you bringing her?"

"He needs to think we're cooperating," Mr. Raspy voice said.

"We're wasting our time," the other man muttered, this time in quieter tones, almost sulky sounding.

"The woman isn't part of this. She hasn't seen our faces. Once we get Andre and his money, we let her go. And no one else will strike him but me. Andre is mine." Venom dripped from the man's voice.

"Then what's the fucking point? We're going to get rich off this guy so who gives a shit about that bitch? Some of the guys are getting pissed you won't let us touch her."

"I'm not a rapist. And your men are thinking far too small if they're concerned about one woman. This is a huge score. They can buy plenty of women after this."

"You know who she is though. Not every day a prime piece of ass like that—"

A sharp thud rent the air, as if flesh had met flesh. A man grunted.

"Do you want to stand around and bitch, or do you want your money?"

"I want my fucking money."

"Then bring the woman to the vehicle and quit questioning my orders."

The man let out a string of curses in a foreign language. Russian maybe.

No, she wouldn't let them hurt Andre. The frustrating man had proven he wasn't like his father. He didn't deserve to die.

"Nika! Wake up! Can you hear me?"

Nika sucked in a deep breath as her eyes widened and she found herself staring into dark, familiar eyes. "Declan?"

"Are you okay?" Worry lines etched around his eyes.

He looked up and away from her. "Cancel the ambulance," he barked to someone.

Using his forearm as leverage, she held onto him and pulled herself up. "I'm sorry, I..." The realization that they weren't alone made her stop talking. She couldn't tell him what she'd seen in front of others. They'd think she was insane.

Immediately he hooked an arm around her back and helped her sit up straight. "You passed out. How are you feeling?"

Glancing around, she spotted Andre and the other man, Odell something, sitting by the computers and staring at her with concern. She leaned in close to Declan, clutching onto his shoulders. She didn't care what anyone else thought of the action, she didn't want them to hear what she had to say. "I need to talk to you in private."

A frown marred that handsome face, but he helped her to her feet. After a brief murmur to Andre, Declan quickly led her to the kitchen.

She could see the tension rolling off him. "We have to leave pronto, but I'll have one of my men take you to a doctor if—"

"No, but you can't let Andre meet the kidnapper alone. They're going to kill him."

Declan's espresso eyes darkened and narrowed. "Why are you telling me this? Feeling guilty?"

It took all of a second to understand what he meant. "No, you dumbass! Listen to me. Whoever those men are, they are *not* going to let him live. I don't really understand but the man who—the leader—he wants to make Andre suffer." That was the vibe she'd gotten from her vision.

He stepped closer, caging her in against the nearest counter, his big body immovable as he leaned down so that inches separated their faces. "Why are you telling me this? Not getting as big a cut as you'd hoped?" His words were quiet, but they dripped with raw, barely concealed anger.

"A cut of what? Why aren't you listening to me? Whoever these men are, they are going to kill Andre," she whispered the last part, not wanting anyone to overhear. Her thoughts were still a little jumbled but she knew what she'd seen in her vision. Andre might be related to the scum of the earth, but Nika couldn't allow him to go to his certain death in good conscience. When she'd been in that dream state, she'd gotten the sense from her sister that Alena didn't want that either. They needed to save him.

Declan's angry expression faltered. "*Whoever?* You don't know who took your sister?"

"Of course not. You aren't listening to me." She let out a frustrated groan, finally shaking off the rest of her sluggishness. "I saw, just now, what they're planning. Well, heard and sort of saw."

Declan leaned back a fraction, but not much. His hands still caged her in against the counter. "You...saw it? When you passed out?"

"Yeah. Just now. I was in a house that hadn't been finished. Or maybe it's in the process of being finished. There was a lot of dust though so I think it's abandoned or something. I heard two men arguing. Talking about

Alena, I think. They never said her name, but they said Andre's. They're going to bring Alena with them, but they're not planning to let Andre live."

"Why?"

"A man with the raspy voice said he wants him to suffer and he said he was the only one who got to touch Andre. He didn't explain why. Oh, I also saw a crate of what might be explosives and guns. Assault rifles."

Declan's frown deepened. "Did you see anything about these men I can use? Any distinguishing characteristics?"

He believed her. He was different than most people she'd met but she'd still expected some sort of argument. "You believe me?"

"Is there a reason I shouldn't?"

"Well, no. I just expected...an argument or something."

"I can't think of one reason why you'd lie about this. And if you are, you better believe you'll pay." His voice was a low growl.

The hairs on the back of her neck stood up as his words rolled over her, but she ignored the short-lived flash of fear. "I didn't see them. They were behind a half-built wall. They probably thought I—Alena—was asleep. I think but I don't know. It's hard to completely gauge things in that state. One of the men was angry because the man with the raspy voice wouldn't let him," Nika swallowed back the bile in her throat, "touch Alena." For that small miracle, she was so damn grateful that her sister hadn't been harmed in that way. It made it easier to freaking breathe.

"You're sure of all this?"

"As sure as I can be under the circumstances."

"Can you think of anything else?"

She shook her head. She'd had visions before, usually of things about to happen, but she'd never had one of real importance. And not one connected to people she was close to. Not like this anyway.

"Stay here, I'm going to talk to Andre."

Instinctively she grabbed Declan's bicep. His muscles flexed under her fingers but she didn't let go.

"You're not going to tell him about me are you?"

"I'm not telling anyone about this, trust me. I think I have a better idea of who we're dealing with now. And you've been a big help. We're going to get your sister back. Stay put," he ordered. Before he left, he cupped her jaw gently. He opened his mouth, maybe to say something else, but just as quickly he snapped it shut and strode from the room.

* * *

Andre lifted his arms as Odell helped secure the bullet proof vest.

"What the hell is wrong with you, Andre? You barely know this woman." His father paced in front of him, but Andre managed to keep himself from lashing out. He was always in control. Except around his father. Or sperm donor, as he preferred to think of Yasha.

Considering the 'great' Yasha Makarov cared for no one but himself and considered all women disposable, the question was hardly surprising. "I don't expect you to understand."

"This could be a trap. She could be using you."

Andre had thought about that, but if Alena had wanted to extract money from anyone, the last two men she'd been involved with would have been much easier—and wealthier—targets. Yes, Andre had done well for himself, but she'd dated richer men. And she had a very nice financial cushion. He'd had her checked out thoroughly. No, whoever had done this was coming after him personally. He could feel it straight to his bones. It wasn't as if she could have predicted he'd be called away on business. He'd been the intended victim, not her. She was just an innocent bystander. Which made him feel beyond guilty. "Not everyone has an ulterior motive," he snapped.

"Is that too tight?" Odell asked quietly.

He shook his head. "No, but thank you."

Before his father could continue his tirade, the door opened and Declan stepped through carrying a blue windbreaker. Immediately Yasha turned on Declan. "Talk some sense into my son. This is a trap."

"I hate to agree with him, but your father is right." Declan handed him the light jacket. "Put this on."

"So you think this is a trap too?" he asked as he slipped the jacket over his head.

"I think these men are highly trained and might try to take you in addition to your money. This is only partially about the money. I could be wrong, but I think that whoever is behind this wants to take whatever he can from you then he'll likely kill you."

"How do you know that?" Andre asked.

"Instinct."

"So why are you letting my son go?" his father interrupted.

Declan switched his attention to Yasha. "If we don't, they'll kill the woman and come after Andre again. I don't know who's behind this, but if this is personal, he's not going to rest until your son is dead. We can stop him now while he's still cocky enough to think he's planned it perfectly."

Andre intervened when it appeared his father would argue with Declan. "You have no say in this father, so get over it. I'm doing this and you're free to leave at any time."

A muscle tightened in his father's jaw. "Does the name Rick mean anything to you?"

Andre's eyebrows rose at the name. "Why?" He glanced at Declan, who also looked surprised.

"Before I arrived, I spoke with an associate of mine who might have mentioned that name. He *might* have a connection with all of this."

Declan's gaze locked on Andre's. "I think we know who the kidnapper is."

"You can't be sure," Andre muttered.

"He's the only person who makes sense. Whether you want to admit it or not, this is personal. He blamed you for your wife's death. According to *you*, he swore you'd pay one day."

Andre shook his head. "That was a long time ago—"

"Rick is the name of the bastard who was fucking that whore?" Yasha's lips curled up in distaste.

"That's enough," Andre said. His wife might have cheated on him, but Andre took some of the blame. He hadn't exactly been the best husband. Or even a husband at all. Maybe if he'd paid more attention to her or come home before eight o'clock some nights... His throat tightened with painful memories, but he shoved them away. He'd been a fucking ghost in his own marriage.

"Why? She never respected you—"

"I'm not having this conversation again." Andre turned to Declan. "I'm ready when you are."

He might not know Alena as well as he wanted, but he couldn't let anything happen to her. After years of faceless bed partners, he'd finally met a woman who made him feel something again. He'd fucked up his marriage. No matter what anyone said, he shouldered most of the blame for his wife's indiscretions.

Nothing might develop with Alena but he'd already failed one woman, he couldn't fail another. Especially not this one.

"I need to speak to you alone," Declan said, his intent clear.

"Father, privacy please." Andre didn't look at Yasha as he spoke, but knew his use of the word 'father' would work.

After a muttered curse, Yasha left the office.

"We have a lead where Alena's being held," Declan said the moment the door closed. Before Andre could ask questions, he nodded at Odell. "Show him what you've got."

As the computer genius pulled up the satellite feed and other maps, Declan explained to Andre his theory of her whereabouts. "I've already put in a call to my guys. Eight man team I had on stand-by. They're on their way to the subdivision. There are four main exits. Instead of infiltrating I'm going to have them watch the exits and tail anyone who leaves. They'll blend, don't worry," he added. "They're all in armored minivans or cars that look like every day vehicles."

He cleared his throat before continuing. "Since we know that they've got eyes on your place, if their knowledge of Yasha's arrival is anything to go on, we should keep up appearances and head to the meet point. I'm going to order another team to head to the subdivision also as backup. This time these guys don't have the element of surprise. The end goal is for you to never make it to the meet point, for my guys to apprehend and stop them before they arrive. And despite what they think, we'll have eyes on you at all times. You're not alone. I need you to have all the facts before we move forward."

Andre nodded once. There wasn't another option for him. He was doing this. "Let's go then."

CHAPTER THIRTEEN

Alena wasn't surprised when a masked man stepped into the door-less entryway of her room a few minutes after the conversation she'd overheard.

"Time to go," he said, motioning with his hand.

"Where?" She sat on the edge of the mattress but didn't make an attempt to get up. She knew she was in a house and so far she'd only seen one or two captors. Everyone stayed masked though. And she knew there were more men. Maybe a dozen. But they didn't hover in the house. She usually heard them outside, probably as they watched the perimeter of wherever she was.

"You don't ask questions. Come now." He took a few steps in the room, impatience in every line of his body.

At this point she knew she had few options. These men wanted to kill Andre. She couldn't allow that. He was a good man, but the darkest part of her knew she needed him to get to Yasha. The thought alone made her feel shitty, but she would have her vengeance. Right now she had the fact that these kidnappers needed her alive. So even if she failed in her attempt to escape, she didn't think they'd kill her. At least not right away.

Knowing that, she steeled herself for what she had to do and stood. She stuck out her bottom lip in what she

163

knew was a sensual pout. She crossed her arms over her chest, pushing up her breasts in the process. "Where are we going?" She put a little extra whine into the question.

The man let out an exasperated sigh and took another step forward. He held out an arm. "You come now. No more questions."

Sighing, she stepped closer to him but instead of walking past him, sidled up to him, pressing her body to his as she laid her hands on his chest. "No one will tell me anything," she murmured, stroking her fingers down his chest.

He stilled, his eyes going wide. With a mask on it was hard to read him, but his eyes gave him away. "Ah..." He rubbed the back of his neck and glanced toward the entryway, as if looking for someone.

She took the only opportunity she might have. Striking out fast and hard, she punched him in the throat. Collapsing someone's trachea was hard to do and she didn't know if she'd done it now.

The man stumbled back, one hand flying to his throat as he swung out at her with a fist.

She ducked and kicked out at his knee instead of going for his groin. Men always seemed to expect that. She heard the crack, rejoiced in the sound.

A gasping, hoarse noise escaped his throat, but he didn't cry out as he fell. Oh yeah, she'd damaged his throat good.

Adrenaline pumped through her as she attacked again, jumping onto his back as he started to fall forward. Despite his injuries he was reaching for his holstered weapon.

She wrapped her arm around his neck, cutting off his blood supply. Her uncle had taught her this move. One of many he'd taught her.

The man grabbed onto her arm, digging his fingers into her skin, but she tightened her grip. Ten seconds was all she needed and he was too weak to truly fight.

Eventually he fell limp against her, but she continued holding him, needing to make sure he was down. He might regain consciousness after this, he might not. She wasn't sticking around to find out.

After another thirty seconds she let him go. As he slumped to the floor she pulled his weapon from the side holster and chambered a round. She'd only have a small window to get the hell out of here now.

Moving quickly she patted him down and found a set of keys for a Chevy. SUV she guessed. Palming them, she jumped to her feet, pistol in hand. Her heart was a wild thump against her chest as she stepped into the hallway. It was lined with more open beams of wood.

She hurried down it, looking for a way out. Going on foot wasn't an option, she needed to find the vehicle. It would be armored. These guys had planned this kidnapping well and wouldn't leave something like that to chance. Not after that insane attack on Andre's vehicles.

The layout of the house was easy enough. As she reached what would be a kitchen given the cutouts in the frames, she heard a door open somewhere.

"Where the fuck are you? Come on man!"

Damn it. She didn't want to use the gun because it would be loud and draw attention, but she would if she had to.

Blood rushing in her ears, she pushed open a door without a knob and breathed a sigh of relief to see a black SUV sitting in the three-car garage.

Moving quickly and quietly, she stepped into it and shut the door behind her. Not bothering to try the garage door opener since she doubted this place had electricity, she raced to the SUV and slid into the driver's seat.

Her hands were shaking as she put her foot on the brake and pressed the start button. She liked the newer model vehicles that didn't need keys. The engine roared to life and she gunned it, flying through the shut garage door without pause.

No one was in the driveway as she barreled through, sending debris flying everywhere. Someone shouted behind her, a man, as she flew into the street. Someone was running after her from the busted up garage.

She swung a sharp left and pressed the OnStar button. She was getting help.

* * *

Declan answered his cell when he saw Odell's number. "You got a visual on the satellite yet?"

"Alena's escaped," Nika said. "I'm using Odell's phone because she's on my line."

His fingers tightened around the steering wheel. "Are you sure?" His gut told him she was telling the truth, but the last woman he'd trusted had turned out to be a bigger liar than he could have imagined.

"Of course I'm sure. She just called me. Odell's talking to one of your guys. He said you have a team or something near a neighborhood you thought she was being held at." There was a hint of accusation in her voice, but he ignored it.

"Let me talk to Odell. Now." He turned to Clay who was in the passenger seat. "Contact the team. Tell them potential change of plans—Odell, what's going on?" he asked as his friend came on the line.

"Alena called her sister from a vehicle. It was easy enough to trace the number. It's linked to an SUV's communications system. She doesn't know where she is, but I located the vehicle through the GPS. She's about two blocks from London and Cash. Same area we thought she was being held. I've told them to find and follow her. She's either got men after her or will soon."

"If you can trace that vehicle, her kidnappers can too. If they're not already on her trail. Nika needs to tell her to go with our guys. She won't listen to anyone but her sister."

"Agreed. Hold on."

After Odell relayed the information to Nika, Declan called London and Cash just to confirm. They already had a visual on Alena. Said an SUV had come barreling out of the neighborhood and they'd followed.

As soon as they disconnected, he radioed the team driving behind him. "Head back to base now. Mission aborted." He'd explain everything later, but for now that was all anyone needed to know.

Declan met Andre's gaze in the rearview mirror. The man had been unusually silent. "Looks like these guys made a mistake."

Andre simply nodded, relief in his expression.

Declan was relieved too. Unfortunately Yasha had been brought into this equation now. The last thing Declan could afford to do was leave either sister alone with Yasha. Now that the opportunity had presented itself he doubted the sisters would pass it up if they truly intended to go after the criminal. If he could get Yasha out of the house without any further contact with the women, he might be able to neutralize whatever Alena and Nika's plans were.

CHAPTER FOURTEEN

Nika waited in the marble foyer of Andre's home, barely able to contain herself. Energy hummed through her at the thought of seeing her sister in a few minutes. Alena was alive and safe. Odell hadn't told Yasha, who was apparently making himself at home in Andre's place. He was in the pool house she'd heard, but she didn't care.

Odell, who was standing next to her, was talking into his mic. He had an earpiece in and had been conversing with someone. Maybe Declan, she couldn't be sure.

"Your sister is here. Pulling down the drive now." He placed a reassuring hand on her shoulder and squeezed once.

"Thank you for tracking her down. What you did back there," she said, referring to the magic he'd done on the computer, "was freaking amazing. Thank you sounds stupid, but it's all I have."

To her surprise he seemed flustered and just grunted a non-response. He rubbed a hand across the back of his neck as if embarrassed.

Before she could say anything else the front door opened. Alena stepped inside, looking rumpled but okay.

A smile split her face when she saw Nika. Nika didn't care if she made a scene as she raced for her sister and pulled Alena into a big hug. "I thought I'd lost you!"

"I'm okay."

"You're sure?" she asked quietly, mindful of the men who were spilling into the foyer. "I know what you said, but...did they hurt you? I saw the video." Nika's voice broke on the last word. She'd been so damn terrified.

A harsh laugh escaped as Alena pulled back. "That was all for show. They bound my wrists and strung me up in a garage for about ten minutes. After that they dumped me in a room. I had to pee in a bucket and they didn't even let me take a shower," she grumbled.

Nika snorted. "It could have been worse." Even thinking about how bad it could have been made her stomach roil.

Expression turning grim, Alena nodded. "Yeah."

"Come on ladies," Odell said, motioning to both of them. "I'm sure you're hungry or thirsty. Or both." It was directed at Alena, concern in the man's face.

"Water would be really good," her sister said gratefully.

He started to usher them in the direction of the kitchen, but paused. Nika could tell he was listening to someone on his earpiece. "Head to the kitchen. Declan and Andre are almost here," he said almost absently, turning away from them and heading back for the front of the mansion.

Once they were alone in the kitchen, Nika grasped Alena's hands. Instinctively she lowered her voice. "Yasha is *here*. He's in Andre's pool house right now I think."

Alena's expression went hard, her body pulling taut with tension. "What?"

"From what I can tell, Andre and his father do *not* get along, but he had to borrow some of the money for your ransom from Yasha."

Surprise flickered across Alena's face. The bruise on the side of it had turned a faint shade of purple, but did nothing to distract from her beauty. "How much were those guys asking?"

"Twenty million in cash and bonds."

She lifted an eyebrow. "And Andre was willing to pay it?"

"Yes. We've got to call this off or find another way to get to Yasha. This is getting to be insane. We can't use Andre anymore." Nika's conscience could only handle so much. Not to mention her recent involvement with Declan.

"Forget it. This is perfect," her sister whispered through clenched teeth.

"Andre was willing to pay twenty *million* dollars to get you back. We need to walk away, now. I've got a bad feeling about this." The man had been willing to save *her* sister. Nika didn't like owing anyone anything, but she owed Andre everything. He might not have actually saved Alena, but he'd been willing to. That meant something.

Alena ignored Nika's plea. "Are you having...dreams?"

"No, well, yes, visions." She'd never imagined that she'd consider her dreams of Declan more disturbing than dreams of the future.

"About Yasha?"

She wanted to lie but the truth was she hadn't had any about the man. And she couldn't tell if the sick feeling in the pit of her stomach was pure guilt or more than that. Her emotions were on too much of a rollercoaster. "No."

"Then I don't see what the problem is. If we do this right, Andre will never know anyway. It's going to look like an accident. You worry too much."

"And you don't worry enough." Nika hated the feeling of utter powerlessness surging through her. She'd just gotten Alena back, she didn't want her sister to willingly put herself in danger now.

Before she could continue the door opened and Declan and Andre walked in. Her chest constricted when she made eye contact with Declan. There was something raw and possessive in his gaze and she felt it all the way to her core.

Yasha Makarov be damned. At this point, she was ready to pack up and leave. Everything about this was too personal. When her sister had poisoned the Lazarev brothers, the two of them hadn't spent any time with the men. They hadn't gotten to know them. Not that it would have mattered if they had. She wasn't sorry they were dead, but she didn't like using someone the way they were using Andre. It made her feel dirty. So far she'd been able to compartmentalize their actions, but this...this was different. Andre wasn't the monster his father was. She wasn't sure if using him made them just as bad as Yasha. No, they weren't even on the same level, but it still felt wrong.

Not to mention Declan was involved in this and she wasn't sure what to do with her feelings for him. There was no way she could compartmentalize what he made her feel.

"Alena." Andre said the word like a prayer as he crossed to her. "I'm so sorry. This is my fault—"

Alena cut him off almost immediately. "Stop, please. I'm okay and that's all that matters."

While Andre murmured a few soothing words to her sister, Nika took a step in Declan's direction. She didn't want to eavesdrop on something that was so personal. As she neared Declan she felt more grounded. For some inexplicable reason, she was more in control of her senses around the sexy man. Sure, he made her nervous as hell, but he knew about her gift and he didn't think she was crazy. "Did you find out anything about the kidnappers? Where they are?"

"No, but we're searching the area your sister escaped from now." He cleared his throat and focused his attention on Alena. "Ms. Brennan, I know you've been through a lot but I have some questions for you."

With Andre hovering protectively over her, Alena pushed back a stray lock of hair and nodded. "I'll tell you whatever I can."

"Do you need medical care?" he asked.

"No, but I should tell you that I killed someone. A man. When I was escaping. Or I think I did, I don't know if he's actually dead. I didn't stick around to find out."

Next to her, Andre stiffened, looking surprised right before guilt bled into his expression.

"How?" Declan asked.

"I punched him in his trachea. I might have collapsed it but I'm not sure. After choking him into unconsciousness I stole his gun and keys and ran."

For a moment Declan looked thoughtful, but just nodded. "Do you know where you were being held?"

"Not really. It was a house, but not finished. I drove an SUV right through a garage door. There wasn't anyone out on the streets and all the yards had wildly overgrown grass. I guess the neighborhood was abandoned. I drove a little like a crazy person trying to find an escape. Then your guys found me." She pressed her face against Andre's chest for a moment and Nika knew her sister well enough that she wasn't acting.

Nika could tell that Alena actually cared for him, even if she didn't want to admit it.

Declan didn't pause in his questioning. "Did you see any of their faces?"

"No, they were very careful to wear masks but I did overhear them talking before I escaped. One man was angry that the guy in charge wouldn't let the other men, well, rape me. He didn't say the actual words, but I understood the intent. More than once I heard the men talking outside the house I was in. Sometimes in another language. I don't know what it was, but it was harsh sounding."

Nika's vision funneled for a moment after the word rape. The thought of anyone hurting her sister like that made her want to vomit.

"Do you remember any of the words?" Declan asked.

"No, but I think it was possibly Russian. The man I think was in charge was angry at Andre for something. He didn't explain it, but it was obvious he hates him— you." She glanced at Andre, who remained silent. Alena quickly looked back at Declan. "I don't think he planned to kill me, but he definitely wanted Andre to die. He told the other man he wanted to take his money and make him suffer. His voice was really raspy too, like he was a smoker."

"What you said about punching one of your captors in the trachea, can you run through everything from that point?" Declan asked.

They all listened quietly as she relayed everything.

Declan glanced at Nika as Alena finished. And Nika could practically see the wheels turning in his head. Her sister's story was similar to what she'd told Declan from her vision, at least right up until Alena had escaped. Nika had never had visions about people in her life before, at least not that she knew about. It worried her that she was now.

"Is there anything else you can think of that might be important?" Declan asked.

"Yeah." She reached behind her and pulled out a gun she must have had tucked into her jeans. "I took this from the man I..." She cleared her throat. "I took it when I left. Maybe you can use it to track the serial number or something?" Alena placed it on the marble island and slid it a few inches away from her.

Andre picked the gun up by the edges and walked it over to Declan. "You can ask her these questions later. She needs rest and I'm going to have my physician look her over," he murmured.

Nika started to speak, but caught her sister's eye. Alena shook her head once, telling Nika not to say anything. Biting her tongue, Nika watched as Andre ushered Alena from the room, practically carrying her. A stab of pity cut through her for Andre. Even if Alena did care about the man, they were both using him and it made Nika feel sick.

As they left Declan hurried to one of the cabinets and opened it. She frowned as he placed the gun in an oversized freezer bag.

"What are you doing?" she asked.

"I might be able to get some prints."

"Oh right, that's smart." Nika shifted from foot to foot, unsure what to say. Her uncle had erased every trace of her and her sister from the system so she wasn't worried about her sister's prints. "Are you... uh, are you going to call the police about the man Alena might have killed?"

Declan shook his head. "We don't know where the body is, if she even killed him and honestly, I'm not involving the fucking cops in this."

A healthy dose of relief settled over her. She definitely wasn't going to argue with him.

"You want to sit?" Even though it was phrased as a question, it somehow sounded more like an order coming from him.

"Sure." She settled on the high-backed stool at the island. She wished she could be with Alena right now but it was clear Andre wanted to take care of her and at this point she'd give the man that much.

Instead of staying on the other side of the island and keeping distance between them, Declan sat directly next to her and swiveled her seat so their knees barely touched. The expression on his face was undeniably predatory. He was completely invading her personal space but he obviously didn't care. The truth was, she didn't care either.

"I think it's time you tell me exactly what you are."

"I don't know." The words were a faint whisper on her lips. She hated feeling vulnerable but by admitting this to him she was opening herself up. She still wasn't positive.

For a split second, he faltered. "What?"

"I…see stuff. When I'm awake or sometimes dreaming, I get visions of people, places, things, you know…stuff. Sometimes it makes sense but sometimes—usually—it doesn't. Occasionally I'll get…" She trailed off, unsure what his reaction would be.

"You'll get what?" He scooted those final inches closer so that their knees touched.

It was hard to concentrate with Declan so close. His earthy scent enveloped her, sending most of her coherent thoughts scattering in all directions. Other than her sister and one friend, Nika had never told anyone else about her gifts. Not even her uncle. It was too weird and she hated the thought of Declan looking at her like she was a freak. Though that wasn't a real fear considering he walked through her dreams.

"Nika," he persisted.

Just the sound of her name on his lips heated her body. "I get flashes of things that haven't happened yet. In a future tense sort of way. I'll touch someone or walk by someone and just *see* what could happen to them. Like, if they might get in a minor car accident, or get stuck in traffic or pick a winning lottery ticket. It's usually small stuff though. And it's not always like that. Sometimes I just have dreams that don't make any sense." When he didn't respond, she inwardly cringed, but kept her face impassive. Maybe she'd overestimated his ability to believe everything.

"Yesterday you said you had a dream, like someone had shot you."

"Yeah, so?"

"Can you describe it?"

"There's not much to tell. I entered the vision or dream, whatever you want to call it, in a hospital bathroom. I didn't realize it was a hospital at first, but once I adjusted to my surroundings I saw there was an IV attached to my arm and I was really groggy. When I stepped out into the room someone was waiting for me. He shot me. I didn't see a face though, the man was in the shadows." She wrapped her arms around herself to ward off the sudden shiver that racked her body.

"How long have you had these visions?"

She fought back the painful memory of her accident. "Almost five years."

"And you just started dreaming out of the blue five years ago?"

"Sort of. I was in a really bad car accident. I broke both my legs, a few ribs, and had substantial brain swelling. The doctors had to induce a coma and when I came out of it, I was different." Panic punched through her as she thought back to that torturous time in her life. Back then she'd thought her dreams were just nightmares after enduring such a horrific accident. Then, she'd worried she'd been losing her mind.

Directly after the accident, she'd had dreams—or nightmares really—all the time, which she'd chalked up to PTSD. Asleep or awake, it didn't matter. She'd gotten awful visions of people dying and spirits had appeared everywhere. When she was in the shower, when she was sleeping, when she was undergoing physical therapy. And they'd always wanted to talk. About what happened to them, who they'd been when they'd been alive, what they hadn't gotten to accomplish. Freaking nightmare. She'd continued to pretend they weren't there and they'd finally left her alone. And once she'd realized what was going on she'd kept her mouth shut about it.

Then about a year after it had happened she'd met a woman, Ariel, who'd been like her. Ariel had tried to help her understand her visions, but Nika hadn't wanted to listen then. She hadn't wanted any part of the paranormal. Even after all the research she'd done on her own, she still had a problem accepting some things.

"Will you do me a favor?" Declan asked.

If he looked at her with those dark, intoxicating eyes, she was likely to do anything he asked. "Maybe."

"Any more dreams you have, no matter how small, will you tell me about them?"

"Even the ones that star you?" The almost flirty question slipped out before she could stop herself.

A slow grin spread across his fallen-angel face. The man just looked as if he wanted to do wicked things—and she'd let him. "Especially those."

She should run fast and far away before she fell into his trap but she couldn't seem to stop herself. Didn't want to stop herself from wanting him.

When he suddenly frowned at her, her stomach muscles tightened. "What's wrong?"

His jaw tightened and she watched as his Adam's apple bobbed once. "If I don't leave this room right now I'm going to do something stupid. Like kiss you. And I won't stop once I start." The words were a soft promise.

"Who said you'd have to stop?" The question popped out before she had a chance to analyze it.

A low burn started deep in her belly as her gaze fell to his lips. She couldn't look away, no matter how hard she tried.

Declan leaned in closer, taking her off guard and not giving her time to stop him. Not that she wanted to. When his mouth crushed against hers, she slid out of her seat so that she was standing between his legs. Wrapping her arms around his neck, she leaned into his body, savoring his strong embrace.

A tiny voice in the back of her head told her that she needed to be convincing her sister that they should be on the next plane out of Miami but all she wanted was to feel Declan's naked body against her.

In real life.

She wanted more than his fingers inside her or his mouth on her this time. She desperately wanted to feel his thick cock filling her. To see what he looked like as he climaxed. He'd already given her so much pleasure in her dreams and she wanted to give it back to him. It was stupid when they had no future, but she wanted to experience what being with him would be like at least once. If she didn't, she knew she'd regret it for the rest of her life.

As she clutched his shoulders, he roughly grasped her hips. His embrace was hard and demanding. When one of his hands crept underneath the hem of her shirt and skimmed her skin, her inner walls clenched involuntarily. What she wouldn't give to feel him push into her right now.

The sound of the kitchen door swinging open caused her to jump away from him. It was one of the security guys whose name she couldn't remember. Hell, she could barely remember her own name at the moment. With wide eyes, he turned on his heel and disappeared back through the door.

"Shit," Declan muttered.

Nika took a step back from him, needing to put distance between them.

"Nika..." He shook his head and she was disappointed to see he had his game face back on. The intimacy was over and it was back to business. "I need to find out who took your sister. When you had that vision of those two kidnappers, was it like you were yourself or were you your sister?"

It amazed her that he could switch back to business mode so fast but if he could, she could too. She knew it was important to find out who had taken Alena, but the frustration she experienced was acute. She'd rather be kissing him than talking. And that wasn't like her. "It was me. It felt exactly like I was there and was watching those guys."

"And at the hospital was the same?"

"Yes. Why are you asking about that dream?"

"Just curious."

"Don't lie to me," she snapped.

For a second she wondered if he'd respond, but he scrubbed a hand over his face. "What I'm about to tell you doesn't leave this room." He held her gaze and only continued when she nodded. "One of my men was shot last night in his hospital room. Very similar to the way you described. I refuse to believe that's a coincidence."

Nika held a shaky hand to her throat. The past few months, even before Declan had started visiting her dreams, her visions had become more vivid. She hadn't known what to do about them though. For all she'd known, they weren't even real. Her dreams were often so jumbled she couldn't make sense of them. But that dream—vision—had been *real.*

Declan's strong voice pulled her out of her thoughts. "That's why I need you to keep me informed of your dreams."

She nodded. "I will. Why was he killed?"

"I don't know, but I think it had something to do with the kidnapping." He stood then, putting some distance between them. "I've still got a lot to do, but uh…would you like to have dinner with me tonight?"

"Yes?" She wasn't sure why it came out as a question.

A small smile tugged at the corner of his lips, softening his features. "Don't sound too excited. I just figured your sister would be resting or spending time with Andre. Neither you or I are targets and I can take an hour away from here to eat. If you don't want to, you're not obligated."

"Are you asking me because you want to discuss the kidnapping?"

"No." The answer was automatic.

Something inside her eased at that. "Is this like a date?" She really hoped it was.

"Yes, but don't expect to get lucky." The unexpected humor in his voice made her smile.

A real one. The action was so relaxing, it surprised her. It had been so long since she'd let her guard down around anyone. For the past year she'd been pretending to be having a good time everywhere she traveled with Alena, but everything about her had been fake. And she hated that. "I'd like to have dinner with you then." More than she would admit.

In return, he smiled too. The crinkling action around his lips and eyes made her breath catch. An almost imperceptible dimple appeared on his left cheek. It was out of place, but so...adorable. "I'll meet you in the foyer at seven."

"Okay. Do you know which room Andre put my sister in?"

"Her room is the one directly next to yours, but I doubt she's in there right now."

"Oh, right." That nauseous feeling was back, but she ignored it. "Of course. Well, I guess I'll see you this evening." Nika slid off the chair and hurried from the kitchen before she could say something stupid.

She couldn't believe she'd admitted to him what she could do. In her gut she knew he didn't trust her, but she wasn't sure why. There was no possible way Declan could know what she and Alena were planning, but he *had* been in her head poking around before they'd met. She remembered his visits but she wondered if somehow he'd seen something he wasn't supposed to. That didn't make sense though. He would have said something to Andre if he had.

Shelving those thoughts she hurried up the stairs in search of her sister. Whatever Alena was planning next, Nika needed to know.

At this point, she wasn't sure she could go through with their plans. Without even realizing it, Declan had knocked her world off its axis. Most men, even if they knew Alena wasn't available, didn't hide their attraction to her sister. Declan was different, though. When he looked at Nika, she knew she was the only woman he wanted. More than that, he knew what she was and believed her and... she genuinely liked him. He'd kept her included in what had happened during the kidnapping, treating her as if she mattered and had a right to know what had been going on.

* * *

He slipped one of his many throwaway phones out of his pocket and ducked into one of Andre's empty guest rooms.

Rick picked up on the first ring. "What the hell is going on?"

"Why don't you tell me? How did the woman escape? I thought you had everything planned perfectly," he whispered.

Rick muttered a string of violent curses. "She attacked one of my men. It was...unexpectedly violent. And precise."

"Does she know anything...about me or you?"

"We've never taken off our masks and I haven't spoken about you to anyone here."

He took a shaky breath, letting an ounce of calm invade him. Maybe he was still safe. Declan hadn't acted like he knew anything, but at this point, he couldn't afford to get careless. "What's the plan?"

"I've had to change a few things, but keep your ear to the ground. Is Yasha still at the house?"

"Yes. Why?"

"I've been in contact with Yasha regarding the sale of some items he's acquired."

He didn't even want to know what those items were. It could be people or weapons or drugs. "He's doing business with *you*?"

"It's not as if he knows my real name." Rick's words were clipped.

"Right, of course. Yasha's still here but Andre isn't happy about it."

"He's angry at his father?"

"As far as I can tell, he hates his father. Until today, I don't think they've spoken in a while."

There was a slight pause on the other end. "Call me if you hear anything."

"I will...Are you still planning to target Andre again after this?"

"One way or another, he will die, but his father is my primary target."

When they disconnected, he wiped the sweat from his forehead. This cloak and dagger shit was going to kill him. He had no problem hiding in a swamp for three days or being dropped off in the middle of the rainforest with no supplies or communication equipment, but this...sucked. Lying to Declan and the rest of his team made him want to rip his own throat out.

Unfortunately, he had no choice.

CHAPTER FIFTEEN

A lena wrapped the plush cotton towel around herself and stepped from the bathroom into Andre's room. She'd already towel dried her hair and smoothed on lotion. Now all she wanted to do was sleep, but doubted that was possible.

As soon as she entered Andre's room, he pushed off the bed. His expression was concerned, but there was no hiding his desire. The man wore it right out in the open. "Are you okay?"

"I'm not going to break down if that's what you're worried about." She smiled and tried to fight the sudden overwhelming wave of insecurity she experienced. It was ridiculous. She modeled for a living and had no problem walking around in skimpy clothes in front of a crowd. So why was she hesitating at what she was about to do? Andre was a means to an end. *Nothing more.* Something she felt she was constantly reminding herself of over the course of the last few weeks. The man had been willing to sacrifice a lot of money to save her. A woman he'd been seeing less than a month. She didn't want to hurt him.

"Here." He pulled back the rich gold and blue comforter and sheet.

In response, she let her towel drop and it took all her control not to instinctively cover herself. Her nipples tightened as air rushed over her breasts. It was as if all the air sucked from the room as Andre's pale blue eyes darkened. His gaze raked over her body in blatant appreciation, his breath hitching in his throat.

Wordlessly she took a few steps toward him, covering the small distance. Guilt slid through her like ice, but she ruthlessly shoved it aside and pulled up unwanted, violent memories. Memories of her beautiful mother's broken, bloody body. Those bastards had practically ripped her jaw from her face. The image was forever seared into her brain. It was buried deep in her psyche. No matter how hard she tried, she couldn't get rid of it. Even counseling hadn't helped. Alena had protected her little sister from seeing what those monsters had done to their parents, but she remembered. Even when she didn't want to, she always remembered. Every fucking detail. And it reminded her of what had to be done.

Andre's strong hands settled on her hips. "Where'd you go just then?"

Feigning a smile, she wrapped her arms around his neck. "What are you talking about?"

"Just then. You were here, but you weren't really *here*. What were you thinking about?" The concerned look on his face made what she had to do even harder. How this man was even related to Yasha was beyond her. She'd assumed he'd be a monster just like his father, but he was so different.

"Nothing important." She pressed her naked body up against him so they were hip to hip, making her intentions as clear as she could. Using her body this way to get what she wanted wasn't something she'd ever done. Sure, she'd gained a reputation for sleeping with rich playboys, but she'd only slept with less than a handful of the men she'd been linked with in the media. And the men she actually had slept with, she'd wanted *them*, not something from them. This was a new experience and she didn't know what to make of it. She really *liked* Andre. He was smart, funny, sexy and she could tell he liked her sister too. Not just for her benefit but he'd seemed to enjoy Nika's company as well. That went a long way in her book. Alena wished she didn't like him so damn much.

His erection pushed insistently against her lower abdomen, but his blond eyebrows pulled down. "I don't want you doing this out of a sense of obligation."

"I'm incredibly grateful for what you did, but I want you. Very much." At least that much was true. She was very attracted to him. She'd have to be blind not to be. He looked like a Nordic god. But that wasn't all. The man was just...good.

"I don't want your gratitude," he murmured as one of his hands strayed to her breast.

When he lazily rubbed a thumb over her nipple, she instinctively arched her back. On one level, she knew she was using him, but nothing could dilute the fact that she still desired him and was growing to care for him.

Far too much. In a way, she almost wished he was like his father. It would make things so much easier. She could use him, walk away, and never look back. Unfortunately, nothing was happening like she'd originally planned.

She leaned closer. "Then what do you want?"

He covered her mouth in a gentle, almost reverent kiss. Unbearable heat pooled between her legs as he continued stroking her breast. His unhurried movements sent a shot of pleasure straight from her nipple to the building heat between her legs. It was as if her pleasure points were connected and each time he teased her, the more damp she grew between her legs. When she clutched his shoulders, he moaned into her mouth, the sound urgent. His tongue rasped over hers with a barely contained hunger. The raw energy humming through him ratcheted up her own desire about a hundred degrees.

She gasped when the backs of her knees hit the bed. Andre's arm wrapped around her waist as he laid her on the silky sheets. For a brief moment she wondered what it would be like to allow herself to melt into Andre's strong embrace. She'd spent so many years protecting her sister and choosing relationships where she was in control. For once, she wished she had a decent man like Andre in her life. Maybe someone she could love. When he suddenly pulled away from her, her entire body mourned the loss.

"What are you doing?" she asked as he drew the comforter up until it covered her bare breasts.

"You need rest and I want you to have time to think about this. You've been through a lot in the past couple days." His voice was hoarse, strained.

"But I want—"

He placed a firm finger over her lips, but she didn't miss the heat in his eyes. "Sleep and we'll talk later. Do you want me to send your sister in? I know I stole you away earlier."

Her entire body ached, both from her escape and from an unfulfilled need, but her mind was also exhausted. If she spoke to Nika now, she might give in to her sister's demands that they call the whole thing off. Denying her little sister what she wanted was the hardest thing Alena had ever done and she was dangerously close to breaking. "Not right now. You're right, I am tired. I'll just take a little nap."

As he strode toward the door, she sat up. "Andre?"

"Yes?"

"I know we haven't gotten to talk about everything yet, but Nika told me that your father was going to help pay part of the ransom. Is that true?"

Something dark flashed in his eyes as he nodded. "Yes."

"I'd love to thank him later. Do you think you could ask him over for lunch or dinner tomorrow?" She bit back the guilt and nausea that pushed up. Her original plan had been to seduce Andre, then somehow get his father invited over. In a strange way, the kidnapping had worked in her favor. Now she'd be able to take Yasha out a lot sooner than she'd expected.

"I don't know—"

"Please? It would mean a lot to me."

He sighed, but nodded. "I'll ask him."

"Thank you." Alena fell back against the fluffy pillow as the door shut behind him.

He obviously hated his father too. Something she hadn't counted on. But, she'd just have to work around it.

* * *

"What the *fuck* is going on?" Yasha shouted the moment Andre stepped into his office.

Andre rubbed a hand over his face. Everything about this scene was so typical. "What are you shouting about *now*?"

"Nice of you to come see me now that you're back."

"I didn't realize I needed to check in with you." Andre stared at his father and for what felt like the millionth time in his life, he wondered how they could be related. He didn't even think of the man in front of him as his father. He thought of him as Yasha, as if that somehow separated their blood relationship. If only it was so simple.

Yasha glanced at two of his guards and nodded, indicating for them to leave. Once the door shut behind them, he sighed. "Your girlfriend is alive, yes?"

She wasn't his girlfriend. Hell, he didn't know what she was but Andre didn't correct him. Instead he nodded and gritted his teeth. The thought of Yasha knowing anything about his personal life brought out protective instincts for Alena. The man brought death and heartache wherever he went. He didn't want this man anywhere near her. "She's here and resting."

"What happened? I heard whispers that you didn't meet with the kidnappers."

"She escaped so your money is untouched. You may take it when you leave."

"Don't you think that's convenient?" he sneered.

"What's convenient?"

Yasha tapped a finger on the desk. "Her escaping so easily."

"If you saw her, you wouldn't say that." He bit back a sharper retort. Giving his father the details would be pointless. Yasha trusted no one. He never had. He treated people as if they were objects, especially women. In Yasha's world, women were for sex only. Whether they wanted it or not.

"I want to know how you met this woman and who she is," Yasha persisted.

Andre tempered his annoyance. If he showed emotion, his father would pounce and push him until he gave something away. "I'm not having this conversation with you. Who I date is none of your concern. However, if you'd like to have dinner tomorrow, Alena would like to thank you for offering to help pay for her return."

"I did not do it for her."

"I know that and you know that. She no doubt thinks you're my loving, concerned father. Since we both know *that's* not true, I'll tell her you're unable to make it." That way he wouldn't have to lie to Alena.

His father's head cocked slightly to the side and his eyes flashed with something Andre couldn't put his finger on. "No, I will dine with you tomorrow. I would like to meet this woman you're so infatuated with. Hopefully you haven't fallen for another whore." He practically spat the words.

Instinctively Andre started to argue but thought better of it. Might as well get it over with, then get his father out of his life once again. For good this time. "Fine. Be here at six sharp."

Instead of moving, Yasha still lounged against the desk. "I need a favor."

Of course he did. "What is it?"

"I need to use one of your marina warehouses in a few days, just for a couple hours."

Andre shook his head. "No. No way. I'm not helping you move drugs."

"This is not about drugs. I simply need a place to meet with some associates. I'm being watched by the FBI and I can't afford to be seen at any of my establishments."

"You swear it isn't about drugs…or women?" He narrowed his eyes. His father was a criminal, but for the most part he was honest with Andre.

"Neither. I need privacy and considering our relationship, they won't be watching you."

Andre couldn't tell if he was lying, but he had given him the money for Alena. "I'll think about it."

"When you do, think about the money I gave you with no strings attached."

No strings except the favor he wanted. "I'll let you know tomorrow evening."

Yasha nodded once. "I will see you then."

As the door shut behind his father, Andre called Declan.

He picked up on the first ring. "Everything okay?"

"Where are you?" Andre asked.

"In the kitchen, going over some things with Odell. Your father is in your office and I don't want him to know what we're doing."

Andre scrubbed a hand over his face. "He's leaving but he'll be back tomorrow for dinner."

"Do you think that's a good idea?" Declan asked.

"No, but he's up to something dirty. I can feel it. I want to talk to you. *Alone.*"

"Be there in a sec."

Andre collapsed into his leather chair after they disconnected. His father was an evil man. He understood that on every level.

It was time he did something about it.

CHAPTER SIXTEEN

Nika looked at herself in the mirror for the tenth—okay, fiftieth—time, then rolled her eyes at her reflection. Declan was just taking her to dinner, nothing more. She hadn't dated much as a teenager so maybe the ridiculous excitement humming through her was normal.

Growing up with an uncle who worked in foreign intelligence and with a sister who looked like, well, a model, dating hadn't been easy. Her uncle had basically vetted anyone who had asked her out, not caring that they were sixteen-year-old boys. To him, everyone had been suspect. And on the off chance some guy passed his stupid tests, they ended up falling for Alena anyway. Turning eighteen and leaving for college had been the best day of her life. Not that she didn't love her family. She did more than anything. They were small and tight-knit, and they seriously had issues, but her sister and uncle were all she had.

She shook her head and turned away from the mirror. If she allowed herself, she'd be lost in her memories forever. By the time she got to the front door, Declan stood in the foyer talking on his cell phone. When he saw her, however, all speech stopped and his eyes glittered with pure, heated desire. And it was all directed at her. She clutched onto her purse as if that could somehow ground her.

He'd wanted her before, but this was something entirely different. The primitive waves rolling off him sent a jolt of hunger and feminine awareness spiraling through her entire body. She swallowed once, but couldn't seem to break contact. Those dark eyes of his held her captive. If he kept mentally undressing her, they'd never make it to dinner. Not that that was such a bad thought.

"I'll call you later," he muttered into the phone before sliding it into his pocket. He didn't take his eyes off her. He wore dark pants, a black sweater that stretched perfectly across his oh-so broad chest and shoulders. For the most part he'd been wearing suit jackets that didn't exactly hide his muscular build, but the lack of a jacket showed everything off.

Masculine.

Powerful.

Dominant.

Three things she normally avoided in a man. Not with Declan. It was as if she was drawn to those qualities.

"You look...perfect," he murmured.

Self-conscious, she glanced down at her simple black dress. It didn't even show off any cleavage with its boatneck cut, but he certainly liked it. Which made her feel ridiculously happy. "Thanks."

She didn't know what to expect from him, but she was certain of one thing. Whatever was going to happen with him would inevitably be short term. A fling might break her heart, but she was going to take the chance and enjoy it while it lasted.

"I should have asked before, but are you a vegetarian?" he asked as he held open the front door for her.

She shook her head because she didn't trust her voice. Outside the house stood four armed guards that she could see, but she was certain there were more that she couldn't. Separated from the line of black SUVs, an older model Land Rover sat in the front of the circular stone driveway. "Is this yours?"

The lights flashed when he hit the key fob. "I figured this would be a little lower key than one of the SUVs."

Nika was surprised he didn't drive something flashier, but she was secretly pleased. Everything about him was just so...male. Including his vehicle. Since she spent a lot of time traveling with her sister, the men they often hung out with had horribly entitled attitudes. Declan was understated. More importantly, he was the kind of man she knew could and would protect her if the need arose. He'd protect anyone that needed it.

"So you don't think we need any extra security?" she asked as soon as they were headed toward downtown Miami.

He glanced in the rearview mirror. "We've got a small team tailing us, but if I actually thought you were in any danger, we wouldn't be leaving the house. You were never a target and you're not involved with Andre."

She'd figured, but had needed to ask. They'd brought in even more security to Andre's house and that place was locked down tighter than a fortress. She knew it was the only reason Declan was probably even leaving for an hour or so. "Did you manage to find out anything about the kidnappers?"

"We're working on it. We found the house where they kept your sister."

"Really?"

He snorted. "Hard to miss with the garage door splintered apart."

A short laugh escaped even as that same sense of relief spread over her. She was so damn grateful Alena was okay. "I'm guessing you didn't find anyone though since you haven't said."

"No one. So even if your sister did kill someone, he wasn't at any of those houses. We found evidence they'd been staying at a couple of the homes but they'd all cleared out. My guys had four of the exits blocked, but they found another way to get out undetected." She could hear the anger in his voice and had no doubt he'd make it his mission to find those men.

"Are you guys ever going to involve the police?"

He lifted his shoulders again, not answering one way or another. And she wasn't going to push.

"As a precaution," he continued, "we're going to keep your sister under basic lockdown along with Andre, but the real target was always Andre. It would be stupid to make another attempt so soon, but I'm guessing whoever wanted to kidnap him will try again."

Nika wished she could somehow feel better about that, but it was still scary. Alena wanted to use Andre to get to Yasha. And someone wanted to hurt Andre. It would be too easy for them to get caught in the crossfire. The thought of Declan getting caught in anything made her blood turn to ice.

And what happened when Alena killed Yasha and they tried to leave? What if some crazy kidnappers followed them and tried to take her sister *again*? Nika doubted that scenario but there were too many variables and Nika didn't understand why her sister couldn't see that. She'd tried talking to Alena again after her nap but her sister hadn't wanted to listen to a word. If anything, she was even more determined to kill Yasha now. And Nika had been too afraid to ask if Alena had actually slept with Andre. Her sister liked to put on a façade for the world, but she was very particular about her bed partners. Still, Alena planned to seduce Andre and if things had already gone that far, Nika knew her sister would never back out once they slept together. It was as if Alena was completely blinded by her rage.

"Andre's father is coming to dinner tomorrow night." Declan's voice interrupted her thoughts.

She stiffened, but forced herself not to outwardly react any more than that. Even though he wasn't looking at her, she was under the distinct impression that Declan was testing her. Or maybe she was just reading into it too much. "Yeah, Alena mentioned something about that."

"What do you think about him?" Again, his face was impassive, but she could almost swear he was baiting her.

More likely, it was her own guilt clawing at her. "I know he was giving Andre the money, but he seemed like a dick."

Declan let out a sharp bark of laughter. "That's an understatement."

Nika mentally shook her head at herself. She was totally overreacting. He wasn't testing her. He was just making conversation. "How long have you lived in Miami?"

"Two years. I moved here to be closer to my family and start Gallagher Security."

"You have a brother, right?" she asked.

He nodded. "Three, actually."

"Are you close to them?"

"Very. What about you? Other than your sister are you close to your family?"

She shrugged and tried to choose her words carefully. "We have an uncle but other than that, we don't really have anyone."

He cleared his throat and she guessed what he was going to say before he said it. It was that standard date talk, she thought. You talk about work, family and hobbies. "What about your parents?"

"Dead." The word stuck in her throat. She couldn't tell him the real way they'd died and she didn't want to lie about that. It just felt wrong on too many levels.

"I'm sorry. I lost my mom too. Car accident." His words were quiet and sincere.

She glanced at him but he didn't take his eyes off the road. "I'm sorry you lost your mom. How old were you when it happened...ah, if you don't mind me asking?" She knew she shouldn't continue down this path because it would likely invite more questions about herself, but she wanted to know everything about him.

"This summer it'll be four years so...I was about thirty at the time. What about you?"

"I was five so I don't really remember much about either of them. Alena does though and she..." Nika fiddled with her seatbelt as she trailed off, her throat tightening.

"She what?"

Nika shrugged. "She just tells me stories. I imagine it was harder on you because you at least have memories of your mom."

He didn't respond, just glanced in the rearview mirror and frowned.

Her heart beat quickened as she took in his body language. "Is everything okay?"

"Yeah." His short, one word answer didn't leave much room for discussion.

Nika self-consciously smoothed down her dress as silence descended in the vehicle. The little voice in her head told her to guard her heart, but with Declan she didn't want to. He was different, like her, and she enjoyed that she could be herself around him. Well, to an extent anyway.

"What are you thinking?" His intoxicating voice sent shivers to all her nerve endings.

"I'm just thinking about last night and wondering if the next step will be just as good." She wasn't sure where the words came from, but with him she wanted to put everything out there. She couldn't be honest about everything with him, but this attraction between them, this inexplicable pull, she wouldn't deny it. Didn't want to. It was obvious he wanted her as much as she wanted him so while she still felt a little insecure around him, she felt comfortable being herself. It was freeing.

His fingers tightened on the wheel. "It'll be better." The words came out as a soft rumble.

Her breasts grew heavy with need at the thought. The things he'd done with his mouth and fingers had already surpassed her expectations. And that had been in her dreams. She knew the reality would be better. So much better.

As they drove deeper into the heart of Miami her curiosity got the better of her. "Where exactly are you taking me?"

"A steakhouse not far from here."

"And that's all you're going to tell me?"

His mouth pulled into a small, sly grin. "Patience."

That was something she normally had in abundance, but not with him. She started to ask another question, but he beat her to it.

"So, what do you do when you're not traveling with your sister?"

Back to the date talk. "I do a lot of freelance web design. I've built up a decent portfolio but it's nowhere near where I'd like it to be. Eventually I'd like to start my own company and do it full time, but for now…" Shrugging, she glanced out the window. She couldn't focus on work the way she wanted to until she and her sister had finished what they'd started.

"For now, what?" he persisted.

"Well, Alena wanted to travel some while she had the chance. Last year she was busy modeling and since I didn't have any pressing contracts I decided to travel with her." The practiced lie rolled off her tongue with frightening ease. The part about the web design wasn't a lie, but the traveling part was all bullshit. The words left a bitter taste in her mouth.

"I've been looking to have my company's website redesigned. Think you might be interested?"

Despite everything going on, she actually wanted to. The life of a socialite was boring as hell and when they traveled so much, she missed working. Missed staying in one place. Alena liked to travel, but Nika wanted roots. Wanted real friends. Wanted a place that she called home and meant it. So much so, it sometimes hurt to even think about it. They had their place in New Orleans and she loved visiting there, but it had never felt like home. They'd never stayed long enough to get truly settled in. "I'll let you look at my portfolio and if you're interested, maybe we can work something out." The answer was vague and she knew it wouldn't happen because as soon as Yasha was dead she and Alena were leaving Miami. They wanted to put as much distance as possible between themselves and anything related to the man.

Declan steered up to a restaurant with two giant lion statues out front. Without pause, a valet driver rounded the vehicle.

"Good evening Mr. Gallagher."

Nika grabbed her purse as another valet opened her door. But the man's words stopped her as he addressed Declan. "I think your friend is still inside, Mr. Gallagher."

Declan frowned, his body going almost preternaturally still for a moment before he turned back to the other man. "What friend?"

"I'm not sure. I overheard someone asking the maitre d' if you were on time for your reservation."

The hair on the back of Declan's neck tingled. He'd only made the reservations a few hours ago. And he sure as hell wasn't expecting company. "Nika, shut your door."

Her eyes widened but she did as he said without question.

Both valet drivers' eyes widened and the one closest to him spoke. "Mr. Gallagher—"

Declan took the keys from him. "Cancel my reservations and apologize to Eduardo for me." Without waiting for a response, he slid back into his seat and pulled away from the curb.

"What's going on? Is it something to do with the kidnappers?"

"I'm not sure but I'm not taking any chances." Only a handful of people knew where he was going tonight, including the small security team he'd had follow them. Half of his men weren't aware he'd left and most of Andre's regular guys didn't know either. It might mean nothing that someone had shown up and was asking about him, but Declan didn't believe in coincidence.

He keyed his radio, choosing to use that over phones. "Croft, fall back, but don't lose us. See if we've got a tail and get their plate."

"On it."

He watched in the rearview mirror as the SUV turned off down a side street. He glanced over his shoulder, then in both side mirrors. From what he could tell, he wasn't being followed, but since he had Nika in the vehicle, he couldn't take any chances. He headed toward Fifth Street until he made it to Brickell Avenue.

Lined with a cluster of high-rise buildings, it was probably one of the worst places to be stuck, but since it was late, there was little traffic and he wanted to make it to the highway quickly. If someone was after them, it would be easiest to put distance between them and lose them on a crowded freeway.

Keep Nika safe. The words rattled around in his head. Nika was everything he hadn't realized he wanted and needed in a woman. She was soft and sweet and he didn't have to lie about what he was with her. It was hard to remember that he'd been assigned to check her out. He might try to deny it, but something about her called to his most primal side.

"Boss."

Declan picked up his radio, keyed it. "Yeah?"

"Spotted a Humvee that looks like it might have been tailing you, but I think the driver made us. Got the plate. He turned off a couple streets back, heading for the highway is my guess," Croft said.

"Send the plate number to Odell now. We're headed back to base, everyone follow."

"On it."

"It could be nothing," Declan said to Nika. "We'll know more once we run the plate, but you're officially under lockdown now too."

Her electric green eyes widened, seeming bright against her smooth, caramel skin. "Excuse me?"

"Unless you have an armed escort, you're not going anywhere." He figured he probably sounded like an overbearing dick, but until he found out if they'd actually been followed or not, he intended to keep her safe.

CHAPTER SEVENTEEN

He quietly shut the guest bathroom door behind him and turned on the faucet before answering his cell phone. "Yeah?"

"Is Gallagher back to the villa yet?" Rick asked.

"Yeah." He'd been surprised to see Declan back so soon, but he was fairly sure he hadn't shown it.

"Do you know if he's figured anything out?"

"No. I haven't said two words to him since he got back. If I start asking too many questions, he's going to know something's up. And to be honest, I think he already knows something is going on. After tonight, I guarantee he gets rid of the team and brings in new faces."

"Can you throw suspicion on someone else?"

"I can try, but what's the point?" He opened the door and glanced out to find the guest bedroom still empty.

"The point is, I'm paying you a lot of money and you'll do what I say."

"I'll do what I can, but you made a mistake going after Declan. He has a lot of powerful friends. Even if he didn't, if you fuck with him, his entire family will come after you. There will be nowhere on this planet you can

211

hide." Which was why he hated what he was doing. But he had no choice.

"I wasn't trying to kill him. I just want to talk some business with him. He must have made us tonight."

"Then call him on the damn phone. If you try to corner him again, he'll put a bullet in your head. I'm telling you though, if you want to bribe him, it won't work."

"That's what I thought about you."

He gritted his teeth at Rick's words. The other man knew exactly why he was helping. It wasn't as if he had a choice. "Go to hell."

Rick laughed, the sound harsh and devoid of humor. "I'll be in contact."

The phone went dead before he could respond. Sighing, he shut off the sink, then eased open the door once again. All this sneaking around was going to give him a heart attack if he wasn't careful and then he wouldn't be able to take care of his daughter.

The thought of his sweet little girl was the only thing that gave him enough resolve to do what had to be done. He knew he was beyond redemption and he'd do whatever it took to save his daughter.

* * *

Declan shut his eyes and tried to concentrate on Nika, but it was no use. He figured she might not be asleep yet. Once they'd returned to the house he'd had to follow up on more work. At this point they were running down leads and it was tedious. Normally that wasn't what his guys did, but for this job, it was necessary. He'd contemplated handing everything over to the cops, but Andre didn't want to and he couldn't involve them anyway since he was doing an off the books favor for Vernon.

After trying to get into Nika's head again, he scrubbed a hand over his face. He hated that he hadn't even been able to take a break with her, but that was the job. He'd thought about going to her room, but... fuck, she had him all twisted up. He was on the job and shouldn't even be involved with her. For more than one reason.

Right now he wanted to know who the hell had been following them and what they wanted. There hadn't been any aggressiveness so it stood to reason whoever it was hadn't wanted to kill him. Yet. After making a list of the people who were aware that he'd left with Nika, he'd narrowed it down to exactly eight—including Andre and Alena. Since they weren't suspects that left a small pool to choose from. Considering Odell and Clay were also on that list, he was starting to second guess his entire team. He could bring in all new guys but that wouldn't solve his problem in the long run because there would still be a traitor working for him on future jobs. He needed to solve this problem *now*.

Leaning against his headboard, Declan closed his eyes and focused on Odell. It was after midnight so he should be sleeping. The black wave of the dream state slowly rolled over him with a familiarity he'd fallen into.

Bright lights...a Blackjack table...a man wearing a dark suit placed a hand on Odell's shoulder. The silver nametag read Roberto. A picture of a pyramid in the background.

"I need you to come with us, sir."

"What about?" He didn't glance up from his cards.

"The bet you made on Southern Dancer."

The scene dissipated and was replaced with a new one. Fists against ribs...a river of blood across a tile floor...a bloody tooth lying in a small pool of crimson liquid...

Declan jerked awake at the sound of his phone ringing. He'd taken his cell off vibrate and now he regretted it.

"Southern Dancer," he muttered to himself. Sounded like the name of a horse. He grabbed the pad on his nightstand and jotted it down before answering his cell.

He frowned when he saw Riley's number. "What's up?"

"Hey. You all right?"

"Yeah, why?"

"Haven't heard from you about that thing."

Declan snorted. "Still working the job."

"Staying safe?" his brother asked, a trace of worry in his voice. Riley might be younger but he always looked out for his family.

"I'm good. Have you talked to Maden lately?"

"Last I heard he was somewhere in the Middle East with Dad."

Much to Declan's annoyance, their youngest brother had been recruited by the CIA as soon as he'd finished college. He didn't have any military experience but he spoke nine languages and had the ability to blend in almost anywhere. Not to mention he was basically a human lie detector. His clairvoyant capabilities had gotten him far in the world. Despite that, since he was the youngest it was unavoidable that the rest of the Gallagher brothers worried about him the most.

"Yeah, same here. Wish he'd get his ass home for a break." He couldn't wait until they were all in the same city again.

"Me too. I'm about to crash, but just wanted to check in."

Once they disconnected Declan laid back down, all his focus on Nika again. He could feel himself hitting obsession level with her. The need to see her, touch her, talk to her. Tonight on the way to dinner he'd enjoyed just being with her, getting to know her better. Everything about her seemed real.

Dark curly hair, flawless skin. Bright, emerald green eyes. Petite, lean body with just enough curves to hold onto. Damn it, she had to be asleep. Unless she was blocking him from her dreams. But he didn't think so.

After changing into jeans and a pullover sweater, he tucked his SIG into the back of his pants. If he didn't talk to Nika now, he'd never get any sleep and he wouldn't be able to do his job at full capacity. Or at least that's what he told himself as he started to leave. He paused at the door, then returned to his nightstand. He grabbed a couple of condoms and headed for her room. His chance of using the condoms was probably slim, but he wasn't taking a risk that they got started and she changed her mind because he wasn't prepared.

One of his guys guarded her door but disappeared down the hallway when he saw Declan.

He knocked once.

"Who is it?" Nika's called out softly.

"It's me."

"What do you want?"

He tried the handle, but it was locked. No surprise. "Can you open the door?" he asked through gritted teeth, then immediately regretted his tone.

The door cracked open a few inches, but she didn't offer to let him in. That just annoyed him. He'd been losing sleep over her and she was blocking him out. Without giving her a chance to refuse him, he pushed the door open and quickly stepped inside. The thought of anyone else seeing him begging her to let him in was embarrassing.

"What are you doing?" She placed her hands on her hips and glared at him.

His lower abdomen tightened as he drank in the sight of her. In addition to form-fitting yoga pants, she also wore a skin-tight tank top that stretched across her breasts, perfectly accentuating her soft curves. If he stared hard enough he could just see the outline of her nipples—

She crossed her arms over her chest. "Um, hello per-vert?"

He stifled a smile. Hell yeah he was where she was concerned. He felt no shame. "I want to talk."

"In the middle of the night?"

"I want you," he rasped out, then inwardly winced. *Real smooth.*

Her eyes widened, but she didn't respond. Just swallowed audibly, her gaze trailing to his mouth for an instant.

"I'll go back to my room right now if you tell me to." And take a long, cold shower.

She bit her bottom lip as she eyed him, her green eyes flashing with...lust. "That dream we shared a few weeks ago, the one where you tied me up... Are you into that kind of stuff?"

A slow smile spread across his face. She wasn't telling him to go. "Not normally, but I liked having you restrained."

Her eyes flared with heat again. She liked that thought too. She shifted slightly, almost as if she was pressing her thighs together.

Oh yeah, she wanted him to stay.

Moving slowly, he removed his SIG from his waist-band and laid it on the nightstand. Then he stripped his sweater off.

Nika's breathing hitched, her chest rising and falling just a little faster as her gaze tracked over his bare chest.

The raw hunger in her eyes made everything inside him go still for an instant. To be on the receiving end of that look made him feel ten feet tall.

He'd already tasted her and felt her come against his hand. Now he wanted to feel her slick walls around his cock. To feel the warmth of her climax rushing over him.

Covering the short distance between them, he cupped her cheeks in his hands and crushed his mouth over hers. She tasted minty, sweet, as if she'd just brushed her teeth.

Declan wanted to devour every inch of her. He might have started entering her dreams to get to know her, to find out more about her, but this had nothing to do with that now. It had everything to do with her and the electric pulse that seemed to permanently exist between them.

As his tongue tangled with hers, her fingers trailed up his chest. He shuddered at the feel of her short nails scraping against his skin. She stopped at his shoulders, digging in and pressing tightly against him, as if she couldn't get close enough.

He didn't want a barrier between them.

Feeling frantic, like a randy fucking teenager, he grasped the hem of her top and tugged, only breaking away from her mouth to pull it over her head. He got a brief view of those gorgeous breasts and pale brown nipples before she grabbed onto his face and pulled him back to meet her.

Her kisses were hungry and frantic, mirroring how he felt. He grasped onto her hips and without pause, she lifted up, wrapping her legs around his waist.

Grabbing her ass, he rolled his hips against hers, walking until they fell onto the bed, her underneath him. It would be so easy to tug her pants down and get her off with his fingers before thrusting into her, but he felt that familiar need well up.

Ever since that first dream he'd been consumed with the need to taste her outside of a dream. Now to be able to do it in reality... He managed to tear his mouth from hers.

"If you stop I'll kill you," she rasped out, fingers still digging into his shoulders.

"Need to taste you." It was pretty much all he was capable of getting out. Crouching between her legs, he tugged her pants off. His breath caught in his throat when he realized she didn't have anything on underneath.

It was like she was trying to kill him.

Feeling possessive, he cupped her mound, sliding his middle finger along her slit. She was so wet. His cock pressed painfully against the zipper of his jeans.

Jeans he didn't want to be wearing.

But he was keeping a barrier on. Had to have something between them since he was barely holding onto his restraint. The woman made him feel unhinged, out of control.

Her eyes closed and her head fell back as she rolled her hips into his hold. It was probably the sexiest thing he'd ever seen. She was splayed out like some sort of offering and it was... There was no word for it. All he could think was that she was his, that he had to claim her.

Pressing his hands against her inner thighs he bent between her legs and flicked his tongue over her clit. The little bud peeked out from her swollen lips, begging to be touched.

The moment he made contact, she moaned his name.

"Declan." She slid her fingers through his hair, holding onto his scalp as if she was afraid he'd leave.

Not happening. The reality of this was a hell of a lot better than dreams. When he flicked his tongue over her clit again, her fingers tightened, her moans growing louder.

Right then he was thankful for the sound-dampening insulation in this place. Finding a rhythm, he teased and stroked her with his tongue. Though he wanted to drag this out longer, he was desperate to be inside her, to feel her sheath wrapped around his cock. He slid two fingers inside her, knowing she needed the extra stimulation.

Moving in and out slowly, he slid his fingers along her inner walls, savoring the way she clenched around him tighter and tighter.

Nika knew she shouldn't be surprised by how fast Declan got her worked up, not after their shared dreams. But still, it was a shock to her senses to be so close to climax already.

His tongue was pure heaven as he stroked against her sensitive bundle of nerves. It bordered on pain, but was just pleasure right now, the way he flicked against her with the right amount of pressure.

The way he'd learned her body so quickly stunned her. She arched her hips against each stroke, her inner walls gripping him tightly.

When he sucked on her clit, she lost it, her orgasm slamming through her like a sharp punch to all her nerve endings. Pleasure shot through her and she forced herself to let go of his head. Clutching the sheets beneath her, she rode out the waves of her climax.

As they spiraled through her, it was too much and not enough at the same time. "Inside me." It was a miracle she was able to rasp out those two words at all. Her brain was in pleasure overload but as he sat up and stripped off his jeans, she watched the man she'd come to think of as being so precise and economic with his movements actually tremble.

It was subtle, but through heavy-lidded eyes she saw his hands shake as he stripped of his jeans. When he pulled up a condom from his discarded pants she was glad one of them was thinking clearly.

Pushing up, she went to reach for the packet, but he was faster, ripping it open and rolling it over the most gorgeous cock she'd ever seen.

"Next time." The words were a sexy growl from an even sexier mouth.

She wanted to ride him, to feel all that strength pulsing beneath her, but the most primitive part of her brain knew that this first time, he was going to be on top. A man like Declan was dominant to his core.

The knowledge sent a shiver through her. Later she'd feel him under her. Now she wanted to experience every inch of this sexy man. Right now it was as if nothing else existed. She could pretend that for a little while anyway.

His mouth covered hers as his body did the same. As she wrapped her legs around his waist, his cock nudged her entrance. Thick and long, he pushed into her slickness. On instinct she arched into him, taking every inch of him.

Her abdomen clenched as he thrust hard once, filling her completely. Surprising her, he didn't start thrusting, but remained still inside her as he continued kissing her.

She could kiss the sexy man for hours, be consumed by the taste and feel of him.

"Move, damn it," she gasped. She was aware the demand sounded a lot like begging. She was beyond caring. She needed more, more, *more.*

He made this sexy, growling sound, but didn't say anything as he started thrusting. Caging her head in with his forearms, he stared down at her, pinning her with his dark gaze as he sank into her over and over.

There was something painfully intimate about the way he watched her. Even if she wanted to tear her gaze away, it would have been impossible. She was completely ensnared.

One of his hands claimed her breast, almost lazily, definitely possessively, as his thrusts grew erratic. She knew he was close and knew it wouldn't take much for her to climax again either.

Reaching between their bodies, she tweaked her already over-sensitive clit and just like that, fell into another orgasm. "Declan." It was all she could say.

His name on her lips seemed to push him over the edge. Or maybe he was finally able to let go of his control.

"Mine," he growled, claiming her mouth again as he found his own release.

She wasn't sure how much time passed, but their climaxes seemed to go on forever. The pleasure spiraled through every inch of her until he stopped driving into her with that franticness.

That raw desire quickly slid into something else as his kisses grew sweeter. He slid one of those big hands through her curly hair, holding her with a surprising gentleness until finally he pulled back an inch. But he didn't draw away completely.

Instead he laid his forehead against hers, his breath warm against her face. "Can I stay with you tonight?"

She ran her hands down his muscular back, loving the feel of his strength beneath her fingertips. "Oh yeah." Because they weren't done. Not by a long shot. There was no way this thing between them would ever work out long term so she was going to squeeze every ounce of pleasure from this experience that she could.

Deep down she knew she'd never meet another man like Declan and she wanted to remember this always.

CHAPTER EIGHTEEN

*N*ika's body tingled and sang with electrifying energy. She knew what was coming and forced herself to open her eyes. Sitting up in bed, she glanced next to her. Declan was a blur, as if he were part of a fuzzy photograph, but at least he was there and that comforted her. Her own body was curled up next to him and while it freaked her out a little, there wasn't a thing she could do about what was going to happen. Even though she'd wanted to deny what happened the other night, when that little girl had visited her, she'd known bone-deep what was to come. The visits were about to start again.

She hadn't talked to an actual spirit in a couple years, but she could feel it straight to her core that all that was about to change. In dreams when she communicated with spirits, she could still see the living, but it wasn't their world. She was on a different plane right now, in between the worlds. She saw the living as if through a distorted looking glass.

Sometimes the dead dragged her to other places, but more often than not, they just visited her wherever she happened to be. Usually her bedroom.

A little girl dressed in a pink, frilly nightgown with a cartoon character Nika didn't recognize finally appeared at the foot of the huge bed. And she was holding a tattered teddy bear. Blonde corkscrew curls surrounded the girl's soft, round face. She couldn't be more than ten. It was the same girl as before. She looked afraid.

Nika spoke first to ease the little girl's fears. "Hi, I'm Nika."

"I'm Selina." The tiny voice penetrated the still air and she clutched her bear tighter to her chest.

"Why are you here?" Nika asked.

"They told me you could help me."

"Who did?"

"The other children."

Nika's heart stuttered. "I don't understand. What other children?"

"They told me you're finally listening and that you'd help me."

Okay, not exactly an answer. Nika focused on what she did know. "You're obviously afraid of something. Do you want to tell me what it is?" Because the truth was, she might not like talking to the dead, but she couldn't deny helping a kid.

Her small shoulders lifted. "The dark."

"Whatever hurt you can't do anything else to you." More often than not, the spirits understood that, but kids were still kids no matter what form they were in. It broke her heart that some children couldn't find that closure they needed to move on from this plane.

"I know, but I'm still afraid."

The vise around Nika's heart tightened and twisted. The child was so young, she should have no problem finding peace. Unless she'd been the victim of a violent crime. Nika really hated this part. "How can I help you?"

"I just want my mommy to stop crying. I want her to be happy again."

"Who's your mommy?"

The little girl's eyebrows knitted together tightly. "She's mommy...but daddy calls her Anne."

"What's your last name?"

"Reynolds."

Nika made a mental note, but the girl continued. "They keep fighting all the time. I need mommy to know it wasn't her fault. I was playing hide and seek with my teddy bear. I knew I wasn't supposed to leave her..."

Selina was fading slowly, but it was fast enough that panic took root inside Nika. It took so much energy for spirits to visit her in her dreams and it might be a while until she saw her again. If she even saw her at all. She couldn't wait that long to help.

"How did you die?"

"I drowned. We were camping and I was playing hide and seek. I fell down a hole near a funny looking tree. I tried shouting for help, but it was dark and wet..."

And then she was gone.

Nika blinked as the bedroom came into focus.

Declan propped up on one elbow staring at her with concern. "You okay?"

"Yeah. I uh...just had a dream. Sort of."

"What was it?"

"It's not important," she muttered, not wanting to bother him with it.

He splayed a comforting hand over her bare stomach. "Tell me."

She scooted closer to him, liking the intimate way he touched her. It felt right, natural. Talking about this was harder than her other gifts, but maybe it would be good to share it with him. He seemed to know more than her about all this stuff. "A little girl came to me. She was very young, probably under ten. She told me she fell down some kind of hole on a camping trip with her parents and drowned. She wants her mom to stop crying."

His entire body went rigid, his hand tightening against her skin the slightest fraction. "Are you telling me you talked to a spirit?"

She stiffened at his tone. It wasn't as if she *asked* the dead to talk to her. "Yeah."

"Is this the first time it's happened?"

"No. Why?"

His jaw clenched but he answered. "You didn't mention it before. You said you had visions of people and places, but you didn't say anything about talking to dead people."

Nika sat up and tugged the sheet to her chest, needing an extra barrier. She didn't understand why he seemed so upset. "It's not like I was hiding it from you. I *just* told you."

"I know..."

"But what?"

"That's a big thing to keep from me." There was something in his tone that raked against her senses.

Now he was starting to make her mad. "I've told you more about myself than I've told *any* man before. I haven't talked to a spirit in years so *excuse me* if I didn't think about it before. I've had a lot on my mind lately." It wasn't like he was so damn forthcoming about his own gifts. She knew he was a dream walker but that was about it. And she hadn't pushed him on it out of respect.

When he didn't respond, she shoved the sheet away and swung her legs off the bed. Before her feet touched the ground, his arm snaked around her waist and he had her pinned on her back underneath him.

"I'm sorry." His deep voice enveloped her, sending little tremors of awareness rolling through her body.

"You're kind of being a jerk." She wiggled underneath him, trying to put space between them.

"I know and I'm sorry." He still didn't budge.

She knew if she truly wanted him off of her, he'd move. "You don't sound very apologetic."

"Well I am," he murmured, his gaze dipping to her mouth. She recognized that look.

When she felt his erection beginning to swell against her lower abdomen, she pushed at his chest. "You better not think—"

His mouth curved into a half-smile, definitely unapologetic now. "I don't think anything. I just can't help this reaction when I'm touching you. Now what's the girl's name?"

She paused. "What?"

"The girl from your dream."

"Oh...uh, Selina Reynolds. Why?"

"I'll see if I can find out some more information. If what the spirit said is true, then there's probably a missing persons report filed on her."

"Oh, God, I didn't even think about that...Thank you." She'd just been hoping she could help the girl pass over, but it would be better if she could help the parents find peace somehow.

"Is there anything else that might be helpful?"

"She said she fell down a hole near a funny looking tree."

He watched her quietly for a long moment, his expression almost thoughtful. "The last woman I was involved with lied to me. She was special, like you, and she...almost got me killed because of her lies."

Guilt detonated inside her. She wasn't doing anything that could get him killed. And yeah, if she was getting technical she wasn't lying to him. She wasn't being straightforward either. Ugh. "Did you work together?" she asked.

He nodded, his warm breath feathering over her shoulder as he dropped a light kiss there.

"What happened?"

He didn't answer. Instead, he cupped one of her breasts and teasingly rubbed her nipple before dipping his head to her other breast. When he gently pressed down with his teeth, she shoved all her questions to the side. If he didn't want to talk about his past that was fine with her. She didn't want to talk about hers either.

CHAPTER NINETEEN

Yasha unsnapped the wrist wraps of his boxing gloves and tossed them onto his workout bench. His chest and arms were sore, but at sixty-five, he had to keep in shape. He knew better than most that there would always be those younger and stronger trying to make a name for themselves. Killing him would immediately give someone street credibility.

He should know. Decades ago he'd done the same thing. After years of working as a thug for minimum pay, he'd taken out the entire Belov family, established himself, then eventually moved to the United States.

The land of the free, indeed. As a criminal, he had more rights in the States than as an upstanding citizen in Moscow. Not that he'd ever *been* an upstanding citizen.

The door to his private gym opened. Out of habit, he glanced up and reached for his weapon, though he already knew no one but Dima would bother him during his workout.

"You done for the morning, boss?" Dima asked as he handed him a towel.

"Yes. Is my appointment still a go?"

Dima nodded as he glanced at his watch. "He should be calling in half an hour."

231

"Good."

"What about...the other stuff?"

"Good as well. I'm going to change the meeting place."

Dima's expression barely changed but Yasha could tell he was surprised. "Why?"

He opened the door and nodded at Dima. "Walk with me. A source tells me some high ranking members of the FBI and DEA are in town."

Now Dima frowned. "For you?"

"Hard to tell. It could be unrelated." As far as he knew, no one had a clue what his plans were, but he wasn't going to take the chance. Not with a deal this big on the table.

"I'll keep my ear to the ground too. I was going to put this on your desk, but I got the results back regarding the Lazarev brothers' deaths." He held out a thin manila file.

Yasha bit back his annoyance. He had to shower and prepare for his call. He didn't have time to read something that probably didn't matter anyway. "What does it say?"

"They died of heart attacks."

Yasha paused in the hallway. "All of them?"

"Yes. It is strange. They each had unnaturally dilated pupils and according to reports, two of them were acting odd before they died."

"That part is not so strange." All of the brothers had been involved in drugs. One of the many reasons Yasha had cut ties with them years ago. It was one thing to sell drugs, but using one's own product was bad business. Any addiction was a weakness.

"Maybe, but I found something else strange. I was looking into the Brennan sisters as you asked. On the surface, everything about them looks normal. They were raised in London by an uncle but moved to New York when the oldest was twenty for her modeling career."

"What's strange about that?"

"Other than the fact that I can't find much information on their uncle—nothing. Just a name, but no property holdings or bank accounts. At least not under his name. It's as if he's a ghost. However, I was looking into their travel patterns and they were in Frankfurt, Cairo, and Nassau when each Lazarev brother died. At the exact dates for each death. I probably wouldn't have noticed it otherwise, but I was researching them at the same time."

Wasn't that just interesting. "You're certain?"

"I cross-referenced their flight logs. It could be a co-incidence, but…"

Yasha took the folder from Dima as the other man held open his office door. "This is good work. Make sure you confirm with my son that we're having dinner with them tonight."

"You're sure you still want to go?"

"I definitely want to meet these women." He shut the door behind Dima and opened the file. If the women had been in only one city, he might have been able to write it off as coincidence, but all three? Impossible.

It wasn't such a strange concept that a government agency would use a beautiful woman as a means to an end. Hell, the KGB had done the same thing and he was positive the FSB was still doing it too. If the women did work for the government, he guessed this was the CIA's doing. One way or another, he was going to find out who the sisters were working for and what the hell they wanted with his son. Then, he would kill them.

* * *

Declan stared at Nika's still form. It was impossible to tear his gaze away. She looked so peaceful. Unlike when she was awake. She seemed...worried all the time. Like something was constantly weighing on her mind. When her sister had been taken he understood, but he saw it now and he'd seen it even before Alena had been kidnapped.

Opening up to people wasn't second nature to him, but he wanted to admit things to her he'd never told anyone. If he did, he hoped Nika would too. And it wasn't just for the job. He could admit that much to himself.

After that monster Madelyn had nearly killed him he'd kept a certain distance from women. *Especially* bed partners. Not that he'd had many in the past couple years. And from what he could tell, neither had Nika. He knew he shouldn't care, but the most archaic part of him was insanely pleased. He didn't want anyone in her bed except him.

He was still trying to wrap his mind around the fact that she talked to spirits. He'd heard of a few psychics with that particular ability but they were few and far between. With that kind of power, Nika had to be stronger than Madelyn.

He shook thoughts of that treacherous bitch away. He had to stop thinking about her. She was dead and Nika was nothing like her. She might be keeping secrets from him, but she wasn't evil. He traced a finger down her arm. She stirred slightly under his touch, but didn't open her eyes. She still had her back against his chest so he pushed her curtain of dark hair out of the way and lightly raked his teeth over her neck. Her exotic scent rolled over him with a subtle intensity. Everything about her was irresistible.

Although she didn't open her eyes, he felt the exact moment she woke up. Her breathing and heart rate increased the slightest fraction.

"What are you doing?" Her voice was barely above a whisper.

"What do you think?" he murmured against her soft skin.

She groaned and rolled over to face him. "Don't you have work to do?"

He glanced at the clock on the nightstand, then turned back to her, his grin wicked. "I don't need to be up for another twenty minutes. We could do a lot in that time frame."

He could tell she was trying to keep a straight face as she asked, "Aren't you tired yet?"

He'd woken her twice in the middle of the night, but he wasn't even close to being satisfied. Something told him he would never get tired of her. That scared him. "I don't think that's possible."

A small, seductive smile played across her lips. She threw her leg over his waist and inched closer. "You're like a cyborg."

Only with her. "Complaining?"

Her green eyes flared a shade darker as she shook her head. He'd been a little rough last night, but she hadn't minded. Still, he wanted to be gentle with her this time. Take care of her.

Reaching between her legs, he rubbed his finger over her soft folds. He didn't want to break contact and put on a condom just yet so he kept his movements measured. Watching her take the pleasure he gave was more of a turn on than he could have imagined. Everything that had happened between them felt more than casual.

This was supposed to have been just another job. He wasn't sure when his objective had changed, but now he wanted to find a way to make sure Nika and Alena didn't do something stupid. He didn't care about that piece of garbage Yasha, but he understood why Vernon wanted him alive. At least for now.

When Nika fisted his cock and stroked him once, twice, he groaned. He wanted her in his bed on a permanent basis. He rolled his hips into her grip as he stroked her with his fingers.

He wanted to give her more foreplay than he had the last few times. When he increased pressure against her most sensitive spot, she began moving her hips faster against his hand.

At the sound of the door opening, she froze. Her eyes widened and she scrambled to pull the sheet up. While he didn't care about a little nakedness, instinct and the job kicked in. He rolled over, grabbed his weapon, and aimed at the door as he blocked her from view.

Light flooded the room as the overhead lamp was switched on. "Nika...oh...oh, crap..." Alena stood in the doorway, eyes and mouth wide open.

He immediately lowered his weapon, but didn't move off Nika.

"Hey, Alena." There was a trace of nervous laughter in Nika's voice.

"I'm sorry. I didn't know. I'll, uh..." Holding a slim gold key she'd likely used to open the door, Alena backtracked and shut it behind her.

"Shit," Nika muttered under her breath.

Declan frowned as he laid the weapon back on the nightstand. "Does it really matter that she knows about us? I already let Andre know."

"You did?"

He nodded once. What he was doing wasn't professional. He'd never slept with anyone on the job before.
Ever. Never wanted to. Even if she wasn't part of his
security detail, not in the technical sense, it still
shouldn't have happened. But he couldn't pretend to be
sorry about it.

"Oh, well, good I think." Averting her gaze, she
cleared her throat, seeming at a loss for words.

"Is there something you want to tell me?" *Just tell me
what's bothering you.* He wanted to shout it at her but
knew it wouldn't do any good.

"Like what?"

When he laid a hand on her stomach, her muscles
tensed. She started to lean into him, but just as quickly,
rolled back.

He felt the subtle rejection like a punch to his gut. He
wanted to push her, to see what was bothering her, but
pulled back himself. Declan grabbed his clothes off the
floor and slipped his pants on. "It's almost daylight. I'm
going to grab a quick shower."

"Okay." She sat up and clutched the sheet against her
chest. He could practically see the wall she was putting
up between them.

"Want to join me?" He cursed himself for asking
even as the words spilled out.

She shook her head. "Maybe next time."

Sharp disappointment punched through him, shred-
ding his insides. Without looking at her, he put his shirt
on and left. He doubted she was ashamed of their rela-

tionship considering her sister was sleeping with Andre, but he didn't like her reaction. He scrubbed a hand over his face as he returned to his room. This was just a job. He repeated the words over in his head, but it didn't matter. It was bullshit and he knew it. Somehow Nika had gotten under his skin and now part of him wanted to call the entire job off.

Unfortunately, he couldn't. Not only did he owe Vernon his life, but if Yasha was moving human cargo, he couldn't look the other way. No matter how much he cared for Nika.

CHAPTER TWENTY

A s soon as the door shut, Nika let the sheet drop and cursed at the empty room, the words all directed at herself. The hurt that had flared in Declan's eyes sent a knife through her heart, but she didn't go after him. She probably should but... God, she was no good with this kind of stuff.

After tugging on her discarded pajamas, she rushed to her sister's room. She knocked once, then opened the door to find Alena stretched out on the bed staring at a muted television screen.

Nika sat down on the edge of the queen-sized bed. "Why aren't you in Andre's room?"

"I couldn't sleep so I left him. I figured you might be awake too, but..." Alena propped up against the pillows and drew her knees to her chest. "So, what's going on with you and Mr. Security?"

"His name's Declan. And I don't know. He's..." Nika stopped herself. Declan hadn't exactly told her she couldn't tell anyone about his gift, but of all people, she understood the need for privacy. She'd never kept anything from her sister before, but it's not as if Alena *needed* to know he was a dream walker. He wasn't walking in her sister's dreams. Or Nika assumed he wasn't.

241

Alena's eyes narrowed a fraction. "He's what?"

"He's...I don't know, different. I really like him." It sounded lame, but she wasn't sure how to explain to her sister what Declan meant to her. Especially when she didn't understand those feelings herself. He made her feel special.

"Are you sure he's not using you?" she asked quietly.

There wasn't any hint of malice in her sister's question, but the words stung just the same. Nika pushed off the bed. "Why? Because he's interested in me and not you?"

Alena jerked back as if Nika had punched her. "No! I've seen the way he looks at you. It's obvious he's attracted to you. I swear I didn't mean it that way."

Wincing, Nika sat back down. She wanted to kick herself as the old insecurities bubbled to the surface. She wasn't sixteen anymore. "Sorry, I know you didn't. I...I don't want to talk about him, okay? Whatever I'm doing with him won't affect anything we're doing here."

"I wasn't worried about that."

"Really?" she asked dryly.

The corners of her sister's mouth curved up. "Well maybe I'm a *little* concerned."

"Don't be. It's just sex, anyway." As soon as the words were out of her mouth, she wanted to take them back. It wasn't true and she knew it. Worse, she *knew* her sister was aware it was a lie. Even thinking, much less saying, what she'd shared with Declan was just sex made her stomach twist into a painful knot. As if she was some-how betraying what they'd shared together.

Somehow Declan had figured out the exact nuances of her body. How she liked to be touched. Where she liked to be touched. It was maddening that he'd figured her out so easily. And the fact that he could literally get into her dreams when he wanted gave her an extra rea-son to feel connected to him. She didn't know if that was such a good thing either.

"I'm going to do it tonight." Alena's words cut through her thoughts.

"Do what?" For a moment, she'd forgotten what they were doing at Andre's house. God, she felt like such an idiot. "Wait, do *it*?" Panic surged through her that her sister was talking so freely about this especially since they'd agreed not to talk about anything. She mouthed the word 'surveillance'.

Alena shook her head. "I've already scanned for bugs. This room is clean. He's coming to dinner tonight. It might be the only chance we ever get."

"There are going to be so many people around. Yasha's people, not to mention Andre's own security." Terror sank its talons into her and dug deep.

"I've done this three times before. I'm not going to get caught. Besides, I'm going to take care of him a little differently than the others. No one but Yasha will be affected. I wouldn't risk hurting someone else. Not now."

Nika hadn't questioned Alena before, but she'd already guessed that Alena would kill Yasha differently than the others. With the Lazarev brothers, she'd given them massive doses of atropine. The first two had been easy enough. She'd lured them alone under the pretense of having sex. One she'd killed in the bathroom of a club, and the other, she'd killed in his hotel room. It was the only time she'd been sure they'd leave their bodyguards. With the last brother—Kirril—it hadn't been so easy considering his tastes ran to younger girls. So, she'd injected it straight into one of his vodka bottles. They'd both expected him to die later, once they'd left the Bahamas, but he'd managed to kill himself the day before they'd flown back to the States. It placed them there at the time of his death, but there was nothing they could do about it now. And it was unlikely anyone would make the connection. Why would they?

"I'm going to spray it on his plate and utensils. No matter what he touches, he's sure to ingest it." Alena smiled, but it didn't reach her eyes.

Which made Nika wonder if her sister's heart was even in it this time. "Will it be enough?"

"It's a very concentrated dosage."

"But what if someone else touches his utensils instead? What if Andre does?"

Alena's eyes narrowed. "I have it worked out. Trust me. There will only be the four of us at dinner and if Andre makes a move to sit in Yasha's spot, I'll create a distraction."

"A distraction?"

"I'll spill something. Have a wardrobe malfunction and flash a breast. Whatever it takes. I won't let anything happen to Andre. I'm fast with my hands, you know that. I'll switch the silverware if I have to. This will work. *It has to.*"

There were so many things Nika wanted to say, but she would be wasting her breath. Alena knew how she felt. When it came down to it, Nika couldn't leave her sister no matter how much she wanted to call this thing off. Alena had been more than a sister, she'd been the only mother-figure Nika had ever had. Their uncle might have raised them and provided a roof over their heads, but Alena had been the one to tuck her in every night when she'd been younger. Alena had slept with her when she had nightmares. Had taught her how to drive a car, how to apply makeup, hell, how to flirt. She'd been a mother and sister combined.

Sighing, she pushed off the bed and faked a yawn. "I'm going to grab another hour of sleep, okay?"

Alena frowned for a moment, but nodded. "Okay. Meet you downstairs for breakfast?"

"Sounds good." She dropped a quick kiss on her sister's cheek and hurried back to the safety of her room.

If her sister attempted to kill Yasha and failed, they'd both be dead. If Yasha didn't kill them immediately, he would eventually. She had no doubt that the man would hunt them down and make them pay. Of course, that was if Andre didn't do it first. Nika didn't think Andre was like his father, but in her experience, family tended to stick together no matter what.

She laid against her pillow and even though she'd gotten little sleep the night before, there was no way she could rest now. She had to think of some way out of this. After tonight they could be dead. Or Yasha could make it so they wished they were.

* * *

Yasha looked up from his computer as his second-in-command stepped into the office.

Dima quietly shut the door behind him. "You called?"

"The meet has been moved to tomorrow morning." It changed his plans, but everything could be adjusted.

Dima frowned as he took a seat across the desk. "Why the sudden urgency?"

"My client is feeling pressure from some outside sources. CIA or FBI, I think. His window of travel is small and he will not send anyone else to pick up his merchandise." Yasha understood because he would do the same. Especially considering the price the man was paying for them. Young virgins to the highest bidder. Some men cared about that kind of thing. And it was going to be very good for his bottom line.

Dima shrugged. "The men are ready."

"I know that." His men were always ready. He'd handpicked them. Most of them came from Moscow or Odessa, and while they were little more than brainless thugs, they were well trained and they feared him. That was all that mattered.

"Is there something else?"

"I want to move our other merchandise tomorrow also." In the end, he would decide, but he trusted Dima's opinion. Moving drugs and women was all the same. He had buyers for both lined up all along the East Coast. It was easier to unload everything at once.

His dark eyebrows rose slightly, but Dima nodded. "That could work. Only if your son allows us the use of one of his warehouses."

"That won't be a problem." After reviewing the file on the Brennan sisters, Yasha had a strong suspicion the women were most definitely working for someone else. And they were using Andre for an unknown purpose. If Yasha could use that knowledge against them, he had no doubt he'd be able to convince his son to help him. As a favor.

"If you're sure, I'll contact Mr. Carter's assistant and set up a time."

"No, I will speak to Mr. Carter myself."

Dismissed, Dima nodded and left.

Once Yasha was alone in his office, he called the man he only knew as Richard Carter. Other than a name, he didn't know much else about him. He'd heard whispers that Carter was the go-between for warlords and various third world dictators. As long as he paid in cash and wasn't law enforcement, Yasha didn't care who the man worked for.

"Yes?" He answered on the second ring.

"I believe we have some business to finish, Mr. Carter."

"Is this my Russian friend?" He had a faint trace of a British accent.

Friend. He nearly snorted. "Yes. Are you still interested?"

"I have a couple clients who are very interested, but we never settled on a price."

He started high, knowing he'd have to go lower. It was always the way of things. Just business. Once they settled on a price, they also agreed that tomorrow evening would be choice to meet. Perfect for him. He'd do all his business over the course of one day. And be millions upon millions wealthier.

"Location?" Mr. Carter asked.

"I'll let you know closer to the meet." In case the man wasn't who he said he was, Yasha wasn't taking the chance of a sting operation. He'd done his research, but he could never be too careful. Not when so much money was at stake.

"I'll be expecting your call."

After they disconnected, Yasha poured a small shot of vodka. It was never too early to celebrate adding to his wealth.

CHAPTER TWENTY-ONE

Declan rubbed a towel over his damp hair one more time before heading downstairs. It was insane to feel rejected simply because Nika hadn't wanted to have sex a fourth time in the past few hours. His head told him one thing, but a part of him he didn't even want to admit existed stung.

And he knew she was holding back from him. Vernon had been right about that. The women both knew Yasha. The only thing Declan knew without a doubt was that she wasn't lying about her attraction to him. Nika wasn't faking that. She'd have to be the best actress in the world to pull that off. Their first time together last night had been...intense.

He couldn't ever remember being so driven with the need to be with a woman. To absolutely fucking possess her. Being inside her last night had been the most important thing. The *only* thing that mattered. He'd needed that connection like he needed air.

"Hey, boss. Was just coming to get you." Odell's voice tore him back to reality as he reached the bottom stair.

He glanced at his watch. It was a little before six. "I didn't expect anyone else to be up."

Odell held up a mug with steam rolling off the top and shrugged. "I've been up since three. I followed up on a hunch and I think you'll be happy with what I found."

Declan glanced around the foyer and into one of the living rooms as he followed Odell toward Andre's office. There were guards posted outside and throughout the house, but the place was quiet.

In the office, Odell nodded at the flat computer screen as a driver's license picture popped up. "When we picked up Alena I got the license plate of the vehicle she'd been in."

"Yeah, another stolen plate." Odell had told him this already.

"Well I noticed that the vehicle for that plate, the one following you, or allegedly following you, and the other two from the kidnapping were all from reportedly stolen vehicles taken in this..." His finger clacked over the keyboard before a map appeared on screen. Red indicator markers lit up the screen almost in a square. "They're all from the warehouse district."

Declan stared at the screen. It was interesting. The place had a lot of crime so it made sense.

Before he could say anything, Odell continued. "It was a longshot, but I pulled up that satellite feed again. Check it out," he said, pulling up another feed on screen.

Multiple vehicles and a semi-truck, similar or the same as the one from the day of the kidnapping, were entering a warehouse. "When was this taken?"

"Yesterday afternoon—after Alena was free."

Declan felt that buzz at the back of his neck, like things were shifting in their favor now. "Looks like this could be our guys."

"Definitely worth looking into at least." He'd head down there himself. "Can you get—"

"I'm not done," Odell said, his voice completely smug. "That warehouse is owned by the same corporation that just bought the subdivision where Alena Brennan was held."

Adrenaline shot through him. Oh yeah, this was the lead they'd been waiting for. "Name of owner?"

"Don't have that yet. Still peeling back the layers. And there are a lot," he muttered.

"Can you find a list of other holdings by the same corporation? Specifically in Miami or Florida. But this area first. And check out Homestead too."

"On it. What are you going to do?" Odell asked as Declan headed for the door.

"Set up a team and head down there. This was good work, thanks." Declan hated the wave of mistrust that surged through him. This was exactly why he didn't want to get into his men's heads. Odell *might* have a gambling problem and he *might* be involved with the kidnappers. There was also a chance he wasn't. Sometimes Declan really loathed his gift, but the job was the job. Soon he'd find out if Odell was lying to him or not. He wasn't telling anyone where he was headed. The team would only find out on the way.

Odell tapped his ear piece without looking up from his screen. "I'll call you as soon as I get something concrete."

As Declan hurried up the stairs, he ran into Nika at the top. In jeans and a feminine top with some sort of fluttery material around the hem, she looked good enough to eat. The green color made her eyes pop even more.

Right now they were very expressive. "Hey."

"Hi." Tension hummed through him as they faced each other. He wanted to reach out and touch her but wasn't sure if he should. For the first time since he was a teenager, he felt awkward around a woman.

She smoothed her hands against her jeans in what he'd learned was a nervous habit of hers. "I'm sorry if I acted weird earlier. I guess I got freaked out about my sister walking in on us naked."

"Don't worry about it...I've got to take care of something but we'll talk later." He had a lot more he wanted to say but now just wasn't the time. They might have a lead on Alena's kidnappers and he couldn't waste the opportunity. Not when they could end this thing now.

"Oh, okay." She nodded, but he saw the flicker of hurt in her gaze, there one moment and gone the next.

"Nika..." He wasn't sure what he wanted to say. The woman had gotten under his skin in a bad way and he had no clue how to vocalize his feelings. Talking was overrated anyway.

Cupping her cheeks in his hands, he savored the feel of her silky skin as he covered her parted lips with his. She tasted minty and sweet. As his tongue rasped against hers, his entire body reacted in an instant. His hips jolted against hers, as if he had no control over his lower body. He wanted nothing more than to take her back to his room, strip her naked, and stay that way for hours. Hell, days. Months. Maybe longer.

With strength he didn't know he had, he pulled back on a groan. She sucked in a breath, her lips slightly swollen as she looked up at him.

"Shit, Nika. I've got to go, but we're going to finish this kiss and I'll explain everything later. I promise," he murmured against her cheek. Never in his life had he wanted to put something or someone before his job.

Without glancing back, he headed to his room and tried to clear his head. The job was the most important thing right now and if they could find a solid lead, some of the other puzzle pieces might start making sense.

First, he called Clay, who was sleeping in Andre's guest house, along with his best guys.

"Yeah, boss," Clay answered on the second ring, sounding slightly tired.

"Get two, four man teams together. We're rolling out in ten."

"Where're we headed?"

"I'll tell you on the way. Make sure our guys are wearing vests and have extra ammo."

The men they were after had already proven they had no problem opening fire in the middle of the day. They might have gotten the drop on his men once, but they didn't have the advantage of surprise today. Declan intended to strike hard and fast with no loss of life.

When they disconnected he called his assistant. It was Sunday but she had a computer at home.

"Hey, boss." Blair yawned as she answered.

"Sorry if I woke you."

"No worries. What's up?"

"You mind working from home today?"

"Nope, but you owe me."

"I need you to run a search on a girl named Selina Reynolds. She's either listed as missing or dead. I don't know how old she is, but I think she was under ten when she disappeared. Call your contact with the FBI if you have any trouble." He'd wanted to handle this one personally, but right now he didn't have the time.

"Uh, sure. Anything particular I should be looking for?"

"Information on her parents, where she went missing. Anything and everything you can find. I want to know if the case was ever solved."

"Okay. Anything else?"

"Yeah. Run Odell's financial records, phone records, and anything you can think of."

There was a long pause. "Odell *Dunn*?"

He scrubbed a hand over his face. Until that stupid dream walk, he'd been so sure Odell was above reproach.

"Yeah. And look up a reference to 'Southern Dancer'. I think it might be a horse."

"I'll call you as soon as I've got anything."

"Thanks."

After gearing up and packing extra ammo, he met his team in front of the house. He'd already notified Andre of what was going down, but other than him, no one else knew. The guys on perimeter security would see them leaving, but they wouldn't know anything else.

"So where are we headed?" Clay asked as they pulled down the driveway.

"Warehouse district." His tone and curt answer didn't invite conversation or questions. Exactly the way he wanted it.

Declan glanced in the rearview mirror at Nathaniel and Kevin Croft, friends he'd recruited straight out of the Marines. With eight years of recon training under their belts, they had more than enough experience to handle an ambush. So did the four men in the SUV behind them. He could have assembled more men, but the chance of taking these guys by surprise would have lessened if they'd waited any longer.

Declan called Rico, another of his men, using Onstar.

"Yeah?" he answered.

"Put me on speaker."

When the others were on the line Declan spoke. "We have a lead that the men who kidnapped Alena Brennan might be staying somewhere in the warehouse district. Odell followed up on a hunch and if it pays off, we'll have these guys." Or at least some of them. "Stay close because we're going to park a couple blocks to the south and take them by surprise. Everyone will break down into teams of two. As soon as we disconnect, I'm contacting Odell to send a satellite and ground view of the area to your phones. We'll know more when we have an actual visual. I know this is last minute and we'll technically be going in blind." But he wouldn't apologize for that. They all had the right training and were prepared for this type of situation. "Does anyone have any questions?"

Clay and the other two shook their heads. There was a light murmur on the other end before Rico answered. "We're good on this end, boss."

It was impossible to have everything mapped out until they were on the ground and had a visual, but he wanted to make sure they knew what they were up against.

* * *

Andre stared at his rumpled, empty bed, and berated himself. Alena was free to do what she chose. Still, it irritated him more than he could have imagined that she'd left in the middle of the night. He supposed a lot of men would be happy to have their space, but he didn't like the way she'd left.

Everything about the woman was a mystery. Even during sex, she held something back from him and it was driving him fucking crazy. She was there, in every physical sense of the word and definitely enthusiastic, but she was keeping something from him.

He stepped out of his room to find one of Declan's security guys—Ramon something—standing at attention against the wall near Alena's room. "Is everything all right, Ramon?"

The man's eyebrows raised slightly, no doubt because Andre knew his first name. "Yes, sir. Mr. Gallagher wants me to watch the women until he returns."

"Thank you and whatever Declan asked you to do, keep doing it."

"Of course, sir." He nodded and kept his gaze straight ahead as Andre knocked once on Alena's door.

Without waiting for an answer, he opened it. It was rude, he knew that. He just didn't care. As he entered, Alena was exiting the bathroom wearing a matching black bra and panty set. A jolt of need swept through him as his gaze raked over her toned body.

Her dark eyebrows rose as she wrapped her arms around herself. "Uh...hi."

He immediately shut the door, not wanting anyone to get a view of her half-dressed. "I knocked and you didn't answer so..." Suddenly he felt like an asshole. "I'll leave."

"No, it's okay." She dropped her arms and strode toward him, quickly reverting back to the sex kitten he'd had in his bed last night.

She wasn't after him for his money. Of that, he was sure. He'd run across more than his share of gold diggers and she didn't fit the mold. She had enough money of her own and she'd dated richer men than him. Several had proposed to her, including a prince.

"Why'd you leave this morning?" he asked, trying to ignore what her mere presence did to his thought process.

She slid her arms around his waist and tilted her head back to look up at him. "I couldn't sleep and didn't want to keep you up with my tossing and turning."

"You're sure that's it?" He tightened his grip around her. She melted right into him, as if she'd been made for him. The thought gave him pause because it was so unlike him.

"Of course." It was almost imperceptible but her voice rose slightly when she answered and he knew she was lying.

He decided to ignore it for now. It wouldn't do any good to grill her like some criminal. For all he knew, she just liked her privacy. And she'd been through a hell of a lot the past few days. "Have you had breakfast yet?"

"No, but I'm meeting Nika downstairs in a few minutes. Did you want to join us?"

"I'll just have coffee for now and I'll be in my office most of the day if you need me." Just because he was in Miami didn't mean his business dealings stopped. He was thankful for the time difference of his west coast and central businesses, though. He actually got some peace in the mornings. Of course, his staff called him later into the night, but it was a fair trade off.

"Well, I can't exactly go anywhere, but maybe you can take a break around lunch time." A playful grin spread across her face as she dug her fingers into his backside.

His abdomen tightened as she slid her hands upward and began tugging at his shirt. He wanted her more than he'd wanted anyone, but if they started something now, he knew he wouldn't stop for a while. He had so much damn work to catch up on. He ran his fingers through her hair and cupped the back of her head as he dropped a kiss on her mouth. "Hold that thought until lunch," he murmured.

She pouted prettily with her bottom lip and he *almost* threw his restraint out the window. Somehow, he ordered his legs toward the door, but paused. "Just so you know, Declan might have a lead on your kidnappers. He's following up right now."

"Thank God." Genuine relief crossed her face and some of the tension he'd been feeling earlier dissipated. "Is your father still coming to dinner tonight?"

Her question stopped him cold. It wasn't the words, but the slight change in tone in her normally seductive voice.

His hand on the brass doorknob, he turned. "Yes. Unless you've changed your mind?"

"No." Something flashed in her gaze, but her toothpaste commercial smile lit up her face and he wondered if he was imagining things. "I'll see you in a few hours."

Nodding, he left, but he couldn't rid himself of the queasiness that settled in his gut. Why would she care about his father? If she did at all? He made a note to have his assistant run her records again. He'd been positive he'd done a thorough job before, but maybe he'd missed something. He might care about her, but he wasn't going to let her make a fool out of him.

CHAPTER TWENTY-TWO

Declan adjusted the microphone in his ear and crouched against the warehouse wall. "Is everyone in position?" He kept his voice low.

Rico was the first to answer. "The perimeter is clear on this side."

Nathaniel spoke next. "Me and Kevin got ya covered too."

The teammates were positioned on two neighboring rooftops, providing extra cover. Considering both men had been Force Recon, Declan knew they'd provide the best backup.

When everyone else gave affirmations that they were in position, he turned to Clay, who was crouched next to him. "I'll go in first, you cover me."

After parking a few blocks away, they'd surrounded the target; a seemingly unoccupied and nondescript warehouse. Under better circumstances, they would have been able to stake out the place for a few days and plant listening devices inside. As it was now, this was going to be more or less a straight assault.

Using a wireless snake video camera, Declan and Clay had gotten a visual of four men inside, but there could be more. Declan nodded once at Clay, then eased open one of the side doors. The locks were worn with age and he'd had no problem picking this one. Weapon drawn, Declan swept inside first.

Dark brownish stains covered the expanse of the concrete floor. Using a large metal container as cover, he ducked behind it.

"You're clear," he murmured into his mic.

Clay followed seconds later and pulled the hollow steel door shut behind him. Their rubber soled shoes were silent against the concrete floor. The layout of the building was fairly standard for a warehouse; a big square box with offices on one side of it.

With the exception of the random metal containers, the base of the warehouse was relatively empty.

Crouching next to him, Clay made a few quick motions with his hands. Declan nodded. There was a green truck sitting in the middle of the warehouse, but the men they'd seen earlier weren't with it. They could be using this place as a stash house of sorts. Since they hadn't seen the men exit, Declan guessed they were in one of the offices.

A low hum of male voices and footsteps grew louder with each passing second. Declan peered around their hiding place, then motioned to Clay to get ready to move.

Two men were loading AK-47s into the back of the vehicle while one man stood guard.

Catching these guys by surprise was their main objective. Weapons drawn, Declan and Clay swiveled around from their hiding place. "Don't move!" Declan's voice echoed throughout the building.

The two men with weapons froze, but the third went for his pistol.

"Don't do it!" Clay took a few steps closer and the guy stopped and lifted his hands in the air.

Keeping his weapon trained on the men, Declan whispered into his mic, "Rico, there's still one guy missing. You and Travis enter from the back."

"Affirmative."

Declan trained his weapon on the man in the middle of the three of them. "Drop your weapons. Now!"

After a short pause, they dropped to the floor with a clatter.

"Now kick them over here."

One of the men muttered something, but they all did as he ordered. "Everyone on their knees." When they complied he tucked his weapon into its holster.

He knew Clay would cover him. They'd worked together long enough to have that kind of trust.

He moved to the right, flanking them from the side. He had no doubt he could handle two of them at once, but if they did decide to attack, he wasn't going to make it easy for them.

Declan nodded at the man closest to him. "Hands behind your back." When he positioned his hands, Declan quickly snapped the zip ties around his hands, then secured the man's ankles. Feet and knees could be just as deadly as a fist and he didn't know what kind of training these guys had.

"Who do you work for?" he asked as he secured the next man's wrists.

"Go fuck yourself," the first man snapped.

After he'd secured the third man's wrists and ankles, he started to speak into his mic when Rico said, "Caught a guy trying to jump out a window. He's secured. We're sweeping the offices upstairs. So far they're clear."

"Good work." He turned his focus on Clay. "You remember Belgrade?"

The corners of Clay's mouth pulled up in a knowing smile. Without pause, Clay took a few steps toward the men. "Who do you work for?"

Silence.

All three men stared at the floor. Of the three, only one looked scared. Wearing a black beanie, faded jeans, and a black T-shirt, he couldn't be more than eighteen or nineteen. He kept his mouth shut just like the others, but noticeable sweat rolled down his face.

"All right. Which of you is willing to die for your boss?"

That got their attention. All the men stared at him. Two with hardened defiance. One with terror. Declan cut the bindings on the youngest kid's feet, then grabbed his collar and yanked him to his feet. "Let's see if you can fly."

"What the hell are you doing, man?" He tried to struggle against him, but Declan kept a firm grip on his shirt.

"In case you guys haven't figured it out, we're not cops." Another reason he hadn't involved law enforcement. He didn't mind working in shades of gray sometimes. "You don't have any rights. One way or another, you're going to answer my questions." He shoved the kid toward the door that read *STAIRS*.

Once they were in the stairwell, Declan made a decision. He could threaten to throw this kid off the roof and hope the information he got under duress was good, or he could level with the kid and maybe cut a deal. Fear would go a long way in getting the guy to talk, but Declan's gut told him he'd get better information if he played a version of the good cop role. "What's your name, kid?"

"Jeremy," he muttered.

"What are you doing with these assholes?" Declan pushed open the door leading to the roof.

When he didn't answer, Declan motioned with his pistol. As they walked outside, the kid's face paled to an ashen gray. The gravel beneath their feet crunched as they made their way to the ledge. No doubt he was thinking all sorts of bad things now. Like how he wouldn't survive a drop.

"You didn't answer my question." Declan peered over the edge of the roof and whistled. "Long drop." Sometimes the fear of the unknown was worse than torture itself.

"Man, what do you want from me?" Jeremy took a small step away from the ledge.

"I want to know who you're working for."

"Man, I don't know. One of my buddies asked if I'd help out with transferring some weapons today. I barely know those guys."

"So who's their boss?"

"Some guy they call Rick. That's all I know. I swear! I just got here two hours ago. Some heavy operation they were running went wrong and they needed more manpower to haul this stuff out. They're paying me a grand for two hours work. What am I supposed to do, say no?"

"Where are the rest of the weapons?"

"They left in *my* van and a semi-truck like half an hour ago. This was supposed to be easy money." He stared down at his boots and Declan was struck by how fucking young he looked.

When he'd been that age, he'd been in the Corps. "Where'd they take the weapons?"

"I don't know the exact address but it's plugged into the truck's GPS."

Declan couldn't believe how stupid this guy was. "You know they were probably planning to kill you right?"

"What? You're crazy." He shook his head and took another step away from the ledge.

Yeah, he was the crazy one. "Were they wearing masks earlier?"

"Well, yeah..."

"And now they aren't. They took them off because they don't care if you see their faces. Whoever asked you to help out, isn't your friend." Declan shook his head at the kid's naiveté. If this guy wasn't connected to the kidnappers, he'd be the perfect distraction for Declan and his men. Rick had to know Declan would eventually figure out more about him, especially after Alena's escape. If Declan had to guess what the original plan was, they'd probably planned to shoot the kid and leave him for dead with some of the weapons. It would send Declan on a pointless chase trying to figure out who the kid was connected to.

"Clay? You okay down there?" He spoke into his mic.

"Yeah."

"Check the GPS in the vehicle. Copy the last few places it's been and whatever location it's currently set to go to, then erase everything."

"On it."

Declan grabbed the kid's collar again and dragged him toward the stairs. "Why'd they kidnap Alena Brennan?"

"Kidnap who? What the hell—"

"Never mind. Listen, I'm going to pull out your wallet so don't try anything stupid." He still had his hands bound, but Declan wanted to put the warning out there. Declan plucked the kid's worn leather wallet from his back pocket then memorized the address on his license. "This is a pretty nice neighborhood you live in. What do you do for a living?"

His neck turned red as he stared at the ground. "I go to the University of Miami."

"You're a student?" God, he really was just a kid. Declan tucked the license back inside. "You live with your parents, kid?" When he didn't answer, Declan bit back a groan. He couldn't allow this guy to be locked up with the men downstairs. They'd kill him in general holding just because he'd talked to Declan. Before he could change his mind, he pulled out his pocket knife and cut through the zip ties.

Jeremy stared at him with wide eyes, but the kid didn't move.

Declan shoved the wallet into his hands. "What's your friend's name? The one who told you about this job?"

"Louis Wesley. I know him from school but we're not best friends or anything. I...I bought some weed from him at a couple parties."

"Stay the hell away from him and stay out of trouble. I'm going to run your information and you can expect a visit from me or one of my associates next week. If I find out you lied—"

"I didn't. I swear! This is a fucking nightmare, man. I just wanted to make some quick cash, that's all."

"Come on. You can leave out the side door." He gave the kid a nudge with his weapon.

"You're really going to let me go?"

"Yeah. Don't make me regret it." When he'd been younger all he'd cared about was fast cars and girls. Cliché, but true. Thanks to a protective older brother, Declan had gotten out of more situations than he cared to remember. He couldn't let this kid do jail time for being an idiot. Hopefully this would be a wakeup call.

Under different circumstances and with more time, he might have been able to get more information from the two men downstairs. They both had prison tats he recognized, and after four or five days of an intense psychological operation, *maybe* he'd have been able to get some viable information from them. Of course, he could try to get into their heads later—and he planned to—but he'd have to wait until they fell asleep. Either way, he couldn't find out shit from them now.

Instead, he was going to leave them tied up and call the cops. Let the locals deal with them. He'd bet all those weapons they were hauling around were hot. Not to mention the fully automatic AKs were illegal anyway. They could try to play it like they don't know anything about them, but their prints would be all over them and this warehouse. No matter what, these guys were screwed.

CHAPTER TWENTY-THREE

"Why'd you let that guy go?" Nathaniel asked from the backseat of the SUV.

Declan glanced at him in the rearview mirror. Nathaniel and Kevin had both seen him from their rooftop perches. "He was just a kid in the wrong place at the wrong time. He told me everything he knew." *Which wasn't much.*

Tonight things were going to change. He'd tried to get into Alena's dreams once, but he was going to have to try again. There might be something about the kidnappers in her memory she wasn't aware was helpful. Then, he was going to get into Clay's head and dig until he found what he needed. After him, he was hitting all his men's dreams.

He pulled out a burner phone he kept for emergencies from the center console of the SUV and called the cops and reported what he'd just seen, leaving out a few details of course. Once he was done, he took the battery out and handed it to Clay.

"Wipe it down for me?"

Clay nodded and got to work.

Declan's own phone buzzed in his pocket as he pulled up to a stoplight. When he saw his friend Ronnie's name on screen, he answered. "Tell me you've got good news."

"You alone?" Ronnie asked, his voice tense.

"No."

"Can you meet me soon?"

"Half an hour work?"

"I'll be at that diner you like. Don't tell anyone where you're going."

When they disconnected, he noticed Nathaniel give him a curious look, but he didn't ask questions. Not that Declan expected him to. His men were all professional and while they were friendly, Declan tried to keep a certain amount of distance from everyone. His years with the CIA had ingrained that in him. Of course, he'd ignored it once and almost gotten killed.

Looking back, he realized he'd ignored all the signs because he hadn't wanted to see them. Madelyn had been calculating. A killer for hire with no remorse. Even though he knew Nika was holding a lot back from him, she was nothing like Madelyn. Nika had a vulnerable streak a mile wide that was driving him crazy with the need to protect her. Which was insane. No matter what, she was still up to something. Yet he wanted to protect her anyway.

The drive back to Andre's place was quiet. When they pulled through the gates of his driveway, Declan left the SUV running as the other men got out.

"You coming?" Clay hoisted his backpack out of the front seat.

"I'll be back in an hour or so. Got my phone on me if you need me."

"Want some backup?"

"Nah, but thanks."

"All right." Clay shrugged and shut the door.

As soon as Declan put the vehicle into drive, his phone buzzed again. He smiled when he saw Blair's name. "Declan here."

"I've got good news and bad news," she said by way of greeting.

"Bad news first."

"I don't know exactly why you wanted me to run Odell's records, but it looks like he's run up a substantial gambling debt. Got in deep with a casino up in Jersey."

"Okay, how bad?"

"I'm emailing the information to you now. He's paid a lot of it down, but he owes about fifty grand."

"They're letting him pay it off?"

"I'm not sure why, but it looks that way."

"Make sure you include all the contact information of the casino." He was going to take care of this, then he was going to take care of Odell. "What's the good news?"

"Maybe good was too strong of a word. I found the information you wanted on the missing girl. Selina Reynolds, age ten, went missing five years ago in southern Georgia. She was out camping with her parents when she just disappeared. Apparently there was a known pedophile in the area, but his preferences ran in the other gender direction so he was eventually cleared."

"Can you find out who was in charge of the case, if it's still open—"

"Already done it. I've sent you all the information you'll need."

"Thanks for all the help. I know today was supposed to be your day off so if you don't have anything pressing to work on, don't worry about going to the office tomorrow."

"Okay, I'm probably going to take you up on that. I'll be hanging out with friends tomorrow but I'll bring my phone and laptop if you need me."

As they disconnected, he pulled into the parking lot of the diner. Ronnie's truck was already there. Once he was inside, Declan found him sitting in a booth. "What's going on?" he asked, sliding in across from him.

Ronnie was a wiry man with bright red hair, freckles covering his entire face and sleeves of Celtic tattoos. His long-sleeved shirt was pushed up to the elbows. In front of him was a package with brown wrapping and a cup of coffee. He slid the package to Declan. "This is the gun you had me run prints for. I don't want it anymore."

Scanning the restaurant, which was mostly empty, Declan took it and placed it on the seat next to him out of sight. "What did you find?"

"Whatever it is, it's not good. I had a buddy of mine run these as a favor. He got a hit almost immediately from a top-secret *flagged* file." Now Ronnie glanced around.

Shit. "What agency?"

He shook his head. "I don't know. The only thing I do know is that the computer locked up and kicked us out of the system for half an hour."

Declan scrubbed a hand over his face as the reality of Ronnie's words sank in. "I'm sorry man. I wouldn't have asked if—"

Ronnie snorted. "It's cool."

Declan wasn't so sure. "That shit will trickle down eventually. They'll figure out who ran the prints if they don't already know.

"My buddy ran the prints using a recently deceased cop's access code. This won't be traced back to either of us, so I'm in the clear. Where'd you get that thing from anyway?"

"I can't exactly say."

His friend gave him a half-smile. "I probably don't want to know anyway."

"Probably not," Declan murmured.

After paying for a to-go cup of coffee, Declan settled into the front seat of the vehicle and turned on his tablet. He knew he could call Vernon and send him a copy of the prints. Even though the prints were flagged, the FBI director would have no problem getting the clearance to view them. Something told him to hold off, however. If the prints could somehow throw Nika's sister to the wolves, he had to talk to her first. Even if she was still holding back from him, he felt like he owed Nika that much.

As the main screen flared to life he called the one man he knew he could count on to be discreet. Carlisle Williams, his former handler with the CIA.

Carlisle picked up on the third ring. "Declan Gallagher."

Declan grinned at the familiar voice. "That would be me."

"Been a while, son." Carlisle's deep voice had a distinctive cadence to it that Declan would be able to pick out anywhere. There was just a hint of a southern accent in it.

"Last time I called, you were too busy to talk."

"Yeah, yeah. I'm busy now and something tells me this isn't a social call. How big is this favor anyway?"

He snorted. "You assume it's for a favor."

"I recognize the tone," he said dryly.

Yeah, he would too. "It's big. And no one can know about this."

"Lay it on me."

"I need you to run a set of fingerprints. A thumb and forefinger. I already know these prints are flagged, but I don't know by which agency."

"So you've run these and been denied access?"

"Not me personally, but yeah."

"Anything else?"

As he spoke, Declan forwarded two emails to Carlisle. "Yeah, and it's going to sound weird—and these two things aren't related. I'm sending a missing persons case to you right now. The missing girl in the file is dead and she passed away not far from her parents' campsite. From what I've read, the locals thought she was kidnapped. They spent a lot of time and energy hunting down suspects, but she drowned in some kind of hole—not man-made from the sound of it."

"A hole?" He sounded skeptical.

"Yeah. Near a funny looking tree. Those aren't my words, but it's all I've got to go on."

"Did you get this information from one of your dream walks?" Carlisle was one of the few people who knew about Declan's gifts. He'd taken full advantage of Declan when they'd worked together.

"No. And I can't say more than that."

"What's my approach with the missing person's case?"

"I need you to make some calls, get people on the ground. I don't care what it takes, but I need that body found. Call in a favor, whatever you've got to do."

"Is this about a woman?" His former boss's voice took on an edge, subtle as it was.

Declan ignored the question. He didn't have to help Nika with this, but if spirits were visiting her dreams, there was a reason for it. And fuck, it was a missing kid. The parents had a right to know what had happened to her. "Are you going to help me out or not?"

"You know I will. Which favor is more important?"

He didn't have to think about it. "The prints."

"I'll get back to you as soon as I know anything."

"Thank you. I owe you one."

Carlisle grunted then disconnected.

Sighing, Declan turned off his tablet and headed back to Andre's. Now it was just a waiting game. There were too many possible reasons for those prints to be flagged and he needed to see the results for himself before he confronted Nika or Alena about anything.

Unfortunately, Declan wasn't so sure what he was going to do with the information when he got it. Weeks ago, everything had been so clear. Find out who the women were and what their true objective was. Now his main objective was keeping Nika safe from harm. Even if that meant keeping her safe from herself.

* * *

Alena held onto the edge of the heated swimming pool and waited for Nika to surface. As her sister reached the deep end, Nika stopped at the wall a few feet from Alena.

"You done?" Nika asked.

"Yeah. I'm going to go find Andre. Do you want to have lunch with us?"

Nika's expression darkened as it seemed to do so often lately. "No thanks."

"So, what, now you're pissed at me?" She couldn't keep the annoyance out of her voice.

"I want to walk away from all this. I don't know another way to say it. Uncle—" Nika stopped abruptly and glanced around the enclosed pool room. It was still empty, but she wasn't taking any chances. She lowered her voice. "I spoke to *him* earlier and he agrees. He said he'll be home soon and he'll find another way to take care of this."

Alena pushed back her temper, not wanting to take anything out on her sister. For so long she and Nika had wanted the same thing. Suddenly things had changed. She didn't understand why her sister wasn't supporting her anymore. It wasn't because she cared if Yasha lived. "Is this about the security guy you're sleeping with?" She didn't want to even say his name aloud. It made things much too personal.

"*Declan* has nothing to do with it." The look in her sister's eyes told a different story, which surprised Alena. Nika almost never got involved with or slept with anyone. "This is about you. I'm worried about *you*."

"I'm not going to get caught." If she thought she might be putting Nika in danger, she'd send her sister packing. She'd been a little nervous before, but the plan to take out Yasha was perfect. As if it had been dropped into her lap.

Yasha's men and even Andre's security would be more focused on outside threats or more obvious weapons. They wouldn't expect someone to poison Yasha. And especially not the woman whose life he'd attempted to save. On the outside she was just a silly socialite. He'd never suspect her. Things were going perfectly according to plan. No one else would be hurt and the world would be saved from a monster. Yasha was an absolute waste of space and his death would never weigh on her conscience.

"That's not the point. How can you be so callous to Andre?"

Alena's stomach twisted at her sister's words. Nika didn't understand. She hadn't seen the carnage Alena had witnessed. Nika was too young to remember, but Alena wasn't. Thinking about her mother's broken body always made her sick so she pushed the visions away. Instead of responding to her sister, she hoisted herself up out of the pool and strode across the tile. Without a backward glance, she wrung the water from her hair, then grabbed a towel and wrapped it around her bikini-clad body.

Behind her she heard Nika's splash and knew she'd started laps again. Nika would thank her in the long run. Once Yasha was finally dead, maybe she could have a normal life. Normal relationships. Just knowing that man was alive and her parents weren't made it impossible to think about anything else. Her whole life had been building up to this moment. She wasn't going to waste the best opportunity they might ever have.

Alena hurried through the expansive house, ignoring the covert looks from some of the security guys. Holding her breath, she knocked on Andre's office door. It swung open a few seconds later. His harsh expression softened the second he saw her. In that moment, she actually hated herself. Not because of what she was going to do to Yasha, but because Andre was exactly the kind of man she'd always wanted. Kind, protective, intelligent and very sexy. She didn't want to use or hurt him but she couldn't see another way around it.

CHAPTER TWENTY-FOUR

Declan stared at his computer screen. *Shit, shit, shit.* He wished what he was seeing wasn't true, but he knew it was. It had to be. His former handler for the CIA wouldn't make a mistake. Not one like this. And he wouldn't have passed on this information lightly. Carlisle had to be risking a lot by giving him this file.

As the door to Andre's office opened, he automatically snapped his laptop shut.

Odell smiled when he saw him. "Hey, boss. I just heard the cops busted those guys down at the warehouse. That's great."

"Yeah it is. We're one step closer now."

"I'm still working on running the backgrounds of everyone you asked." Odell glanced over his shoulder at the closed door then back at Declan. "I think I might have found an interesting connection with Andre's assistant in Vegas and some low-level thugs here in Miami."

He straightened. "You're sure?"

Odell quickly shook his head. "I'm still running financials and other records so don't get too excited. I *might* have found a connection, but I'm still following up on some leads. I'll have something very soon. I just wanted to give you a heads up."

Declan wanted to stay and wait until Odell was done but knew how long Odell's searches could take. "I've got to take care of something but I'll be back downstairs soon. Don't tell anyone what you found, including Andre. He's still…"

"Upstairs with Alena, I know." Odell smothered a chuckle and sat in front of his computer screen.

Gathering his laptop and the pictures he'd printed before Odell had come in, Declan headed upstairs. According to the reports his men had given him, Nika should be upstairs. She'd made a few phone calls—and he planned to find out to whom—then she'd spent most of the morning in the swimming pool. But they said she'd settled in her room and hadn't left in the past hour.

Bracing himself for what he knew was going to come, he knocked on the door. A few seconds later it swung open. Her dark hair was pulled into a damp ponytail and she wore faded jeans and a three-quarter sleeve blue sweater. As he drank in her appearance, he realized she wasn't wearing a bra. Every protective and primal instinct inside him jumped to attention, but he pushed it back down. That wasn't why he'd come to see her.

"Hey, I thought you were Alena." She sounded almost out of breath. Or maybe she was just nervous. He reached out to touch her, kiss her, he wasn't exactly sure what, but stopped himself and ignored the hurt look that flitted across her features when he pulled back.

He had to do this now. He needed to hear the truth from her lips and he couldn't let his lust or anything else get in the way of that. "Can I talk to you in private?"

She frowned, but stepped back and let him enter. He shut the door then set his laptop on the nightstand. Instead of putting the pictures down, he held them against his chest. She stood by the edge of the bed, arms crossed over her chest.

"I'm going to ask you this once. Who are you and what are you and your sister doing here?"

She went still, her breath catching just the slightest fraction. "What are you talking about?"

"Tell me your real name, damn it." He thought he had his emotions under control, but he couldn't stand the thought of her lying to him. Not Nika. After what they'd shared, he expected...he didn't know what he expected, but he wanted the truth.

"You know my name." She tried to take a step back, but there was nowhere for her to go. The backs of her knees collided with the bed.

"I ran the fingerprints on the pistol your sister gave me."

She stuck her chin out. "So?"

"There were only one set of prints. *Female prints.* Want to guess what they turned up? I got a hit on a flagged, top secret, CIA file."

Her face paled but she didn't respond.

"Want to tell me what your name is now?"

"Nika Brennan," she whispered.

He took a few steps closer to her so that barely a foot of space separated them. For his own sanity he should keep his distance, but he wanted to intimidate her. Maybe he should be ashamed of that, but he was going to hear the truth from her one way or another.

"The name on the file I received said the fingerprints belonged to an Angel Aston. Missing at the age of ten. Her five-year-old sister went missing too. Her name was Sasha."

Nika swallowed hard, but still didn't respond.

"Say something," he demanded. He wanted her to say something. Anything. Scream at him. Just tell him the fucking truth.

Her gaze flickered around the room and he knew she was gauging if she could dart past him and make an escape. Where the hell she thought she could go was anyone's guess.

"Don't even think about running. You won't make it out the front door." Now, he stepped forward until his body was pressed against hers. Heat and fear rolled off her body, nearly suffocating him.

The small movement propelled her into action. In a surprising move, she shoved at his chest. "I don't know what you want from me! Whatever you think you know, you're wrong!"

When she pushed him, he grabbed her wrist. In doing so, the pictures he'd been holding fell from his hands. "Shit," he muttered. He'd printed the pictures out as proof for his records, but hadn't planned to show them to her unless he had to.

Her gaze tracked the fallen photos. "Oh my God," she gasped.

When she yanked and wrenched her wrist away, he let go of her, not wanting to hurt her. She collapsed on-to her knees and grasped the picture of the entire Aston family. Anya and Blake Aston and their two children, Angel and Sasha. It must have been taken at Christmas time. Despite the differences in their ages, the two little girls wore matching red and white frilly dresses. And they looked happy. Normal. The perfect American fami-ly.

He kneeled next to her but she didn't seem to notice. Underneath the few family photos was a picture of the crime scene of the dead Astons. He yanked it away and folded it before shoving it in his back pocket. No matter that she'd been lying to him, he wasn't cruel enough to show her that. No one needed to see something like that.

"I don't even have a picture of all of us," she whis-pered. As soon as the words were out, she sucked in a breath, no doubt realizing what she'd confessed. Unshed tears filled her bright green eyes. "What do you want from me?" she whispered.

When she looked at him with that broken gaze, something sharp and jagged twisted in his chest, punc-turing deep. He might have promised Vernon he'd keep an eye on the Brennan sisters, but he'd only promised to make sure they didn't harm Yasha. And he didn't know if they planned to. He didn't have to turn Nika and Alena over to anyone. He wasn't going to. *He couldn't.* He wasn't sure what his feelings were for Nika but if he betrayed her, he knew he'd regret it for the rest of his life. He'd done a lot of things that he wished he could take back but this...hurting her in this way would be the one thing he wouldn't be able to take back.

"Nika..." His words trailed off. What was he supposed to say now?

Looking away, she stared at the floor. "What's that?"

When he realized what she meant, before he could stop her, she'd snatched up one of the crime scene photos.

"Oh my God." The words came out as a soft, ragged, whisper.

"Don't." He tried to take it from her hands but she was fast.

Lightning quick and picture in hand, she sprung to her feet and raced for the bathroom. As he raced after her, he could hear her retching in the other room. She probably wanted privacy but he didn't care. He found her bent over the toilet. Her hair was pulled back but stray wisps fell around her face.

He gathered the loose strands and held them back. A low keening sound came from her, like a wounded animal might make, so he rubbed her back in gentle little circles as she clutched the edge of the porcelain ring.

"It's okay. Get it all out," he murmured.

She did until finally she shut the toilet seat and buried her face in her hands. He spied the picture she'd grabbed next to her knee so he quickly shoved it in his back pocket to join the other one. No wonder she'd reacted this way. It was a picture of her mother's naked bloody body so brutalized it looked as if she'd been attacked by wild animals. He wanted to throw up himself.

"Come on." Declan helped her stand, then brought her to the sink. He turned on the water and even though she didn't look at him, she seemed to understand. She washed her hands, rinsed out her mouth, then patted cold water on her face.

"How did you get those pictures?" she asked in a monotone voice that tore razorblades through his chest.

The last thing he wanted was for her to close herself off from him. Not now. "It's not important."

"Tell me." She finally looked at him. The raw pain he saw in her eyes nearly made him stumble.

"I…when I got the hit on those fingerprints and realized who your sister was, it wasn't hard to figure out who you were. Your parents were more or less legends in The Agency and when their children went missing…" He shrugged, hoping she wouldn't press much harder. He couldn't tell her he'd been sent to spy on her and that he'd gone dream walking inside her head intentionally. Not yet anyway.

It was hard to fathom that she was one of the missing Aston girls. Many in clandestine circles knew about the Aston *incident* and it wasn't pretty. Twenty years ago, two of the CIA's best double-agents had been murdered in their own home on Christmas Eve. The husband had been killed first, and the wife had been raped repeatedly before she'd been beaten to death. The two children were never found. It was assumed someone had dumped their bodies—or worse.

"You know who my parents were?"

He nodded. "They were very good at what they did and their deaths affected a lot of government agencies."

"Really?" The sad note in her voice pulled even harder at his heartstrings and he realized she probably didn't know much about her own parents.

"Yes. They were very respected. There's a memorial dedicated to them." He probably shouldn't have told her the last part but he didn't care.

"I don't know anything about them other than what they did for a living. And I only learned after they died. Growing up, we didn't talk about them. Ever." She collapsed onto the bed so he sat next to her. A few tears spilled down her cheeks. Not caring about the consequences, he cupped her jaw and rubbed his thumb over her soft skin, catching her tears.

"Are you going to tell anyone?" she whispered.

"Not right now." Later, yeah, but for now he wouldn't.

She bit her bottom lip and eyed him warily. "After my parents were killed, a relative took us in and changed our name."

A burst of relief coursed through him that she trusted him enough to tell him that much. "Why?"

"If you know who my parents were, you know that someone murdered them. My...relative didn't think it would be safe for us. I was so young, I don't really remember much. I just know that when I was five-years-old, I became Nika Brennan and I've never thought of myself as anyone else."

"It's been two decades, though." He tried to push for information without seeming like he was interrogating her. Especially when all he wanted to do was comfort her.

"So? If we do admit who we are, how would we explain how we changed our names without hurting...our relative? What good would it do? Those girls died that night and it needs to stay that way." There was a desperation in her voice now.

Declan frowned as some of the puzzle pieces clicked together. It was possible Yasha had been involved in the murder of her parents. Twenty years ago the man had worked with the Lazarev brothers. Now that they were dead—possibly at the hands of Nika and Alena—Yasha could be on their hit list.

He paused, waiting for her to continue, but it was obvious she had no intention of telling him more than she already had. He wondered if she actually knew who'd killed her parents but that left the question of how the hell she even *would* know. If he had to guess, he'd say the 'relative' or whoever had taken them in worked in covert ops or something similar. It was the only thing that made sense for how well they'd completely and utterly gone off the grid.

Declan knew he should grill her, push her now when she was vulnerable, but fuck him, he couldn't do it. Just couldn't.

She watched him carefully now and he could see the shock and adrenaline fading to be replaced by a bone-deep weariness. He'd seen it more times than he cared to count on the battlefield and when he'd been with The Agency. Adrenaline dumps of a certain magnitude could leave someone feeling as if they'd gone twelve rounds in a ring.

The shock of seeing those pictures and the revelation that someone knew her true identity had taken a toll. He scooted closer on the bed until their knees were touching. "I won't hurt you, Nika."

"And you won't tell Andre or anyone else who we are?" she whispered.

Unless it was necessary. But, he didn't say what he was thinking. It would only upset her more. Instead, he shook his head. "I can only promise that I will never intentionally hurt you."

She reached out a tentative hand and cupped his cheek. The gesture surprised him. It must have shown on his face.

"Thank you," she whispered.

"For what?"

A small smile teased at her full lips. "For everything. *No one* knows who we are and...just thank you for not saying anything. Seeing those pictures...it's a shock."

A knot twisted in his stomach. He placed his own hand over hers and squeezed. Against his better judgment, he leaned close and kissed away the remaining tears on her cheeks. "Why don't you get a quick nap in before dinner?" God knew she'd need to take the edge off.

For a second it appeared as if she might argue, but she laid back against the pillow and curled onto her side. She looked so damn fragile he ached watching her. "Is it okay if I keep the pictures of my parents? When we left...it was in a hurry and we weren't allowed to take any reminders of our lives."

Even if he'd wanted to, he couldn't deny her request. The pleading note in her voice made it impossible. "For your sake, hide it somewhere safe."

Nodding, she clutched the photo against her chest. He picked up the rest of the fallen photos and slid a couple of the family shots into the nightstand drawer facedown. "We have more to talk about, Nika."

"I know," she whispered.

He dropped a kiss on her forehead before gathering the rest of his stuff and leaving the room. They had a hell of a lot more to talk about than she realized. She no doubt assumed he meant about them, but one way or another he was going to have to tell her the whole truth.

If she and her sister went after Yasha he'd be forced to stop them. And if he had to expose their true identity, so be it. He just hoped she'd be able to forgive him if it came down to that.

CHAPTER TWENTY-FIVE

*N*ika *opened her eyes and at once knew she was in a dream state. The earthy tones of the bedroom were muted and dull in that old photograph style. A slight movement by the door made her turn.*

It was Selina, the same little girl who'd visited her before.

"Hi," Nika said, giving her a soft smile.

"Hi. I just want to say thank you." Selina's voice was so faint Nika could barely hear her.

"Thank me for what?"

"For helping them find my body. My mommy's still sad, but she seems better now."

Nika wasn't sure who 'them' was but knew the little girl didn't have much time to talk. She was already fading. "I didn't do anything."

"Yes you did...that man you were sleeping next to did."

Nika wasn't sure what Declan had done. He said he'd look into it but she hadn't been sure what to expect of him. It amazed her that the little girl knew Declan had even helped. And made her wonder how much spirits were aware of. A sudden knowledge settled in her chest as she realized the reason Selina was here. "Are you coming to say goodbye?"

Selina nodded and lightning fast she was at the edge of the bed, barely a foot away from Nika. "You're special and you need to stop denying it."

She wasn't sure how she felt about being lectured by a ten-year-old ghost. "It was too much before." When all those spirits had wanted to talk to her all the time and all at once, she'd felt fucking crazy. They'd done it everywhere. It hadn't mattered it she'd been grocery shopping or taking a shower—they'd always wanted to talk.

"You weren't ready then. You have someone strong by your side now. When others come to visit you, you must listen. Filter out the extra noise, the ones who don't need help. Focus on the ones who do."

She sounded far smarter than a ten-year-old should. "Who are they?"

Selina ignored the question. "You helped me so I want to help you." Reaching out, she touched her small, cold hand to Nika's forehead. "Watch."

A shiver skittered over her skin, but it was short-lived. Nika started to ask what she was doing when her entire world shifted. No longer was she in her bedroom. Instead, she was outside. She looked around her and realized she was in Andre's massive backyard. Trees and hedges surrounded her.

And there was a man she recognized hiding in the shadows near an oversized gazebo. Everything happening was so surreal. This was real time, not someone's dream. Somehow she just knew it. She wasn't sure what was going on, but Selina wouldn't have shown this to her if it wasn't important. The man couldn't see her so she walked up and stood directly next to him. It was too surreal.

When she got closer, he fought off a shiver, but continued speaking into his phone. It didn't look like a smartphone though, but like one of those cheap ones you could buy at a gas station.

"...he'll be here tonight. Andre has invited him to dinner. His lover wants to thank him or something."

"As soon as Yasha leaves, contact me," a male voice on the other end said.

"Why don't you just kill him when he's heading to Andre's house?"

"Because I don't know where he's coming from and I've never been able to catch him leaving his house. He has too many decoys and changes his schedule too often to be predictable," the unknown speaker said.

"I'll call you, but this is it. After this, I'm out for good."

"The rest of your money will be wired to you after tonight."

Nika's surroundings started to fade. A hazy mist enveloped her until she was no longer outside, but in her bed.

With a start, Nika threw the covers off, ready to go find Declan, but stopped as her feet hit the carpeted floor. Someone was planning to kill Yasha. Maybe she should just let whoever he was do it.

No. One of Declan's men was a traitor. She *had* to tell him. He'd honored her request to keep her identity a secret. Considering all the lies she'd told him, she had to do this one thing for him. She owed him. She had to let him know that one of his own men was going behind his back. Besides, for all she knew, the traitorous bastard had been complicit in her sister's kidnapping. There was a part of her that told her to tell Alena first, but she silenced that little voice.

* * *

Declan quickly scanned the various phone numbers on the spreadsheet Odell had sent him. Barry Green, Andre's assistant in Vegas, had been making a lot of calls to an unknown number in Miami. To say his call history for the past six months was interesting would be an understatement. The man never seemed to sleep. He received calls at all hours of the day and night from everywhere along the East Coast. Declan highlighted one of the phone numbers and showed it to Odell. "Isn't there a way to track who owns this phone?"

Odell turned back to his computer screen. "The numbers I've looked up so far are from burner phones, but we might get lucky."

The only sound in the room was Odell clacking on the keyboard while Declan continued to scan.

"Sorry boss, this number's a throwaway too," he muttered, frustration in his voice.

Something about the number was familiar. It played in the corner of his mind but he couldn't remember what it was. "What about the connection between Barry Green and Rick Savitch?"

"There's nothing directly linking them, but a handful of these phones can be traced back to a bogus corporation called *Skytri*. It took some digging, but I found a link between an old PO Box address on file for Savitch and *Skytri*. And *Skytri* is linked to the same corporation that owns the warehouse and other property in Miami."

Yeah, not a coincidence. "That's really good work, Odell. I'm going to bring this to Andre now." It wasn't exactly earth shattering news. Declan already had a good idea that Rick Savitch was behind the kidnapping, but now he had something concrete to bring to Andre. The lover of Andre's dead wife was going to pay for kidnapping Alena and killing one of Declan's men.

When he opened the door, he nearly ran into Nika. Her green eyes were bright with worry, but she didn't look as upset as she had earlier. "Is everything okay?"

"Have you seen my sister?"

"She's with Andre. They're—"

She abruptly shook her head. "I don't really care where they are as long as they're not here. I need to talk to you. *Alone.*"

Maybe she'd decided to come clean about everything. He nodded toward the kitchen. "Come on. Kitchen's usually empty."

As they strode down the hall, Clay walked out of one of the rooms, closing the door behind him. He had his SIG in his hand. Clay's eyes widened for a fraction of a second when he spotted them, but then he relaxed.

He smiled easily as he approached them. "Hey boss, just checking the perimeter."

That was when it hit Declan. The phone number he'd been trying to place looked familiar because he'd seen it once before. When Clay had called him from the hospital after Ethan's death, he'd called him from a number Declan didn't recognize. He'd probably used the phone by mistake. "Good. Why don't you meet me in the office in a few minutes? I want to go over the game plan for tonight before Yasha arrives."

Clay nodded, smiled almost sadly, and raised his weapon—pointing it directly at Nika's head.

Declan's heart felt as if it stopped, as if time actually stilled for one long moment. He couldn't drag in a breath as he stared at his longtime friend—holding a weapon on the woman he cared about. He'd never lost his cool before in op situations but this was different. This involved Nika. A cold sweat rolled over him in one icy sweep. Declan's weapon was tucked securely in its holster—under his jacket. His fingers itched to make a move for it, but it would get Nika killed.

For the first time in his life Declan understood what it meant to 'see red'. If Clay had been just a little closer, Declan would break his neck for pointing that weapon at Nika. His hands clenched at his sides and he made a move to stand in front of her, but Clay shook his head.

"I don't think so." With his SIG, he motioned toward the room he'd just exited. "In there. Now."

Nika paused so Declan nodded at her. "Do as he says."

Once they were inside, Clay locked the door and kept enough distance between them so that Declan couldn't wrest the SIG away from him without risking injury to himself or Nika.

Clay swore under his breath. "How'd you figure it out man?"

Declan shook his head, wondering how Clay had even known he *had* figured it out. "I wasn't sure until right now."

"Damn it." He darted a nervous glance around the room. They were in one of the smaller, unused guestrooms that lead to the backyard. Clay pointed his weapon at Nika again and Declan had to restrain himself from simply reacting. If he could just cover the distance between them—

"Make another move and I'll blow her head off." There was a deadly edge to Clay's voice. He recognized it, but he'd never been on the receiving end.

Declan remained still, knowing exactly how something like this could play out if he made one wrong move. Letting Nika get hurt wasn't an option. "What did you get yourself involved in?" Declan needed to keep him talking so he wouldn't do anything stupid.

"My daughter's sick and I needed the money. Simple as that."

"Why didn't you come to me? I would've helped you. You know that." They went back a long way. To their fucking military days. Declan took a small, lateral step so that he was standing slightly in front of Nika, but not making a move on Clay.

A harsh bark of laughter erupted from Clay's throat. "You got two million bucks lying around for experimental therapy in Switzerland because I don't, and my insurance company sure as hell doesn't. You," he tipped the SIG at Nika, "reach under his jacket and pull out his weapon. Slowly." The last word was said with that same deadly edge.

Nika looked at Declan with wide, green eyes. More than anything Declan wished he'd been able to protect her. If he'd gotten into Clay's head before now, he'd have known his friend—*friend*—was a dirty traitor. He'd never relished violence but right now he wanted to rip Clay's head off for doing this.

Nika's hands trembled as she pulled Declan's own SIG out.

"Who are you working with? Rick Savitch?"

With his free hand, Clay rubbed a hand over his forehead. "Yeah, no sense denying it," he muttered. "He wants Andre and his father to pay for the death of Ivy. If Andre hadn't switched vehicles the day of Alena's kidnapping Rick would have taken him but never would have let him live. I'm not sure exactly what Rick has planned but he's going to kill Yasha eventually. He wants Yasha to see his son die though. To suffer. I think he might be targeting Andre's sister too. I, I never meant...It doesn't matter! Nika, put the gun on the floor, then kick it over to me."

She did as he demanded, then sidled up next to Declan.

But Clay wasn't finished. With his free hand, he reached into his jacket pocket and pulled out a zip tie. He tossed it toward Nika. "Secure his hands to the bedpost. I can see what you're doing so make sure it's tight."

"Sorry," she muttered as she tightened the clasp around his wrists.

"Why'd you kill Ethan?" Declan asked.

Clay shot a nervous glance at the door. "I didn't want to, but Rick ordered me. There was no way Ethan could explain why he'd taken the back roads that morning and Rick was afraid he'd spill his guts once he healed."

"Why was Ethan working for Rick?"

"Fucking money, man!" His weapon hand trembled slightly before he regained focus. "You're coming with me." Clay tipped his weapon directly at Nika again and Declan swore his heart stopped. Clay was going to suffer for this.

"You don't need her. No one knows about you but me. Just leave her and get the hell out of here. You already have a head start. No one will find us for a while."

Clay shook his head. "I don't have any more zip ties and I'm not taking the chance. The girl comes with me. Insurance. I'll drop her off as soon as I'm away from here."

Declan yanked once, hard enough the entire bed rattled. "I swear to God if you hurt her, I'll hunt you down and kill you." He'd do a lot more than that, but vicious threats would mean nothing to a man like Clay. Declan just wanted him to understand what he intended.

"I'm not going to hurt her. Damn it, Declan! This wasn't supposed to happen. This isn't personal and I seriously hope you catch that bastard, Savitch. I didn't mean for any of this to happen. I just needed the money." He switched his attention to Nika. "Grab the sash tying one of the drapes and cover his mouth."

Silently she did as he asked, but Declan noticed the trembling of her hands as she untied the fastening and walked toward him. Once she was finished, she still stood by Declan.

Clay waved his weapon at her. "Get over here now."

Nika cast Declan a pleading look but did as Clay asked. Declan grunted but she'd done a good job tying him up. He could only watch as Clay tucked the SIG into the pocket of his jacket and grabbed Nika by the arm.

As they walked from the room, something primal surged through him. Struggling against the bedpost, he yanked with all the strength he had. The ties cut through his skin but the pain barely registered. The queen-sized bed had a canopy frame so even if he managed to shimmy up to the top, he was still blocked.

Using one foot as an anchor to ground him, he lifted his other leg and kicked at the post. It was a difficult balance and the frame was fairly solid, but as he kicked and jerked with his hands and foot, a deep cracking sound split the air.

He experienced a burst of hope. They hadn't been gone that long. If he could just get free, he could save Nika...crack!

The entire frame shifted and the post finally broke free under the abuse. He used his weight to pull the post backward. It slammed against the dresser but he dragged it until he could slip his bound wrists off the broken wood.

His hands were still hooked together, but at least he was free of his anchor. He pulled the sash out of his mouth as he rushed from the room. Heart pounding, he ran into Nathaniel walking from the kitchen holding a sandwich.

"What the hell—"

"Cut me free. Now!"

Without pause, Nathaniel dropped his food, the plate splintering against the hard floor as he pulled a knife from his pocket.

Declan didn't give him a chance to ask questions. "Clay's been working with Rick Savitch. He took Nika less than five minutes ago. They won't have gone far. Radio everyone and tell them to gear up. Tell Odell to pull up whatever satellite views he's got of this area. Give me your weapon and cell."

"Here." Nathaniel was already pulling both out.

Forcing down the panic raging inside him, Declan sprinted for the front door. His vehicle was parked around the side of the house and he had a spare key in it. Before he'd made it around the palatial home, he stopped when a flash of movement caught his eye.

One of the guards who watched the perimeter was jogging down the driveway with Nika next to him. For a brief second, his axis tilted, but he pulled it together and ran toward her.

Nika's eyes were wide as she reached him, but she looked unharmed. "He didn't hurt me. As soon as he was past the driveway, he let me go—"

Not caring that he had an audience, he cupped her face and crushed his mouth over hers. He'd never felt so desperate, so hungry, but he had to convince himself she was real and unharmed. His tongue rasped against hers with a barely contained hunger. He slid his hand around and grasped the back of her head and held tight. His fingers slipped through the curtain of her hair. Her kisses were just as fervent as his. Underneath him, her body trembled slightly and he almost came undone.

"Boss!" Nathaniel's voice made his eyes snap open.

Fuck him, he was out of control. He pulled away from a dazed looking Nika. Her green eyes swirled like a mercurial summer swell off the Atlantic.

Turning, he faced Nathaniel but blocked Nika from the other man's view. "What?"

"Everyone's ready, but..." He nodded in Nika's direction.

"Take your brother, Ramon, and Rico. Stay in contact with Odell and see if you can hunt down Clay." It burned Declan up that he wasn't the one hunting that bastard down but he couldn't leave for two reasons. Nika, being the main one. But Yasha would be there soon and Declan needed to be at the house. "He might have let her go, but we're bringing him in. I'm going to alert the local PD and see if they can put out a BOLO on him." He didn't want to involve them but sometimes he had to go the police route. He'd do it for Nika.

Later, once Nika had a chance to decompress he was going to take her down to the police station to make a statement. Clay had held her at gun point and taken her prisoner. Declan assumed she'd want to press charges because he sure as hell was going to. They just had to catch him first. If she didn't want to, he planned to take care of Clay personally.

He turned back to Nika. "I want you to go upstairs and stay in your room with your sister."

She glanced around to make sure no one was close before turning back to him. "Listen, I was coming to tell you that I had a dream about Clay when he stopped us."

"It doesn't matter now." He already knew Clay was dirty. Nothing would change that.

"No, it *does* matter. The man he talked to wanted him to call when Andre's father left tonight. Whoever was on the other line wants to kill him *tonight*."

Suspicion warred inside him that she was telling him. "You're sure?"

"I know what I saw. What are you going to do?" she persisted.

"Talk to Andre about the man I think was behind your sister's kidnapping and figure out what we're going to do about it."

"You'll come get me though, right?" Her voice was edgy and uneven.

After just having a SIG pointed at her head and see-ing those crime scene photos, he was impressed she was keeping it together so well. He wanted to stay and com-fort her but he had too much to do. "I'll be up there as soon as I can. If I could go with you I would." Not caring if anyone saw, he cupped her cheek gently and rubbed his thumb over her soft skin.

His heart still thumped an erratic drumbeat and he knew no matter how long he lived he'd never be able to get rid of the memory of seeing her with a SIG pointed right at her. Now she was safe and that was what mat-tered. He planned to keep her safe.

Rick Savitch might be smart, but everyone left a digi-tal fingerprint. It was just a matter of time until they found him.

CHAPTER TWENTY-SIX

Nika jumped at the sound of her bedroom door opening, but stilled when she saw her sister.

Alena ducked inside and quietly shut the door behind her, her dark eyes just a little wild. "It's done," she whispered.

An icy chill slithered through Nika, knowing exactly what 'it' was. "How?"

"They've got guards watching the food preparation, but there was only one guy in the dining room. I told him I wanted a drink and I spilled champagne on my top. Since I'm not wearing a bra, it was easy enough to distract him." She motioned to her soaked, white shirt, as if Nika could have missed the dark outlines of Alena's nipples.

Moving quickly, Alena pulled out a small spray bottle and hurried toward the bathroom. Nika followed and leaned against the doorframe, watching as her sister disposed of the rest of the liquid then dabbed at her ruined shirt. "What if someone else sits in that seat?" Nika asked, fear detonating inside her.

"They won't. Andre will sit at the head, there are two seats to the left of him, and one to the right. There are only four of us."

Her sister's reasoning did little to soothe the acid rolling around in Nika's stomach. For a moment she considered confessing everything to Declan, but after all she and Alena had been through together, she couldn't betray her sister.

Not when her sister had been the one to raise her, to protect her from seeing the carnage after their parents' attack. When she'd seen that photo of her mother, she'd finally understood where her sister's rage came from. Alena had only been ten when she'd seen their bodies. That image was probably seared into her brain so deep. Lord knew Nika couldn't get that horrific photo out of her mind. But for Alena to have seen it at such a young age?

Alena turned around, her expression determined. "We'll be leaving in a few days—unless you want to stay and play with Mr. Security—so stop worrying."

Nika couldn't even think about a future with Declan. The sex had been amazing but she'd done nothing but lie to him since they'd met. Well, sort of. He knew her identity now, but he still didn't know they planned to undermine his very job. She reached out and grabbed Alena's arm as her sister tried to leave the bathroom. "Alena—"

Nika stumbled and sagged against the door. Alena caught her before she could fall, but nothing could block out the vision that assaulted her mind.

Declan was pointing a gun at one of Yasha's men. He was tall, dark, scary looking. Andre was shouting. And Alena was on the floor covered in blood and crying.

Nika opened her eyes to find Alena staring down at her. She shifted and realized she was lying on the carpet in the room.

"Nika! Are you okay?" her sister shouted.

"Stop shouting, I'm not deaf," she muttered.

They both turned at the sound of the door opening. Nika sat up to find one of Declan's men standing in the doorway, gun drawn.

He lowered his gun when he saw them. "Is everything all right in here?"

"We're fine!" Alena snapped.

Without pause he stepped back and shut the door behind him.

"What just happened?" Alena whispered.

Nika clutched onto her sister's arm. "I saw you covered in blood. Andre, Declan, and Yasha were there too. Alena, we can't go through with this tonight. We'll find another way." Her voice broke on a sob. She couldn't lose her sister. She *refused* to.

"You saw me covered in blood? Where, when?"

"It doesn't work like that and you know it. Alena, you were on the ground, Andre was shouting at his father and Declan had a gun. I don't know what's going on, but whatever it is, it's not good."

Her sister pulled her into a hug and smoothed her hair down. "You see things all the time and they mean nothing. Stop worrying."

Shaking her head, Nika pulled away from the embrace. Alena couldn't believe the lie coming out of her mouth. The things she saw always meant something. "It's not *nothing*. I know what I saw. I've never seen something happen to *you* before. Not like this. This is a warning."

Alena stood and held out a hand for her. She helped Nika to her feet then placed her hands on Nika's shoulders. "I'm going to change and I suggest you do the same. I'll see you downstairs for dinner."

God, she was so stubborn. "Alena..." But her sister didn't turn around.

Nika raked a hand through her hair and started to follow after her sister, but stopped herself. She waited a few seconds, then opened the door. The same guard from earlier was standing there. She half-smiled at him and headed down the hallway. Once she was in front of Declan's door, she knocked. When he didn't answer, she tried the knob. Locked.

"Are you looking for Mr. Gallagher?" She turned at the sound of a male voice.

It was the same guard. She frowned at him. *Was he following her around?* "Yes, do you know where he is?"

"He's not here."

There wasn't much time left until dinner and she wouldn't trust anyone else with this information. "Do you know where he is?"

"No, but he should be back in half an hour or so." Nice, vague answer.

"Okay, thanks." He hadn't come to see her like he'd promised and now her mind was racing. Was it possible he somehow knew what she and Alena had been planning? No. If he did, he would have told Andre and she and Alena would have been out on their asses by now.

She hurried back to her room and locked the door. If she could get dressed and get downstairs before anyone else, maybe she could get rid of the silverware. And Alena wouldn't be in any danger.

* * *

Declan stood at the end of the stairs. Andre and Yasha were already in the dining room, drinking vodka—which Declan had purchased himself. If anyone tried to poison their drinks, it wouldn't be from the bottles. Now he was just waiting for Alena and Nika to make an appearance.

"Hey, boss, did Ms. Brennan ever find you?" Nathaniel asked as he walked through the front door.

"Which sister?"

"Nika. She was looking for you earlier. Oh, never mind…" He nodded toward the stairs.

Declan turned back to find Nika descending. His heart quickened when he saw her, an automatic response around her now. There were a hundred other things he should be focusing on, but it was hard to think straight with the way her dress clung to her curves in all the right places. She wore an emerald green cocktail dress that matched her eyes and each step she took, he got a peek of perfect, toned legs. Something was wrong though. He could see it in her expression.

When she reached the bottom stair, she clutched his hand. The gesture surprised him, but he didn't pull away. He dropped a kiss on her cheek. "You look beautiful."

"Thank you…I really need to talk to you. It's important."

The panic in her voice made all his instincts go on full alert. "Come on. We'll find some privacy."

"Nika, there you are!" Her sister interrupted the moment and Nika dropped his hand as if she'd been burned.

She swallowed noticeably, her back straightening. As soon as Alena reached the bottom of the stairs, Alena hooked her arm through Nika's.

"Are you eating with us?" She directed the question to him.

He shook his head. "No ma'am."

She gave him a tight smile and steered Nika away. Nika threw him a glance over her shoulder and the sheer terror in her eyes kicked all his senses into high gear. He fell into step behind them, giving them a small berth.

Unless they'd managed to get very creative, neither woman had any weapons. Alena's short yellow dress was practically a second skin. And Nika had come to him about Clay earlier. If she wanted to kill Yasha, why would she have told him everything?

"Ramon, Kevin, Nathaniel, you read me?" He quietly spoke into his mic. When they all answered in the affirmative, some of his apprehension abated. They were trained and these were just two civilians. His men could handle it.

As they entered the dining room, he made his way until he was standing against one of the walls. He blended into the scenery as Alena and Nika were being introduced to Yasha.

* * *

Nika couldn't fight the terror spiraling through her like an out of control avalanche, rolling over everything that got in its way. She stood right in front of the man who had killed her father and raped and beaten her mother to death. She'd met him once and wasn't sure how she'd stand to be near him again, especially after seeing the actual pictures of what he'd done. Sitting through a whole meal with this monster seemed utterly impossible.

As Alena sidled up to Andre, Yasha's gaze narrowed on Nika. "Good evening Ms. Brennan. What's your name again?"

She knew very well he remembered her name but forced a polite smile. "I'm Nika."

"So how are you liking Miami so far?" he asked casually, though there was nothing casual about the gleam in his eyes. He looked like a predator, ready to rip her throat out.

"Apart from my sister getting kidnapped, peachy." Okay, maybe the sarcastic response hadn't been the best idea, but fuck him.

Yasha's eyes narrowed, but her sister laughed a delicate, silvery sound and if Nika didn't know her better, she'd believe Alena was having a good time.

Nika on the other hand was close to puking on her stilettos.

"Would either of you ladies like something to drink?" This time Andre spoke, all smooth charm. Unfortunately it was real. Why did he have to be such a good guy?

"I'd love a glass of champagne and I'm sure Nika wants a glass of pinot noir if you have it," Alena answered.

Nika nodded and pasted that smile on again. "If you don't mind, I'm going to take a seat. I've been feeling a little unwell today." Without waiting for a response, she walked to the seat Alena had directed her to sit at.

They'd gone over their seating arrangement earlier and this was exactly how they'd planned it. The only difference was Nika wasn't faking her nausea. She felt as if she'd vomit at any moment and there was nothing she could do about it without betraying her sister. If she told

Declan now, he'd have to expose them and that would put both of them in danger from Yasha.

The dining room was huge, but she was very aware of the extra security buzzing around. Declan and another man stood against one of the walls and even though her back was to them, she was very aware of Declan's presence. He might not be looking at her, but she felt as if molten hot laser beams were slicing into her back. She wished she was with just him right now, upstairs in one of the bedrooms. Or better yet, far away from this place on a warm beach somewhere.

Two more of his men that she'd seen around the house stood by the mini bar area and near the fireplace was a man she'd seen with Yasha before.

Alena squeezed Nika's thigh as she slid in next to her and a second later, a server appeared out of nowhere with their drinks. She took a sip of her wine and resisted chugging it.

Next to her they were talking about one of Andre's Biloxi casinos and possibly expanding and some other nonsense. She had to resist the urge to stare at Yasha. The tall blond man looked so much like Andre, except his eyes were darker. Penetrating. And empty. Looks aside, seeing the two of them together it was so obvious how different Andre was from his father.

"How is your sister?" Yasha's question to Andre brought an unexpected silence from their host.

The movement was slight but Andre's hand clenched tightly around his glass, his knuckles going white. His grip was so hard Nika was afraid he'd break it. Finally he spoke. "She's fine."

"Please tell her I was asking about her wellbeing."

"Damn it, father," Andre muttered.

Yasha turned his attention toward her and Alena. "He chooses his half-sister over his own father. She's nothing more than the daughter of a whore."

Nika bit back a gasp at the man's crude words and she could feel Alena stiffen next to her.

Andre slammed his fist against the table. The silverware and plates shook dangerously. "Damn it! Can't you just behave like a normal human being for a couple hours? Why are you even here—"

"Andre." Alena placed a calming hand on his forearm. He stilled immediately and she nodded behind Yasha. A man dressed in all black had just stepped from the kitchen and was carrying two salads toward them.

Nika's breath hitched in her throat but she managed a smile as the man placed the plates in front of her and Alena. A moment later another man appeared and he placed plates in front of Andre and Yasha. Apparently they were just going to keep on dining and ignore what Yasha had just said.

Yasha picked up his fork and looked back and forth between Andre and Alena. "Maybe you're just a common whore too, Alena."

Andre stood and shoved his chair back as he did. It clattered loudly against the hardwood floor. "That's it! Get the hell out of here right now."

Alena shook her head and held out a placating hand. "It's okay. He's just being protective of his son. Let's just eat and everyone will calm down."

Nika risked a peek over her shoulder to find Declan staring at her. His expression was neutral and she hated that she couldn't get a read on him. Silently she turned back to find Andre picking up his fallen chair.

Yasha glanced at her as he stabbed a piece of lettuce with his fork. She looked away and picked up her glass of wine. Anything to keep her hands busy. Out of the corner of her eye she watched as he brought the food to his mouth. Everything around her funneled out. This was it. It was finally happening. Maybe once it was all over, they could truly lead somewhat normal lives. His death would look like an accident.

"Stop!" Declan shouted, his voice making the room go quiet.

Everyone turned to stare at him and Nika's heart stuttered when she saw his dark, angry expression.

"Drop your fork, Yasha." Declan's voice was razor sharp.

"You told him?" Alena's voice was accusing, her expression broken.

Nika shook her head, trying to get her sister to be quiet. She'd wanted to tell Declan but unless he'd read her mind, he'd figured it out on his own.

"Told him what?" Yasha asked as he laid the fork down, eyeing both of them warily now.

Instead of responding, Alena picked up her knife and lunged across the table. Plates and glasses scattered everywhere. Nika's wineglass smashed and covered Alena's dress with a giant splash. Before Nika could react, Andre intercepted Alena and snagged her by the waist midair. He tugged her back, but she still struggled against his chest like a wild animal. One of her shoes flew off, sailing past Yasha's head.

"Let me go!" she screamed.

At the same time, Declan shouted again. "Drop it!" Nika looked up to see Yasha's man pointing a gun at them while Declan pointed a gun at him.

Without turning around, Yasha held up a hand. "Dima, drop your weapon. They're not going to hurt me. Are you?" He zeroed his gaze on her and Nika froze.

In her peripheral vision she could see her sister on the floor sobbing, covered in red wine. Declan still held his gun, and Andre was holding onto Alena tightly and shouting something, but Nika couldn't make out the words. All she could focus on was Yasha's dark, hollow eyes.

The same eyes Nika's mother had seen before she'd had the life stolen from her.

"Do you know who we are?" she asked the question, but she felt detached from her body as she spoke. Her voice sounded tinny to her ears.

He shrugged, so arrogantly unconcerned. "You look familiar. Did I sell or fuck your sister, cousin? Someone you love? This is about revenge, yes?"

"Yes." She wasn't going to tell him who they were. He could figure it out on his own. Before she could change her mind, she picked up one of the glass tumblers and threw it at his face. With only a few feet separating them, he didn't have time to react. The heavy glass thudded against his forehead with a loud clunk.

With a surprised cry, he stumbled back and held a hand to his face. Blood trickled down his forehead. "You bitch!"

"That's enough! You need to leave. *Now.*" Declan took a step closer with his gun and that's when she noticed one of Declan's other men had a gun trained on Yasha's security guy.

He'd come with light security tonight, no doubt because he thought he'd be safe at Andre's house. Either that or they were all waiting outside. Probably the latter.

Yasha kept his gaze trained on Nika as he spoke. "I'm leaving, but be warned. You and your sister are dead."

CHAPTER TWENTY-SEVEN

Andre's grip on Alena loosened slightly as his father left the dining room. He wasn't sure what the hell had just happened. Alena shoved away from him and buried her face against her hands as sobs racked her body. Nika knelt down next to her sister and gathered her into trembling arms. Alena didn't fight Nika's soothing.

He wanted to demand that Alena tell him what was going on, even as he wanted to comfort her—though he clearly had no idea who *she* really was. But first he needed to take care of his father. "Declan, take them upstairs," he growled before trailing after Yasha.

Andre stopped him in the foyer where the rest of his men waited. "I want to talk to you before you leave."

"About what? How your girlfriend tried to kill me?"

Andre bit back the anger driving through him and motioned toward the sitting room next to the foyer. "Can we speak in private?"

Nodding, Yasha strode toward the room, his expression calculating. There wasn't a door to shut for privacy but they were far enough away from his father's thugs that they wouldn't be overheard.

Instead of sitting, Yasha leaned against one of the high-backed chairs. Despite the casual stance, Andre knew his father enough to realize Yasha was containing his rage. The red splotch on his forehead would soon leave a bruise, and blood was smeared where he'd wiped it away. It was sure to be a reminder to his father every time he looked in the mirror for a little while. Not that Yasha would need one.

"Did you know about this?" Yasha asked.

"I knew nothing about *that*. What did you do to them?" Andre motioned behind him.

His father ignored his question. "What are you going to do with the women?"

"That's not your concern. I have a proposition for you. I'll give you full reign of the warehouses you asked about if you leave both sisters alone. *Forever*." Andre was filled with rage and another emotion he didn't want to acknowledge that Alena had been clearly using him, but he wouldn't let her die for it. He wasn't a monster, not like his father.

"You think I should let this go? They tried to kill me," Yasha ground out.

"Yet, you're still alive. The decision is yours, but once you walk out that door, the offer will be rescinded."

Yasha paused for just a moment, then nodded sharply. "That is acceptable. I will need the B2 warehouse all day tomorrow and at least twice more this year. Make sure your security steers clear of the area."

"So we have a deal then?"

"We have a deal."

Andre held out a hand. "You'll have the warehouse as early as midnight tonight if you need it. I'll make the call."

After his father had gone, he found Declan in the dining room bagging the silverware and plate where Yasha had been sitting.

"You think they were going to poison him?"

Declan nodded as he glanced up. "There was something about the way they were both looking at him as he picked up his fork. They were tense, on edge. And any woman would have been livid after a man called her a common whore to her face yet Alena sat there and just took it. She wanted him to stay for a reason. I'll know for sure what they were going to poison him with once I run this. What do you plan to do with them?"

"I'm not turning them over to the police." He did plan to kick them out, but not until he got his questions answered from Alena first. And not until he was certain his father wasn't a threat to them.

Declan sighed heavily. "I think I might know why they hate him so much."

Andre frowned. "Why?"

"I need to show you." He reached into his jacket and pulled out a slim manila envelope. "You can't keep these photos, but the people in these pictures were their parents. I think your father had something to do with their deaths." Declan's expression was grim as he handed the packet over. "A warning...they're not easy to look at."

Andre paused, but opened it. As he pulled out the first glossy photograph, his stomach churned. He'd known what a monster his father was, but this... "My father is responsible for this?"

"I believe that twenty years ago he and three other men did that. They raped the woman before killing her." Declan nodded at the picture without looking at it.

"What about the other men involved?"

"Dead."

"Killed by Alena and Nika?"

Declan shrugged. "I don't know."

As he looked at the pictures, something inside him shifted. How could he even be related to someone who could do this? "I know you still have government contacts. I think my father is planning something tomorrow. Probably illegal. Do you know of anyone who would be interested in that information?"

Declan's body went predator-still. "Yasha's planning something *tomorrow*?"

"I gave him unlimited access to one of my warehouses starting at midnight tonight in exchange for leaving Alena and Nika alone forever."

"You're sure it's tomorrow?"

"He was very specific."

"Where?"

"The spread of warehouses I own near the Port of Miami, the exact number is B2."

Declan's head cocked slightly to the side. "You realize what will happen to Yasha when I pass this information on?"

Andre looked at the photo of the dead woman. The woman was so bruised and bloody...there shouldn't have been so much blood. And her face...He swallowed hard then looked back up at Declan. He understood. He just didn't care. Yasha could rot in hell. Jail was too good for him, but if that was the only option, Andre would take it. "I know. He deserves worse than what will happen to him."

"I'll make the call." Declan pulled out his cell on the spot. Andre didn't miss the way his mouth curved up, as if he was trying to hold back a smile.

Andre didn't blame him. Yasha... was beyond evil. Andre could accept it. He'd destroyed Alena and Nika's family. Those photos... his stomach roiled. While Andre knew firsthand the havoc the man had wreaked within his own family, he'd never moved against him. Now he realized he should have. The man was his blood, his father. But seeing firsthand in bright colors, it was too much to turn away anymore. He'd stolen Alena's parents in the most brutal way possible. His father had taken all that from a woman he'd fallen for. Even calling Yasha human seemed to be an insult to the rest of the planet.

After scanning the rest of the pictures, he laid them face down on the dining room table and went in search of Alena.

* * *

"Do you trust your son not to betray you?" Dima asked as they pulled away from Andre's home.

"He wants to save that slut's life. He'll give me what I want." Yasha was positive of that.

"Who were those women?"

"I couldn't place them at first, but I believe I killed their parents. It was many years ago." Almost twenty, in fact. He couldn't be sure, but Alena looked very similar to the Aston woman he and the Lazarev brothers had killed so long ago. The woman had been pale while Alena was darker skinned, but their facial features were the same. They both had that stunning quality truly beautiful women had. The dead woman had been a double-agent who'd gotten exactly what she deserved. Working for the Americans instead of her own country and married to a British-American national. Now that he thought about it, he remembered her well. *Traitorous bitch.* He'd enjoyed killing her. She'd screamed but she'd never begged. Even when he'd told her to.

"For the Belovs?"

Yasha nodded and glanced out the window. It had been so long ago, it didn't matter who he'd killed them for. He'd killed so many after all. If he wanted to move the meet up to tomorrow, he had many calls to make. "Contact Mr. Carter. Our next meeting is at nine sharp, I want the business with Carter finished by then."

"Seven?"

"Make it six. And tell him he may bring three men only. If he doesn't like it, we don't meet and I'll find another buyer."

* * *

FBI Director Vernon Nash scrubbed a hand over his face and exited his last meeting of the day. He grabbed his cell phone from the basket sitting outside the door. As a mandatory precaution everyone had left their phones out during the meeting. The temporary field office in Miami was okay as far as things went, but that wasn't what had him worried. He'd expected results from Declan Gallagher days ago. The man was known for his ability to extract information from people, especially when he got into their heads. Or at least he had been years ago.

Since he'd started his own security firm, his type of work had changed, but his skill of getting people to talk shouldn't have. As far as Vernon knew, Declan had never let a pretty face get in the way of business, but maybe that was what had happened.

Instead of heading for his temporary office Vernon strode toward the stairs. His corner office in the two-story building was secure, but the FBI was working with the DEA and other government agencies. He didn't want anyone overhearing his conversation and the stairwell would provide the perfect amount of interference.

He started to call Declan when his phone rang. "Speak of the devil," he muttered.

"What the hell is going on?" Declan's voice was tight.

"What's happened? Is it Yasha? I heard he was coming to dinner at Andre's."

There was a moment of silence. "How did you know he was coming to dinner?"

Shit. "That's not important."

"It is fucking important! Alena Brennan just tried to kill Yasha and earlier today I found out one of my guys—my friend—is a traitor. I've been trying to call you the past couple hours. I might owe you but if I find out you knew about *any* of this—"

"Whoa, slow down! I have a source within Yasha's organization. I can't tell you his name. That's how I knew about the dinner. What's going on with your security team? You have a *traitor?*" Vernon couldn't hide his surprise. Declan vetted his guys very thoroughly.

"I've got that under control. Do you know who Alena and Nika Brennan really are? And don't lie to me."

Yeah, he knew. By the sound of it, so did Declan. "You said she tried to kill Yasha so I'm guessing she didn't succeed?"

"No. Now tell me what you know."

"A long time ago you'd have already figured this out on your own."

Declan swore under his breath. "You son of a bitch. You know who they are, don't you." It wasn't a question.

Vernon sighed. He should have just told Declan everything he suspected from the beginning, but it hadn't seemed necessary. Keeping the women away from Yasha was all that mattered, regardless of who they were. "I have a fairly good idea they're not who they say they are. You're too young to remember, but you've heard about the Aston incident, correct?"

"Shit. You *do* know who they are."

"Wait, you're sure it's them?"

Declan sighed heavily. "As of a couple hours ago, yeah. I wasn't positive they wanted Yasha dead though. I am now."

"This is above your old pay grade and it's above my current one, but the unofficial rumor is the Lazarev brothers and Yasha Makarov killed Anya and Blake Aston. I wasn't completely sure of the sisters' identities, but after some digging, I made some connections and filled in the blanks myself. Wouldn't have found them if I wasn't looking hard though. So I was right. Give me a SITREP."

"I promised I'd keep them away from Yasha and that's what I've done. When we first met, you said this was personal for you. Why are you interested in these women?"

Vernon paused, but decided on honesty. "I was friends with Blake Aston. I knew if these were his daughters, you wouldn't let them get hurt in the crossfire. It's why I asked you for the favor."

"Why didn't you just tell me all this?" Declan asked.

"It wasn't important and I didn't want it to cloud your judgment. I *need* Yasha alive until we find out where those girls are being held." It ate away at him, knowing so many young women would be auctioned off and sold into hell. No one had the right to own another human being.

"Yasha left this house alive and I know where he's going. According to Andre, his father is using one of his warehouses tomorrow to conduct some *business*." His inflection left no doubt it was illegal. "It's another reason I'm calling."

"How certain of this are you?"

"It's happening. If I was a betting man, I'd say he's probably going to unload the product you're worried about."

Vernon listened as Declan filled him in on all the details of where the meet would take place. When he finished, Vernon sagged against the wall in the stairwell. They had more than enough time to plan an ambush. "We can take him down with this information. Thank you."

"Just free those girls."

After they disconnected, Vernon pulled a pack of cigarettes from his pocket and walked down the flight of stairs. He could worry about quitting another day. Until Yasha was in custody he needed something to calm his nerves.

CHAPTER TWENTY-EIGHT

"I didn't tell Declan about tonight, Alena, I swear. I...I wanted to and I almost did, but I didn't." Nika shifted on Alena's bed and wrapped her arms around her sister's shoulders. She'd already told Alena about the pictures and that he knew their true identity. Her sister's pain tore her up inside.

"We were so close," Alena mumbled against her shoulder. Sniffling, she pulled back and looked at Nika. Her eyes were glassy and puffy. "Do you think Andre will turn us over to Yasha?"

"No." If Nika hadn't been so sure of that she would have been scared to death. But Andre hated his father too. Not as much as they did, but there would be no love lost between them. And, in her heart she knew Declan wouldn't let him turn them over anyway. He probably didn't want to see her again, but he wasn't a cruel man.

"You think he'll call the cops?"

"I...don't know." She didn't think so, but she wasn't going to rule out any possibility. "Do you want to change?" she asked in reference to Alena's ruined yellow dress. The only good thing to develop out of the whole situation was that Nika's vision had been wrong. Well, it had been right, but it had been wine, not blood covering her sister.

"Yeah." She started to push up when the door opened.

Andre looked between the two of them as he closed the door behind himself, his expression hard. All his focus was on Alena, laser-sharp. "Did you originally meet me with the intention of killing my father?"

"Yes." Her sister didn't pause in her answer.

"Was the kidnapping part of your plan?"

Alena shook her head vehemently. "No...It didn't hurt my cause though."

"Why do you want to kill him?" he asked, but Nika was under the impression he already knew the answer.

Alena glanced at Nika before meeting his gaze. "He killed our parents while we were in the house. I was ten when I saw...what he did to my mother. I swore whoever killed them would pay for it with their life. Until a couple years ago I didn't know it was him."

"I'm sorry about your parents." His voice was hoarse.

Her sister stared at him with a guarded expression. "Are you going to turn us over to the cops?"

He raked a hand through his already rumpled blond hair and took a step farther into the room. "No."

"Are we free to go?" Alena asked.

In an instant, his blue eyes hardened as he stared at Alena. "Was everything we shared a lie?"

She shook her head. "Not everything."

Nika knew her sister was telling the truth. She actually cared about this man. Maybe more than she wanted to admit… maybe she even loved him.

His hands were balled into fists at his sides. He seemed so different from the man who'd been doting after her sister the past month. It was like a switch had flipped inside him. Nika wrapped her arms around herself. Even though it wasn't presently directed at her, the angry look in his icy eyes was terrifying.

"I should kick you out on your asses right now," he ground out.

Nika was surprised he wasn't doing just that.

Alena's voice trembled slightly as she spoke. "I'm so sorry, Andre. For everything. I never meant to hurt you. I never meant…"

When she trailed off, he laughed, the sound harsh and angry. "You never meant to hurt me? But you planned to leave after you'd killed him, yes?"

Guiltily, Alena nodded. Nika looked at her feet, unable to meet his gaze.

"Pack your stuff. You leave in the morning."

"We can leave now if—"

"Yasha probably has men watching the house tonight. You'll *leave* in the morning. You can take my plane anywhere you want to go. Then you're on your own." His voice was so bitter, but it was the offer of his plane that made Nika's head snap up.

"What?" Alena asked, the surprise in her voice mirroring Nika's own feelings.

"If you get on a commercial flight anywhere, Yasha will have little problem hunting you down. I'm not my father, I'm *not* a murderer." He spat the last word. "He's sworn to me he'll let you live, but I know him. I saw those pictures. I saw what he did to your family." With those words, he left the room, pulling the door shut with more force than necessary. The resounding slam made them both jump.

"I'm going to go pack," Nika muttered.

"Good idea." Alena's voice was hollow, tired.

Nika wanted to comfort her sister, to ask where they were going next, but she also wanted to cry. Once in her room she folded and packed her clothes with rapid efficiency. She'd traveled enough that she knew how to pack quickly.

Once she was finished she changed into her pajamas and laid her head against the soft pillow. After tonight, she and Alena would have to go into hiding. They couldn't return to their New Orleans home. They'd probably have to sell it. Their contingency plan had always been to escape to their uncle's cabin in upstate New York if anything went wrong. Shit had definitely gone wrong.

As she closed her eyes, a sharp knock sounded on the door.

"Nika, it's me. Open up." It was Declan.

She froze. He knocked again, but she remained immobile. When she heard him mutter a curse, she knew he'd given up and let out a sigh of relief. There was nothing left to say to him anyway. They were over. She'd lied to him in the worst way possible and didn't want to hash everything out. In the end, he still wouldn't want her and she didn't feel like seeing all that sadness and disappointment in his eyes. She knew it made her the worst kind of coward, but she couldn't handle anything else tonight.

As of tomorrow, she was leaving Miami and all this shit behind. She was tired of living out of a suitcase and tired of living for revenge. And she was thoroughly sick of not having a real life and not being able to trust anyone. She had a few friends in New York and London. She'd make a decision later on exactly where she wanted to live, but the one thing she knew for sure, she had to get the hell out of here.

If for some reason Declan could forgive her, which she doubted, even if she got involved with him, he'd have a target on his back simply by being associated with her. Yasha wasn't going to forget what she and her sister had done. She wouldn't put Declan in danger because of her.

* * *

Declan stalked toward his room. He felt like a caged, wild animal. Nika wouldn't talk to him? Fine. He'd simply invade her dreams. He didn't care if she liked it. He was going to make her talk to him. As he reached the end of the hallway, Odell's voice stopped him.

"Boss, you got a sec?"

He turned to find him hovering by the top of the stairs. "What's going on?"

"I need to talk to you about something. It's personal."

"So talk." He was not in the mood for this.

Odell shoved his hands in his pockets. "I don't even know how to say this, but, uh...I have a problem. A gambling problem...addiction. I wanted to wait until after this job, but it's eating me alive inside, especially after the shit that went down with Clay. I owe a lot of money to some people in—"

"Jersey. I know."

He rubbed a hand over his trim hair. "Shit. Why didn't you say something?"

Declan shrugged. "I was going to wait until after this job."

"I just wanted to be up front about it with you and let you know that I'm going to start attending Gambler's Anonymous."

"I'm glad to hear that. I'm going to cover the debt. You've put in a lot of overtime and been with my company from the beginning. I just wish you'd come to me sooner." Declan understood why he hadn't though.

"I know...it's embarrassing."

He tried to smooth past that, not wanting Odell to be ashamed. People had all sorts of vices and reasons for them. He was just glad Odell was taking responsibility. "My brother knows the lady who runs a Gamblers

Anonymous group at Church of God. Want me to put you in touch with her?"

He nodded, relief filling his expression. "Yeah. I'd appreciate it."

"You're a valuable employee but this is a one-time thing. I expect you to attend meetings regularly and if you don't, you're done." Because Declan wouldn't enable anyone. That never worked out well for either party.

"I know. And thank you for..." He rubbed a hand over his face and his voice was tight as he continued. "Thank you for covering it. I didn't expect that by coming to you. I just couldn't take the guilt anymore."

Declan nodded and continued to his room. He'd already called Vernon with the information on Yasha. Now there was nothing any of them could do but wait for the FBI to arrest him. If he really was running women for the purpose of slavery in addition to drug running, he'd be thrown in a deep, dark hole somewhere.

Without bothering to change, Declan took off his shoes and lay on his bed. He was going to get into Nika's head whether she liked it or not.

He ordered himself to focus. Slowing his breathing, he shut his eyes and pushed all other thoughts from his mind except the ones that revolved around her. Wild curly dark hair, smooth caramel skin, bewitching green eyes, small, perfect breasts...

Suddenly he spotted her. She sat cross-legged in the middle of her bed, glaring at him. "Can't you let me get some sleep?" she snapped.

"Why didn't you answer your door?"

She played with the hem of her shirt. "I don't want to see you."

Annoyance flared inside him, hot and bright. "What was I supposed to do, let your sister kill him?"

She didn't respond.

"Is that really why you're angry at me?" He took a few steps toward her, but she erected a mental wall, forcing him to a halt.

Apparently it surprised her too because her eyes widened when he stopped. "Did I do that?"

He didn't want to admit it, but he had no choice. "Yeah."

Her gaze narrowed. "Can I keep you out of my dreams?"

He didn't answer. Only a select number of people could mentally keep dream walkers out of their heads. They could also kill dream walkers if they wanted. If he was killed in his dream state, he'd die in the real world. He wasn't sure he wanted her to know that. "Why are you angry with me?"

She brought her knees up to her chest and wrapped her arms around them. "I'm not angry. I'm...tired of all this. Everything you and I had was based on lies. You knew who I was before we even met, didn't you?"

"I had an idea you and your sister didn't meet Andre by chance. I didn't know what your end game was but once I got your sister's fingerprints, I pieced a few things together."

"Is that why you took the job for Andre—to spy on us?"

He nodded.

"See? You're a liar and I'm a liar. I don't want to start something based on that."

That God awful tightening in his chest started again. He refused to let her walk away from him. "I didn't lie about my attraction to you, a mhuirnín." And he hadn't. She obviously didn't understand how much she meant to him.

"It doesn't matter." Her beautiful eyes brimmed with pain. They seemed brighter in the dream tonight. "I'm done with all of this. Just leave me alone."

"Nika, will you just talk to me? I'm sorry about your parents and everything you two have gone through. I just want to be there for you. I want to get to know you—the real you."

"If..." She pulled in a ragged sigh. "Even if we tried to make this thing work Yasha will always want my sister and me dead. You wouldn't be safe if we're together. It's easier if we end this now."

Fuck that. "Wait—" His surroundings faded only to be replaced with a new scene. He was still in her head, but he was seeing her memories.

For the first time ever. *She must be letting him inside her head.*

A pretty dark-haired girl who couldn't be more than five slid a green and gold wrapped box back under a giant Christmas tree. Sitting cross-legged, she stared at the pile of presents under the sparkling lights and silver tinsel.

"Sasha!" someone shouted.

She turned at the sound. "What is it, Angel?"

"Mom told you to get into your pajamas ten minutes ago. The babysitter will be here soon."

"So? You're not mommy."

The other girl, Angel, rolled her eyes. "Whatever. If you don't change, I'll tell Santa you've been bad."

"You said he wasn't even real." She glared at her sister.

Angel smirked and left the room humming Jingle Bells.

The little girl with short, unruly curls glanced at the giant green tree one more time then ran from the room and up the stairs. After changing into her pink pajamas, she rushed into another room and dove onto a king-sized bed. The fluffy comforter let out a big whoosh.

"Did you brush your teeth?" A woman in her thirties—must be her mother—looked at her through the mirror as she put in a sparkly earring.

"Um... Where are you going tonight?"

"A party." The woman turned around with a huge smile on her face. Her dark hair was piled high on her head and she wore a floor-length black dress. "How do I look?"

"Like a goddess." An ebony skinned man with a slight British accent answered—her father—as he strode out of a bathroom and kissed her.

"Eww." Sasha rolled her eyes. "Why can't me and Angel come with you?"

Her mom pressed on her dad's chest and looked at her. "Angel and I."

Sasha flopped against the pillow and sighed. "Why can't Angel and I come?"

"It's a party for grownups." Her mother sat on the edge of the bed as the doorbell rang.

"Got it," her dad murmured before disappearing out into the hallway.

"You'll have more fun with Angel and Nancy. You like Nancy right?"

"I guess so. She told me that Santa was bringing me presents this year." She bit her bottom lip and frowned.

"Come on sweetie, let me see that smile—"

"Anya! The girls!" The man's shouts were terrified. He sounded like a hurt animal.

"Mommy?" Sasha's voice shook.

But her mom wasn't listening. She headed to the nightstand and pulled a small pistol from the drawer. "Go to your sister's room. Listen to everything she says."

"But—"

"Now!"

Without another word, Sasha raced through the adjoining bathroom and ran right into her sister.

"Angel, what's going on?"

Shouts and loud bangs from downstairs seemed to shake the whole house. Her mother's screams echoed loudly. Tears stung the little girl's eyes. "Is mommy hurt?"

Angel grabbed her hand. "Come on." She yanked Sasha inside the closet then tugged the white doors shut. Sasha watched as her sister pulled back a part of the wall. "What is that?"

"Get in and be quiet," Angel whispered, fear evident in her voice.

She climbed into the little carpeted cubbyhole and waited for her sister to follow. Glass breaking and loud men yelling sounded outside, but her sister shushed her and pulled the wall back into place.

"Why do you have a secret room? What's wrong with mommy?" She clutched her stomach.

"Shh."

Angel grabbed her sister's hand. When their mother's cries grew louder and closer, Angel dropped Sasha's hand. Sasha covered her ears and squeezed her eyes shut tight. Small arms pulled her into a hug, but it didn't block the outside noises.

The little girl jumped when three loud bangs reverberated around them, but her sister grasped her tighter and placed a hand over her mouth. Her mother was crying and saying her father's name. A man shouted vile words in Russian and then he laughed.

Then her mother cried even louder. It was so loud Declan wanted to get the hell out of Nika's head, but he made himself stay put. She was showing this to him because it was important to her. He needed to see it through.

The little girl tried to move but her older sister gripped her tighter.

"I'm going to cover your ears," her sister whispered.

Angel held her hands over Sasha's ears, covering Sasha's own small hands, but it didn't drown out the angry shouts and crying.

When silence descended, Angel removed her hands and wrapped her arms around Sasha. They remained frozen in place, shaking.

He jerked upright in bed. He was covered in sweat and shaking. Nausea rolled through his gut as he lay back down. Closing his eyes, he focused on Nika once again, but it was useless. He couldn't get into her dreams no matter how hard he tried. After seeing that he felt sick. Though that seemed an inept description.

He'd lost his mother too, but not to a violent gang of thugs. He rubbed a hand over the middle of his chest. Alena had been older, she'd likely been the one to contact whoever had helped get them out of the house. And she'd been the one who'd seen what happened to her parents. He wondered how long they stayed in that closet, how long until someone came to help them.

Sighing, he stared at the ceiling. Looked like Nika had figured out how to kick him out of her dreams. That didn't mean she got to kick him out of her life. Because that wasn't happening. Tomorrow he'd find a way to convince her she needed to stay in Miami. Permanently.

CHAPTER TWENTY-NINE

Out of the corner of his eye, Yasha watched Dima stiffen with surprise as they steered up to his son's warehouse.

"I thought we were going to be closer to the pier," Dima said.

"No, that's simply what I told you." Without waiting for a response, he drew his pistol and shot Dima in the head. The small caliber weapon did the job, but it didn't make a big mess.

His driver jerked the wheel slightly, but didn't say anything. As they pulled to a stop, Yasha wiped the blood spots from his face and the right arm of his leather jacket. He leaned forward and spoke to the two men in the front seat. "This is what happens when you try to cross me. Get rid of the body and dispose of this vehicle."

"Yes, sir," they both murmured in unison.

Dima had been ratting on him to the FBI and if he hadn't slipped up, Yasha never would have known. He still didn't know how long he'd been going behind his back, but it didn't matter anymore. As Yasha exited the car, Oleg and five others were waiting to head inside.

Oleg glanced past him and his eyes widened when he saw Dima's body. He quickly averted his gaze. "We've already secured the perimeter."

"Good. Mr. Carter will be arriving shortly." He'd sent his men ahead of him but he hadn't wanted to arrive too early. In case there was an ambush, he wasn't getting taken down with his men. As it was, he still wasn't sure if Dima was the only rat he had.

Sometime in the past few hours, a light fog had descended over Miami. His breath curled like smoke in front of him. The only sounds were the soft squeaking of their shoes across the concrete as they headed toward the side entrance door. After dealing with Dima, the only assurance he had they were safe was the fact that Andre wouldn't betray him. His son might hate him, but blood was thicker than anything.

Huge crates with the product inside lined the walls, but there was enough open space to set up a table for the monetary exchange. Only cash for this deal. And Mr. Carter would no doubt end up much wealthier when he sold the women individually.

Dealing with auctions was too much trouble for Yasha. And too dangerous. A one-time deal like this was perfect.

"They've arrived," Oleg said as he touched his earpiece.

"Search them for weapons and bring them to me." Instead of sitting, Yasha stood next to the table as his man and three others strode out. Out of habit, he glanced around the warehouse, but nothing looked out of place. The rafters were dark and there was no movement. Just as it should be. He felt as if he was being watched, but lately he always felt that way. Like he was in the crosshairs of a sniper. After he was almost killed by that bitch it was no wonder he was on edge.

His heart rate sped up as four men walked through the side entrance, weapons drawn. Three wore black masks but one had his face exposed. Neither Oleg nor his other men were with them.

Yasha reached for his pistol but stopped when the dark-haired leader fired a warning shot at the ground. Thanks to the suppressor the shot itself barely made a whisper of sound, but concrete cracked under the assault.

"Next time I'll shoot your knee. All of you, drop your weapons," the dark-haired man ordered, his voice echoing through the cavernous space.

"This is no way to do business," Yasha growled.

The man trained his pistol on Yasha's head. "Tell your men to drop their weapons."

"*Sdelajte eto!*" He'd been counting on this deal but he wouldn't die for it.

Around him weapons clattered to the concrete floor.

"Now slide them over to me."

Once his men did, one of the masked men gathered the firearms.

"What you want is in the crates. Take it and leave," Yasha sneered in contempt.

"Oh, I'm going to take everything. And I'll be letting all those women go. But not before I kill you. You don't recognize me, do you?"

"I recognize your voice, Mr. Carter. I don't imagine you'll stay in business long if this is how you conduct yourself."

He let out a harsh bark of laughter. "You know me as Richard Carter, but your son knows me at Rick Savitch."

Realization punched into him, a vicious strike. He'd had that whore killed so long ago, it felt like another lifetime. "You were the one fucking his wife?"

Savitch's face contorted with rage. "I loved her and you had her killed!"

Yasha had gone to great pains to cover up that fact. His own son didn't know, would likely have killed Yasha if he had known. There was no use denying it now. "She was a whore and she was making a fool out of my son. I couldn't allow it to continue."

"Does Andre know you killed his wife?"

"Of course not!" he spat. "He would have stayed married to her until she'd left him. It was shameful." His upper lip curled in disgust. "*That* is why you wish to kill me? Over a woman?" He couldn't comprehend that.

"On your knees." The man's voice and hands were steady.

There was no way Yasha could fight his death. With another, he might have been able to bribe his way out, but he was smart enough to realize it wouldn't work with this man. Still, he would never kneel before any man. And he would not beg. "I will not."

"You will do exactly as I say," Rick snarled, taking a step forward.

"FBI! Everyone drop your weapons!" A loud voice boomed.

Lights flooded the warehouse and men swarmed the place like locusts. Men rappelled down on ropes, dropping from the rafters as others rushed through the doors, armed to the teeth. Yasha stood frozen as the masked men dropped their weapons and hit the floor. Everyone complied except Savitch.

"Drop your weapon!" someone shouted.

Never in his life had Yasha thought to be thankful for the government's protection. He smirked, realizing that he'd won after all. The FBI might have overheard everything, but if he could get out on bail, he'd flee the country. There were places in Europe or South America he could hide with relative ease. He might not be as rich as he'd hoped but at least he'd be alive. "You heard the man. Drop your weapon." His mouth curved up tauntingly.

Savitch's dark eyes narrowed. "Don't you think it's convenient that the FBI tracked you here? How do you think they did that?"

Yasha's chest squeezed as the words sank in. Andre, his own blood, had betrayed him. Dima would have given them a different location. No one had known about this place until the last minute except…

"Drop the weapon!" A loud voice shouted again.

Savitch's head cocked slightly to the side as he started to lower his weapon. Then his hand snapped back up and he pulled the trigger.

Yasha fell back against the concrete floor. A coppery, bitter taste filled his mouth. He watched as a Fed slammed Savitch to the ground. His hands were being fastened behind his back with handcuffs but he was smiling. Fucking smiling right at him like he'd just won the lottery.

Someone, another Fed pressed something over Yasha's chest.

"My son?" he whispered.

"Your son gave you up, you piece of shit," the man muttered before cutting his shirt open.

"Open those crates right now!" someone else shouted in the distance.

No! He tried to scream but blood gurgled in his throat.

The wound was fatal. He knew it. They knew it. The only reason they were attempting to save him was so they could prosecute him. Yasha closed his eyes and let blackness overtake him. His own son had betrayed him. As the darkness descended familiar faces swam before him. There were so many of them. How could there be so many?

Horror flooded Yasha as he stared into the face of Anya Aston. Now he remembered her quite well. She'd pleaded for her husband's life, but not her own. "Why are you here?"

She wrapped an icy hand around his wrist and squeezed tight, her grip brutal and unforgiving. "You are coming with us to pay for your crimes."

"Us?" Then he saw them. All of them. The faces of everyone he'd killed. Some were angry and bitter, others glowed brightly, looking at peace. But they were all there.

Staring at him.

Waiting.

Judging.

He tried to run, but it was useless. A dark swirling cloud surrounded him as unbearable pain and fire tore through his body in agonizing waves. "No!"

* * *

Nika opened her eyes and blinked a few times. She looked at the clock, but everything was fuzzy. It was early but the sun hadn't risen yet. As she laid back against the pillow, she realized she was in a dream state. A soft light glowed all around the room and everything was still hazy, muted.

Tensing, she waited for that inevitable visit from a spirit. When a woman wearing a black dress sat on the edge of the bed, all her apprehension dissipated to be replaced by disbelief and joy.

Her mother.

The dress was the same one she'd worn the last night she'd been alive. She looked just as Nika remembered her. Utterly beautiful. Nika opened her mouth, not knowing what to say.

"I can't believe how much you've grown," her mother said. She reached out and cupped her cheek. "You're so beautiful."

It felt more like a soft breeze blowing over her skin than anything else. Tears spilled down her cheeks. She reached up to hold her mother's hand against her, was surprised by how warm she was. "What are you doing here?" she whispered, afraid if she spoke too loud her mother would disappear.

"I can't stay long but I wanted to tell you that Yasha is dead. He will pay for all his crimes." Her voice wasn't triumphant or happy, just matter of fact.

"Dead?"

She nodded, her dark hair swishing around her face. "You and your sister need to move on with your lives. This need for revenge almost consumed Alena. I want you both to find happiness."

"What about you?"

A ghost of a smile touched her face. "I'm with your father. I'm more than happy. I shouldn't even be here right now. My time has passed and I crossed this plane a long time ago, but I need to know you'll let yourself be happy."

She'd say anything if it made her mother stay. "I will, I promise."

"I'm sorry I missed so many years. I hope you know how much I loved both you girls. Your father and I never thought you'd be in danger."

Nika frowned at her words. "We know how much you loved us. What few memories I have are happy ones."

Her mother pushed out a long breath, which seemed an odd thing for a spirit to do. Then she glanced over her shoulder. Nika couldn't see what she was looking at but when she turned back, her face was sad. "I have to go. Tell your sister I love her too."

"I will. I—" Nika bolted up in bed, her heart pounding triple time. Tears clogged her throat as too many emotions choked her. Throwing the covers off, she hurried to her sister's room. She had to tell Alena.

CHAPTER THIRTY

Declan frowned when he saw Vernon's number displayed on his caller ID. He glanced across the table at Riley. They were at their usual diner. "Mind if I grab this?" The sun was barely up so if Vernon was calling this early, something had happened.

Riley picked up his coffee cup and yawned. "Go ahead."

"Yeah?"

"You sitting down?" Vernon asked.

His heart stuttered. "Why?"

"Yasha Makarov is dead and that piece of shit Rick Savitch is in our custody. One of his guys admitted to kidnapping Alena Brennan for a severe reduction in sentencing. Christmas came early this year, my friend."

"Yasha's dead? Tell me you got what you needed."

"We got all of it and more. The girls are safe. It'll be hell figuring out where they were all taken from, but they're alive and relatively unharmed." The relief in Vernon's voice was clear. "As we speak my guys are raiding his house. He had his hand in a lot of shit over the years and we're just at the tip of discovering how deep his connections run."

"I'm glad you got those women."

"Me too. We're more than even, buddy. Hell, I think I owe you now."

Relief flooded Declan. "No, we're even. Thanks for letting me know. I'll tell Andre about his father."

"Thanks."

As soon as they disconnected, Riley's eyebrows rose. "Good news?"

"Oh yeah." Better than he'd hoped for.

As the waitress walked up to their table, Riley shook his head. "We're good with coffee for now." He turned his attention back to Declan. "So tell me the only reason you dragged me out of bed on a Monday morning isn't because your girlfriend kicked you out of her dreams."

Declan's hand tightened around his warm mug. "I don't know what to do."

Riley rolled his eyes. "Talk to her."

"I tried that. She thinks that because we're both liars we don't have a chance." At least now that Yasha was dead she couldn't use him as an excuse. There was no longer a threat.

"Try harder. Be honest with her. Tell her the one thing you're terrified to admit to her."

His eyebrows rose. "Are you serious?"

"Don't look at me like that. You either love her or you don't. If you love her, tell her and hope she doesn't break your trust. If you don't, walk away."

"If she breaks that trust, *I'm dead*."

Riley shrugged and took another sip of his coffee. "Don't ask for my advice if you don't want it."

"I swear, sometimes I wonder—" His cell vibrated again. It was Andre. Frowning, he answered. "Hey. Is everything all right?"

"Where are you?"

"Having breakfast with my brother." The house was completely locked down and he'd left Nathaniel in charge.

"Nika and Alena just left. I thought you should know."

Iciness swept through him. "The plane wasn't scheduled to leave until this afternoon." Andre had said he was going to give them a ride anywhere they wanted to go, but Declan thought there would be time to stop Nika, to convince her that leaving was stupid.

"Plans changed. They're leaving for New York in less than an hour." Andre sounded bitter and angry. Not that Declan blamed him.

His entire body broke out in a cold sweat. "Can you stall them?"

There was a long pause. "I can call the pilot. I'm sure delaying them won't be a problem."

"Thanks. I'm on my way." Later, when it was appropriate, he'd tell Andre about Yasha. Right now, he needed to catch Nika. He threw a twenty on the table and stood. "I gotta go. Nika's skipping town."

"Shit." Riley threw another bill on the table and followed. "I'm coming with you."

His brother was quiet as they drove to the airport. Declan didn't have the energy for small talk anyway.

Right now all he cared about was keeping the woman he loved from walking out of his life. He should have stormed into her room last night and forced her to listen to him. There was no way he was letting her get on that plane. And even if she did, he'd just follow her.

* * *

"Park there." Declan pointed at the dark SUV Nika had probably arrived in. It was parked on the side of the hangar, which would give him the element of surprise. Since Nathaniel and two of his men had escorted the women to the airport, he'd also called ahead. Everyone was under strict orders to keep that Cessna from taking off.

As he turned the engine off, Nika and Alena appeared from the direction of the hangar with Nathaniel. They walked a few feet toward the open tarmac, but their backs were still turned to them. "That's her. The one in the red." The weather had warmed up and she wore a slim-fitting sleeveless cherry red top with jeans and sandals. Her sister wore old jeans, a loose T-shirt and ballet slipper type shoes—a much different state of dress than she'd been in the past week.

Riley let out a low whistle and leaned over to get a better look. "She's a hot little thing."

Declan gritted his teeth. "That's the last time you get to say that." Nika was completely unaware of their presence. They both were. From his position, he could see the plane about a hundred yards off.

Nika had her back half-turned to him and from what he could tell she didn't even seem upset. He was tearing his hair out over her and she was just flitting off to New York. Well fuck that. "Stay here," he ordered Riley.

When he slammed the door shut behind him, she glanced over in his direction. Her eyes widened, but she didn't move otherwise. As he approached, Nathaniel quickly disappeared inside the hangar. He was aware of Alena staring at him, but he ignored her and positioned himself directly in front of Nika.

"I'm going to go...be somewhere else," Alena murmured before hurrying away.

Nika brought her chin up in defiance. "What are you doing here?"

As he started to answer, one of the maintenance guys began rolling their suitcases toward the plane. "You're not going to New York."

"Excuse me?"

"Damn it, Nika. Why are you leaving?"

Her chin notched up another fraction. "What reason do I have to stay?"

"Me." His chest tightened as he put the admission out there.

"You want me to stay here for you?" She wasn't being sarcastic, but her words were like a blow to his face.

The question and her tone stung. "That's right. *Me.*"

She bit her bottom lip and eyed him warily. Then she shook her head. "This is ridiculous. First, I'm a threat to you."

"Yasha's dead."

She blinked once, then seemed to gather herself. For some reason he was under the impression she already knew. "Well, I don't even have a place to stay—"

"You'll live with me."

She snorted loudly. "And third, I have a lot of work to catch up on and—"

"Good. I'm also hiring you to work for me. And we both know you can do your work anywhere in the world."

She eyed him warily, but didn't respond. "So this is about me working for you?"

"Fuck no and you know it. This has nothing to do with work. This is about us, what's between us."

Her eyes filled with tears, but still she said nothing. She swallowed hard, as if she couldn't talk.

God, she made him ache. "You've got a gift you haven't tapped into yet. If you open your mind, I think you'll find you can help a lot more people than that little girl, Selina."

Her expression softened. "Oh...I never thanked you for that. Declan, thank you for finding her. She came to thank me too before she passed over."

"I don't want your thanks. I want you to stay." *Forever.* "There's so much we can do together, Nika. We're different and should embrace that. *Together.* There's so much we can do as... a team. Even if it's not in the supernatural realm, I want to share everything with you, make a life with you."

She shifted from one foot to the other. "Declan, I don't know. There's so much we don't know about each other, and what we do know is based on lies. How can you ever forgive me?"

"We lied to each other, yes, but nothing I *feel* for you is a lie." He waited a beat, then glanced over his shoulder to find his brother staring at them through the windshield. He needed to suck it up and just tell her. Facing Nika, he mentally steeled himself for her response. "You want to know why things ended with my last girlfriend?"

"Why?"

"Because she tried to kill me."

Nika's eyes widened, but he continued. If he didn't get it out now, he might never. "I admitted the one thing to her I haven't told anyone besides my family. In my dream walks, there are only a select few people who actually remember my presence. My ex, Madelyn, was a psychic too. Different than you, but psychic just the same. She worked for the CIA, but she was dirty. I was getting too close to..." He cleared his throat, forcing himself to stop since he couldn't tell her everything. Not yet anyway. "In our dreams one night she used her mental powers to give me a heart attack. If it hadn't been for my partner and a shot of adrenaline, I'd be dead."

"So what happened?" Nika whispered.

"She was on the other side of the ocean when she tried to kill me. Thought she succeeded, too."

"Did you kill her?"

"No." But he knew who had. Once his handler had gotten wind of her treachery, her days had been numbered.

"So you're telling me this because…"

"You have the capability to kill me if you want. I don't know any other way to lay myself bare for you. I don't want any more lies or secrets between us. And if you're through with the stupid excuses of why you can't stay, let's get out of here. Come home with me."

She uncrossed her arms and shoved her hands in her pockets. When she stared at him with those big green eyes, he felt as if he could drown in her gaze. "You know most of my secrets, already."

He nodded. "I do, and I want to start fresh with you. I just want you to give us a chance. Don't leave."

Shadows swirled in her eyes. "You really want me to live with you?"

The vulnerability in her voice made his chest hurt. "After every date we're going to end up in bed together. You might as well save on rent."

Her lips curled up at the corners as she fought a smile. "That's *so* romantic. I don't know how to argue with that."

He took a step closer and when she didn't move away, he cupped her jaw, lightly stroking her soft skin with his thumb. It was too soon, but he decided to take the plunge anyway. "I love you, Nika. That's why I want you to stay. I think I fell a little bit in love with you during that first dream walk and you called me your fantasy man."

She sucked in a deep breath. "Declan—"

He didn't give her a chance to respond. As he crushed his lips over hers, his senses exploded with the taste and touch of her. Her tongue rasped against his, hungry and teasing. He threaded his fingers through the curtain of her thick hair. Energy hummed through him and he tightened his grip. He couldn't lose her. Not when he'd just found her. This was a woman worth fighting for.

She moaned lightly into his mouth and her arms wound their way around his waist as she gripped him tight. He jerked when she pressed her body up against the entire length of his. Through her sheer top, he could feel her hardened nipples pressing against his chest and he realized she wasn't wearing a bra. That was his last coherent thought as he deepened their kiss.

A horn blast tore them apart. Nika's chest rose and fell rapidly as she leaned in to him. Without turning around, he settled his chin on her head and murmured into her hair, "That's my brother and I think he's ready to meet you."

She sighed heavily. "How many brothers do you have again?"

"Three."

"Are they all gifted like you?"

"You could say that." As a telekinetic, a clairsentient and a clairvoyant they were all incredibly different, but in one way or another, they were all gifted.

Her grip tightened around his waist but she shifted so that she was looking at him. "My uncle is MI6. It's how my sister and I were able to get out of the country undetected when we were kids. I was too young, but my parents had given my sister his number in case of any emergency. He broke a lot of laws getting us to safety and if anyone ever finds out, there will likely be hell to pay. He wanted to give us a chance to live normal lives and cut all ties from the CIA. So there you go, that's my biggest secret."

For a moment, he was speechless. The United Kingdom hadn't even acknowledged the Secret Intelligence Service's existence until the last couple decades. It made sense that her uncle was so careful getting them out of the country. And it also made sense why no one had been able to track them. "You come from a family of spies, huh?"

"Pretty much." She bit her bottom lip then looked over to where her sister stood next to Nathaniel. "I need to talk to Alena."

"Okay." He kissed the top of her head before she stepped away, even though the last thing he wanted to do was let her go.

Nika pressed a hand to her stomach as she walked toward her sister. For some reason she felt like she was walking the gallows. Once she reached Alena, she opened her mouth but her sister beat her to it.

"You're staying with him." It wasn't a question.

"Yasha's truly dead," she whispered.

Alena's mouth parted a fraction, tears glistening in her dark eyes. "Really?"

Nika had told her about their mother's visit, but having it confirmed seemed to take Alena off guard. "I didn't ask for the details but I'll get them for you. Why don't you stay in Miami too?"

Alena shook her head, looking miserable. "I can't." For the first time in years, Alena had pulled her hair back into a plain ponytail, wore no makeup, and clothes that were just a little too big for her. Nika started to protest, but Alena shook her head. "I see the way you two look at each other so please don't worry about me right now. I want you to be happy, Nika. That's all I've ever wanted. I just...I can't stay in the same city as Andre right now."

"You care for him."

With tears rolling down her cheeks, Alena nodded. "It doesn't matter now. And I'm not leaving forever, silly girl. I'm going to meet with my agent and see about lining up a few new jobs this year. Work will keep me sane."

They'd never spent much time apart. "I hate this."

"Yasha's dead, we have nothing to be afraid of anymore." Alena wrapped her arms around Nika in a tight hug. "I need to get away from here but I'll call you as soon as I've landed. I just need to be alone right now," she whispered before letting her go and heading for the plane.

Nika watched as her sister boarded it. They'd never spent much time separated before but in her heart she knew it was for the best right now.

She jumped as she felt Declan come up beside her. He threw an arm around her shoulders, the gesture protective and comforting. "Are you going to be okay?"

She nodded and stepped deeper into his embrace. "Yeah. So, where do we go from here?"

"I left breakfast to stop you so how about we start there?"

"That works for me." When she grinned, it lit up her entire face. Declan's stomach tightened with need as they headed back to his vehicle. If she smiled at him like that more often, he'd be likely to do any damn thing she asked.

As they reached the SUV, she jerked to a halt. "Crap. You know I love you too."

The vise around his chest loosened and dissipated completely. He hadn't given her a chance to respond because he'd been afraid of her answer. "I do now."

EPILOGUE

Two months later

Nika didn't hear him approach. He was too stealth for that. But Declan's shadow crossed over the cabana lounge chair she was sitting cross-legged on, hunched over her laptop. "Hey, babe," she said without looking up. She was almost done.

"I don't even garner a kiss?" he murmured, sitting on the end of it.

"What...oh, yeah." She made a kissing sound as her fingers flew across the keyboard, but still didn't look up, just kept him in her peripheral. She'd been working on this project for a month straight and was finishing up a couple last minute things. If she met his gaze she knew what would happen. They'd end up naked and she'd never complete this.

Declan laughed, the sound rich and deep and warmed her straight to her belly. God, she loved the man.

"Done!" She pushed her laptop away and looked up to find him watching her intently, those dark eyes so captivating she still got lost in them more often than not.

"Are you really done?" His voice was wry, his lips curved up just the slightest bit.

She shrugged. "Mostly. A few coding things I need to tweak but you're here and..." Blinking, she glanced around their pool area. "Jeez, what time is it?" The sun was close to setting. She hadn't realized how late it was.

"Time for you to come join me for dinner. I got take-out from your favorite place." He smoothly moved her laptop to sit on the adjoining lounge chair. Wearing black slacks and a button down pale blue shirt that was open at the collar with his tie loosened, he looked delicious. And he was all hers.

That familiar hunger pooled inside her, heating her up. "How about we postpone dinner?" She reached out and tugged on his tie gently, pulling him toward her. Her nipples hardened against the built in cups of her summer dress.

He moved like a sexy, lethal predator, settling between her legs as she opened her thighs for him. She wrapped her arms around him and met him for a lazy kiss. She loved his taste and everything about him. Moving in with him had been surprisingly easier than she'd imagined. They both worked hard so he understood her hours, just as she did his. And he understood her need to work so much which she appreciated. After the insanity of the last couple years, all the planning and traveling with her sister, she loved putting down roots and having a sense of normalcy.

Mainly she just loved Declan. He was helping her with her gifts too and on the sly, they'd helped the police with a couple cases. But she didn't want to think about any of that right now.

"I need to ask you something," Declan murmured, dropping kisses along her jaw as he made his way to her ear.

"Hmm?"

He ran his hands up her arms to where they were linked behind his neck and pulled them apart. When he guided them above her head, she shivered as his fingers skated up her arms, wrists, then linked his fingers through hers.

She automatically arched into him then froze when she felt a ring slip over her left hand ring finger.

Declan lifted his head back to look down at her, his dark eyes sparking with all sorts of emotion. Love, lust and a little bit of worry. "Marry me?"

Nodding, a smile split her face. She didn't even glance at the ring, didn't really care what it looked like at the moment. "Yes." Grabbing his face she met his mouth in a hungry frenzy. "Yes, yes, yes," she said in between frantic kisses.

She already felt so linked to him, on so many levels, but she couldn't wait to show the world that he was hers and she was his.

Thank you for reading Retribution. If you don't want to miss any future releases, please feel free to join my newsletter. I only send out a newsletter for new releases or sales news. Find the signup link on my website: http://www.katiereus.com

ACKNOWLEDGMENTS

It's time to thank the usual crowd. Kari Walker, Carolyn Crane and Joan Turner, thank you ladies so much for all your help. This book has been a long time coming and I'm grateful for all your insight. No surprise, I owe a big thank you to Jaycee of Sweet 'N Spicy Designs for her beautiful design work. This is one of my favorite covers to date. For my wonderful readers, thank you for your continuous support and all those lovely emails, and facebook and twitter messages. You guys rock! As always, a big thanks to my family for putting up with my erratic schedule. To my assistant, Sarah, you keep me sane in so many ways. Thank you! Lastly, thank you to God for everything.

COMPLETE BOOKLIST

Red Stone Security Series
No One to Trust
Danger Next Door
Fatal Deception
Miami, Mistletoe & Murder
His to Protect
Breaking Her Rules
Protecting His Witness
Sinful Seduction
Under His Protection
Deadly Fallout

The Serafina: Sin City Series
First Surrender
Sensual Surrender
Sweetest Surrender
Dangerous Surrender

Deadly Ops Series
Targeted
Bound to Danger
Chasing Danger (novella)
Shattered Duty

Edge of Danger

Non-series Romantic Suspense
Running From the Past
Everything to Lose
Dangerous Deception
Dangerous Secrets
Killer Secrets
Deadly Obsession
Danger in Paradise
His Secret Past
Retribution

Paranormal Romance
Destined Mate
Protector's Mate
A Jaguar's Kiss
Tempting the Jaguar
Enemy Mine
Heart of the Jaguar

Moon Shifter Series
Alpha Instinct
Lover's Instinct (novella)
Primal Possession
Mating Instinct
His Untamed Desire (novella)
Avenger's Heat
Hunter Reborn

Protective Instinct (novella)

Darkness Series
Darkness Awakened
Taste of Darkness
Beyond the Darkness

ABOUT THE AUTHOR

Katie Reus is the *New York Times* and *USA Today* bestselling author of the Red Stone Security series, the Moon Shifter series and the Deadly Ops series. She fell in love with romance at a young age thanks to books she pilfered from her mom's stash. Years later she loves reading romance almost as much as she loves writing it.

However, she didn't always know she wanted to be a writer. After changing majors many times, she finally graduated summa cum laude with a degree in psychology. Not long after that she discovered a new love. Writing. She now spends her days writing dark paranormal romance and sexy romantic suspense.

For more information on Katie please visit her website: www.katiereus.com. Also find her on twitter @katiereus or visit her on facebook at: www.facebook.com/katiereusauthor.

9732

41316715R00228

Made in the USA
Lexington, KY
08 May 2015